MW00856966

A TRINKET FOR THE TAKING

Books by Victoria Laurie

COACHED TO DEATH

TO COACH A KILLER

COACHED IN THE ACT

COACHED RED-HANDED

COACHING FIRE

A TRINKET FOR THE TAKING

Published by Kensington Publishing Corp.

A TRINKET FOR THE TAKING

VICTORIA LAURIE

KENSINGTON PUBLISHING CORP.
www.kensingtonbooks.com

This book is a work of fiction. Names, characters, businesses, organizations, places, events, and incidents either are the product of the author's imagination or are used fictitiously. Any resemblance to actual persons, living or dead, events, or locales is entirely coincidental.

To the extent that the image or images on the cover of this book depict a person or persons, such person or persons are merely models, and are not intended to portray any character or characters featured in the book.

KENSINGTON BOOKS are published by

Kensington Publishing Corp.
900 Third Avenue
New York, NY 10022

Copyright © 2024 by Victoria Laurie

All rights reserved. No part of this book may be reproduced in any form or by any means without the prior written consent of the Publisher, excepting brief quotes used in reviews.

All Kensington titles, imprints and distributed lines are available at special quantity discounts for bulk purchases for sales promotion, premiums, fund-raising, educational or institutional use. Special book excerpts or customized printings can also be created to fit specific needs. For details, write or phone the office of the Kensington Special Sales Manager: Kensington Publishing Corp., 900 Third Avenue, New York, NY, 10022. Attn. Special Sales Department. Phone: 1-800-221-2647.

KENSINGTON and the KENSINGTON COZIES teapot logo Reg. US Pat & TM Off.

Library of Congress Control Number: 2024940936

ISBN: 978-1-4967-4249-0

First Kensington Hardcover Edition: December 2024

ISBN: 978-1-4967-4251-3 (ebook)

10 9 8 7 6 5 4 3 2 1

Printed in the United States of America

A TRINKET FOR THE TAKING

Chapter 1

Stepping out into the sunshine of a beautiful early spring afternoon, I sighed contentedly. I'd always wanted to make it to the bicentennial mark, so today's birthday was a little extra special. And it didn't even bother me that I'd have to meet the boss before I could clear my calendar for the rest of the day of self-care. I badly needed pampering.

Walking down the three brick steps from the back door of my three-level home off Thirty-Third Street in the heart of Georgetown, I headed along the paved pathway to my detached garage, opening the door and flicking on the lights. In the center of the garage was my brand-new Porsche 718 Cayman in arctic gray. She'd been the perfect birthday present to celebrate my two hundredth year.

"Hello, Luna," I whispered, caressing her roof. I name all my cars, just like I'd once named all my horses.

Luna had arrived in my driveway on the night of a full moon, so her name was rather obvious. Her beautiful arctic-gray color also helped to inspire the moniker.

With another contented sigh I opened the door and hopped in, then started her up, hearing the thrum of the engine like a million bees under the hood being awakened from their slumber.

Backing out of the tiny driveway to the street, I spun the wheel and punched the gas, thrilling at the sudden burst of speed.

My grin was wide when I took the tight corner, then slowed down just enough not to attract too much attention. Still, I couldn't help humming a happy tune while I thought about the meeting I was headed to. I had just closed a very difficult caper involving an unbound with a case of sticky fingers, and a talent for disguise. It'd taken me over a week to finally track him down, and he didn't give up his trinket easily. No, I'd had to *persuade* him.

Such an unpleasant experience . . . for him.

Right now, the trinket was safely tucked away in my purse, and it was about to be reunited with its owner.

Weaving in and out of the midafternoon traffic, I was able to gain some speed, once I hit the Washington Memorial Highway. One glance at the clock on the dash told me I wasn't in danger of being late for my meeting, something I have *never* been in the 180 years I'd been working for my employer, Elric Ostergaard.

Elric doesn't tolerate tardiness. He views it as an insult, and I've had the misfortune of seeing what happens to a few of my peers when Elric feels insulted. . . .

Let's just say that it's generally unpleasant and likely to involve a dragon.

Not kidding.

I headed south at a good clip before taking the exit for Alexandria, which is simply the quaintest little town. If I hadn't owned my home since the late 1880s, I might've settled in Alexandria.

Still, it's likely a good thing that I'm not closer to work. There are far too many sniveling, simpering mystics in that town, all vying for Elric's good graces.

They should know better—Elric has no good graces.

Well, except perhaps where I'm concerned.

Avoiding the underground garage, I opted for the sizable parking lot of his headquarters and parked at the back, away from the crowded spaces closer to the building. I wanted Luna to enjoy the sunshine without fear of being scratched.

Grabbing my purse, phone, and key fob, I hurried out of the lot, around the building, and over to the front entrance.

Pushing my way through the revolving door, I came into the lobby and scanned the area to see if there were any familiar faces. There weren't, which was probably a good thing if I'm being honest. Mystics overall are very manipulative creatures, always looking for an angle to work, an advantage to gain, or someone to manipulate. It's wearisome.

Bypassing the information desk, I headed to the elevator where only one other person was standing. He turned when I stepped up next to him and I could feel his gaze traveling up and down my body in a crude, lecherous way.

"You must be new here," I said softly.

"Why do you say that?" he asked, just as softly.

"Because men who stare at me, the way you are right now, don't tend to leave the building in one piece."

He barked out a laugh, and I turned to look him in the eye so that he could see I wasn't making light.

The elevator binged and the doors opened. He waved me forward and I walked into the boxcar, pressing the button for the eighteenth floor, then moved all the way to the rear of the elevator with my back pressed against it in a subtly defensive position.

The lech followed me in and when he turned to the panel and saw what number floor I'd pressed, he immediately headed back out. "It's okay," he muttered. "I'll catch the next one."

I offered him a winning smile as the doors closed.

The ride up was slow as there were lots of people in the building moving from one floor to another. Everyone who entered, however, took one look at the panel of lit buttons and quickly exited the first chance they had.

I couldn't blame them. No one wanted to be responsible for the elevator's slow ascent to the top floor.

At last, the light above the door binged at the arrival of the eighteenth floor, and after the doors parted, I stepped out into the lobby, which was as elegantly decorated as any king's court.

It fit Elric to a T.

Making my way down the corridor, I came to another lobby area, with elegant, high-backed armchairs set in a half circle. Two of the chairs were occupied; one by a woman with short, spiky, blond hair and the muscled physique of an elite athlete, well, except for the section of her upper arm that was missing along with three of her right fingers and much of her left foot. She was barely conscious.

In another chair sat a second woman with long black hair, pale skin, light green eyes, and a beautiful face. She was sporting a sizable bruise to her left eye, a split lip, swollen right wrist, and a long, deep, talon-like cut that traveled across her collarbone over her left shoulder and down the length of her arm. She was also holding herself in a way that suggested she might have a few cracked or broken ribs.

The women had obviously gone a few rounds with one of our in-house dragons.

I would've stopped to offer them each some encouragement, but both seemed to be fighting to stay conscious, so I moved on.

Arriving at the floor's reception area, I smiled pleasantly at Elric's assistant, sitting behind a large, ornately carved white desk. "Hello, Sequoia."

The tall, leggy woman with ebony skin and long silver-white hair regarded me with a forced smile that was more reptilian than welcoming. In a distinctly British accent she greeted me with, "Dovey Van Dalen," while her gaze flickered to the computer screen in front of her. "You're ten minutes early, but Elric is running on time today, so I expect him to be with you shortly."

"Perfect, thank you." Making a motion over my shoulder to the seating area with the two brutalized women, I added, "Is Elric interviewing again?"

Sequoia nodded. "He's looking for a new thief."

I glanced over my shoulder at the pair. "How many did he start out with?"

"For the interviews?"

I nodded.

"Seven."

"How many rounds to go?"

"Two," Sequoia said, and then her smile did appear to be genuine—if you could call "sinister" genuine. "Odds are fifty to one that those two won't last another round."

I looked again at the brunette. There was something resilient about her. Reaching into my handbag, I pulled out a one-hundred-dollar bill, wiggling it playfully. "I'll take a hundred on the brunette to go the distance."

Sequoia's brow arched. "*No one* is taking the brunette, Dovey."

Laying the hundred on the counter I reached into my bag again and pulled out four more hundred-dollar bills. "Make it an even five, then."

Sequoia chuckled and picked up my money, curling it into a roll, then tucking it into the bosom of her blouse. "Results will be in at five. On the dot."

I nodded and was about to ask Sequoia if I should sit to wait for Elric in his office when behind me, I heard, "Tortelduif."

Turning, I found myself looking up into the gorgeous hazel eyes of the most powerful man in the world and offered him a heartfelt smile. "Good morning, Elric."

He stepped close, kissing my cheek. "Happy birthday."

I blushed because he'd remembered. There was no doubt in my mind that the only other birthday Elric had committed to memory was his own.

"Thank you," I told him.

The air around Elric's face sparkled ever so slightly, and as I looked at his warm and affectionate expression, I realized he was masking it with a spell that would keep his ruthless, terrifying reputation intact.

To all the other eyes and ears in the lobby, Elric would appear to have a cool and detached demeanor, but with me, he'd always allowed himself to soften.

He's never been anything but affectionate, generous, and often even gentle toward me, but with everyone else—including, and perhaps especially, his wife—he can be merciless, vengeful, and brutal. And when he wants, he can also be quite deadly.

Elric and I have known each other for nearly two hundred years, and for the first hundred and thirty, I'd been his constant companion, his concubine, his trusted advisor, his spy, and his loyal and faithful servant. My allegiance to him has never wavered, nor has my adoration.

Along with being my frequent lover, employer, and guardian, Elric is also my binder. On this very day 182 years earlier, Elric Ostergaard had won me in a game of cards, and my father had readily given me to the man in exchange for wiping away his gambling debts.

Truth be told, I hadn't really minded. One look at the magnificently beautiful man and I'd fallen head over heels for him.

Perhaps it'd been the same for Elric. Perhaps less so. Still, we'd forged a bonded relationship over the years that felt unbreakable.

In fact, I wasn't even jealous of his wife, Petra, or any of his other women anymore.

Well, not as much, at least.

As a reward for my allegiance, Elric had loosened the bond

of his control over me—something that all binders have over their protégés—and he now granted me a fair degree of agency, for which I was very grateful.

Our current agreement is that I'm allowed to live on my own, keep my own hours, be free of the court politics that plague the territory, and most importantly, I can get paid for the work I do for SPL Inc. As the pay is good, and I have a one-hundred-percent closure rate, it's a neat, comfortable life.

If only a little lonely.

"Do you have it?" he asked, eyeing my handbag.

"Of course I have it."

"Good. Come, we'll talk in my office."

I followed behind him and couldn't help but be flooded with the memories of the first time we'd met—which, coincidentally, had been on my eighteenth birthday.

Nearly two centuries ago, I'd been living a coddled and pampered life in Copenhagen with my wealthy merchant father, his third wife, and my two half brothers.

On the morning of my eighteenth birthday, Father, who'd always called me his little *tortelduif*, had announced that he'd found a suitable match for my hand in marriage in the form of Shem de Groot, the son of an exceptionally wealthy merchant.

I knew Shem, and the thought of becoming his wife made me think wistfully of hurling myself into the Christianshavns Kanal.

The young man was perpetually sickly, five years my junior, painfully thin and with a countenance marred by an unusually prominent nose, hollow cheeks, and buckteeth.

On top of all that, he had the manner and simpering disposition of a boy who, even at thirteen, still cried for his wet nurse.

It was a dreadful pairing, and back then I remember wishing that his sickly disposition would soon be more than his frail, bony body could bear.

Adding to the horror, my father also confessed that he'd invited the boy and his family to my party and that we would wed the next morning.

When the guests began arriving, I was in a state of near panic, and my mood reflected it. After being admonished by my stepmother for being rude to one of her cousins, I headed to a corner to sulk. And I wasn't there but a moment when my future father-in-law arrived with his entourage. I wanted to bolt upstairs when I saw his son, peeking out from behind his mother's skirts, sniffling through a red, runny nose.

But then into the hall sauntered a tall, exquisitely handsome man with light brown hair that fell to his shoulders, and a neatly trimmed goatee. He was dressed in formal attire that must have cost him a small fortune. He wore rings on every finger, including his thumbs, and there was an air about him that was mesmerizing.

We'd locked eyes almost immediately and I'd felt both thrilled and terrified to be wholly taken in by such a man.

Father had motioned for me to come and greet the de Groots, and I'd eagerly left my corner to hurry over, if for no other reason than to get a closer look at this stranger.

Shem's father, Andries de Groot, introduced the man as Elric Ostergaard, a longtime friend of the de Groot family and an influential member of King Willem's counsel.

I'd waited patiently next to my stepmother for my father to make the introductions on our side of the family, and the whole time I'd stood there, Elric had stared at me with an openly smoldering expression.

This would've normally shocked anyone within view, but for some reason, no one appeared to notice. And as for me, I simply couldn't keep my eyes off him, and again, this was behavior that my father would've quickly scolded me for, but he'd carried on as if I weren't openly gaping at the beautiful six-foot-five-inch-tall man, whom I thought was at least fifteen years older than me.

I only discovered later that I'd been off by over a thousand years.

At dinner and by tradition, my betrothed would've been seated next to me; however, for some reason Father insisted that I sit next to Elric. I found the whole affair simply mystical—which is the best way to define that birthday.

After dinner, the men had started up a game of faro—a gambling card game—and, when I'd sat nearby to observe the game, no one had protested.

Long into the night I'd sat there and watched as Elric won hand, after hand, after hand. And all the men at the table had been made considerably poorer.

No one was willing to call Elric a cheat, however. Such influential friends of King Willem would never be called out for such a thing, even if they were doing it blatantly.

But under such conditions, the normal protocol would've been for each of them to end the game early.

And yet, no one did.

Into the wee hours of the morning the men played, and one by one they became mired in debt until there wasn't anything else left to offer up as collateral.

Poorest among them was my father, and normally the horizon of his dire financial situation would've terrified me, but I'd had this strange sense of calm throughout that evening and into the morning hours. I felt no fear.

But I did feel fate.

As the glow of the rising sun began to creep in through the windows, the game was down to only Elric and my father.

Father lost.

And that's when Elric offered him a deal he simply couldn't pass up. Nor did I want him to.

Elric told my father that the next hand would be the last for the two of them, but my father told Elric that he was finished.

He had nothing left to offer as collateral and he was ruined if Elric attempted to collect on his debts.

Elric very pointedly pivoted his gaze to me, and the smile that snuck onto the corners of his lips sent my heart racing.

He told my father that their next hand would be double or nothing, but my father again insisted that he had nothing left to offer. Elric pointed at me and said, "Then I'll take her."

Angered, my father jumped to his feet, ready to banish Elric from his house, but the Viking held up his hand and added, "If I win, I will cancel all your debt and the debt of your guests, taking only your daughter as my prize. If I lose, you may reclaim all that you have lost plus double from my personal coffers for you and your guests."

The only people left at the table were all the men who'd lost sizable sums to Elric, and their attention fixed fully on my father for his decision. The tension in the air was thick, and it didn't surprise me that my own father never even looked at me to gain my opinion.

Instead, he very quickly agreed to Elric's terms.

And he lost.

True to his word, however, Elric released my father and all his friends from their gambling debts, then sent me upstairs to collect my things and meet him at his carriage out front.

After dashing upstairs, I was like a bird trapped inside looking for an open window, fluttering about by bedroom trying to hurry through the task. In my excitement and distraction only a few of my finest clothes made it into my traveling trunk, which two of the servants carried downstairs.

Father had by then retired, and I never forgot that his shame prevented him from seeing off his only daughter.

Elric took me that day to one of his many homes, and that night he took me to his bed, and made me his own.

In the morning, he'd presented me with a gold ring topped with a beautiful silver pearl. He placed the ring on my right ring finger, then laid a dove's feather in my palm. When I eyed him curiously, he took my chin in his hand and whispered,

"Dove so bright,
Dove in flight,
Bird of your feather
Bring us together,
Tap the pearl and make it dance,
You'll never again be left to chance,
The truth of your feelings,
Will be in the sealing,
Of your binding to me,
So shall it be."

And then, something quite strange had taken place. I'd felt a tingling sensation—like a vibrating of every cell in my body. From head to toe it was as if I'd been charged with a current that sharpened my eyesight, enhanced my sense of smell, lit up my sense of taste, and set aflame my sense of touch. From head to toe it was simply this exquisite sensation that I never wanted to end. I'd never felt so giddy. So vibrant. So *alive.*

Elric had taken me once again to his bed and that was a memory that will stay with me to the end of my days. I'd never experienced such pleasure, such craving, such satiated need, before or, frankly, since.

And from that moment on, I'd fallen deeply, madly, and oh, so passionately in love with Elric that I truly felt nothing, *nothing* could ever shake my adoration for him, or the faith in our combined love.

And nothing ever did.

Until Petra came for a visit.

Elric and Petra have been married for well over a millennium. Brought together by Petra's father, who bound them individually into mystics, then bound them together in a matrimonial spell which could never be broken, it was difficult to say whether he gifted them with near immortality or cursed them to coexist.

It was rumored that at points in their thousand years' pairing that they'd been passionate for each other, and it's hard to say when that joint passion had permanently ended and their unyielding hatred for each other began, but hate each other they did with the force of two nearly immortal souls who had nothing better to do with their time than plot each other's downfall.

And yet, their alliance against the five other most powerful mystics in the world remains unshaken to this day. Elric and Petra rule this North American territory united, and if one is called to war, they both go. Even though ruling together is the last thing either wants, they remain united both in wedlock and in commitment to each other's respective power.

And yet, if either had the opportunity to kill their spouse and get away with it without repercussions—and a surety of success—they'd commit themselves to that task without question.

As it is, they often take a swipe at each other's courts, letting the chips fall where they may.

Petra has had me poisoned, beaten, stabbed, stoned, hung, and shot, but each time Elric has used one of his most powerful trinkets to bring me back from the brink of death. And then he's gone after someone in *her* court, many of whom haven't had the good fortune to survive.

And if I'm one of Petra's favorite targets, then Elric's favorite is quite often Petra's son, Marco Sigourney Astoré, whom she bore out of wedlock a hundred years ago, then murdered the boy's father and bound Marco with a terrible curse, which causes a small, ticking spasm somewhere on his body that grows larger and more consuming with every hour. If activated and then left alone to ravage the poor man without the counterspell, Marco's curse would kill him in the span of a weekend.

It's a personal quest of Elric's to discover the exact wording of Marco's cursing. But only his mother knows that, and she's not telling.

To know the exact wording of a bound person's spell is to have total and complete control over them, and Elric has guarded the exact wording of my binding curse with equal fortitude. And, even though I've only heard Elric utter the words once, they remain imprinted on my memory as strongly as my own name.

My binding is far from cruel, which I'm eternally grateful for, because most bindings are quite unpleasant and often painful. Mine is unusual in that it merely forces me to tell Elric how I honestly feel about him or anyone else in any given moment. Every once in a while, Elric will invoke the spell by asking how I'm feeling, and when I look at him, all I feel is love and devotion which, I think, pleases him.

After leading me into his office, he did that very thing. "How're you feeling today, Dovey?"

I smiled and wrapped my arms around his neck, lifting onto my tiptoes to graze his lips with my own. "Happy, loving, and devoted."

He cupped his hands around my face to give me a proper birthday kiss and all felt right with the world.

And because life is just *full* of irony, what happened in the next moment spun my whole world upside down.

CHAPTER 2

Our sweet moment was interrupted by a knock at Elric's door. He eyed it in annoyance. "Yes?"

Sequoia's voice sounded from the other side. "Sorry to disturb you, sir, but Nicodemus Kallis is here, requesting an audience."

At the mention of Kallis, Elric spun me away from him and focused on the door. "Come in, Sequoia."

It hurt my feelings that he'd dispatched me from his embrace so quickly, but I couldn't let it show, so I moved to a nearby chair and sat down, smoothing my features to hide my emotions.

Sequoia opened the door and took only one step inside.

"What does he want?" Elric asked.

"He's demanding an audience, insisting it's urgent."

Elric had his arms crossed over his chest, clearly irritated. "I spent the entirety of last evening entertaining Kallis and the other diplomats and today I have other matters to attend to. Have the applicants gone to their fourth interviews yet?"

"They have."

Sequoia continued to stand there almost expectantly, and Elric regarded her with impatience. "What?"

She cleared her throat. "Mr. Kallis says the matter he wishes to speak with you about concerns one of the Pandoras."

Elric, who'd been leaning against his desk, stood tall. "Which Pandora?"

"I don't know, sir."

The "Pandoras" are a collection of deadly trinkets imbued with incredible power, so deadly, in fact, that the collection had been broken up amongst the seven most powerful mystics in the world. Originally there had been seven Pandora's, but two, Pandora's Pendant and Pandora's Pearl, had been destroyed in the Great War—which had been the last time the world's most powerful mystics had gone to war against one another. It was a war that Elric and Petra had largely come out on top. The five remaining Pandoras had been split up among the five remaining courts that emerged from the conflict.

Elric's brow furrowed as he eyed his assistant. "Kallis is part of Vostov's court, so he must be referring to the Promise."

Sequoia nodded, and the way she shifted her weight from foot to foot indicated she was holding something back.

"What aren't you telling me?" Elric demanded.

"Kallis says that the trinket has been stolen, sir."

My gaze had been pivoting back and forth between Elric and Sequoia and it surprised me when I caught the look in Elric's eyes. He wasn't often surprised, but he appeared to be now. "From where?"

"I believe his hotel room."

My eyes widened. Kallis was a diplomat from the court of Louis Vostov, a twelve-hundred-year-old mystic based in Rome. His court ruled much of Southern Europe, and he and Elric had always held a strong alliance that'd proven quite beneficial over the years.

Still, at the news that a trinket as powerful and as valuable as one of the Pandoras was stolen from within his protected territory, Elric's anger was palpable. "Is Kallis saying the thief is someone from *my* court?"

An accusation like that could have grave consequences if it were true, and even greater consequences if it weren't true.

Diplomats from the various courts were always treated with the greatest respect, especially here in Elric and Petra's court. It was a source of great pride that no diplomat had ever been murdered within the Dobromila-Ostergaard territory. Some had been expelled, but none had ever been murdered, tortured, or overly harmed, which is something none of the other courts could claim.

Within the doorway Sequoia shuffled nervously, no doubt not wanting to be shot for delivering the message. "I don't know what he's been saying, sir. I only know that Mr. Kallis would like a word about his missing trinket."

Elric scowled and waved at her impatiently. "Send him in."

The moment she left, Elric turned to me, holding out his hand. "The trinket you recovered for me, Dovey, please."

I lifted my handbag and wiggled it slightly, then I undid the flap and reached inside for the gold Montblanc ink pen. I held it out for him in the palm of my hand, and he waved his own in my direction.

Instantly, the trinket vanished from my palm to appear in his. "And the mortal who stole it?"

I grinned. "He's back to paying full price."

The pen, which had been charmed by a powerful mystic who owed Elric a favor, had been on its way by bike courier to these headquarters when the courier had been clipped by a car, sending both him and his packages tumbling.

The trinket had somehow ended up on the street where it'd been picked up by a young man named Bill Tate who'd thought it a stroke of great luck to have found such a valuable pen.

He'd had no idea how right he was.

On Tate's way home, another unbound who had just put a FOR SALE sign in his car—a BMW—noticed Bill walking by and offered to sell him the car for a single dollar.

At first, Tate had thought it a joke, but the man had persisted until he'd finally relented and exchanged a dollar bill for the car's title. Within an hour of finding the pen, he'd driven home in the car of his dreams.

From that day forward, if Tate saw something he wanted, as long as he carried the pen with him, he'd be offered it in exchange for a single dollar bill. Within just a few days, Bill Tate had amassed a small fortune in valuable things.

I'd caught up with him just as he was about to enter a high-end jewelry store, and, after a bit of back and forth—mostly back for him and forth for me—I'd relieved him of the trinket that had allowed him so much good fortune.

Tate is a good example of why we keep trinkets away from the unbound. First, because trinkets are created, traded, and, sometimes stolen by mystics to use as a form of currency, either for advancing our own positions or that of the courts we serve. And second, because some of our trinkets are powerful enough to cause *considerable* mayhem in the unbound world.

Elric has perhaps the largest collection of trinkets in the world—but how many he actually has is a number known only to him.

Suffice it to say that within the walls of SPL Inc., Elric has an entire floor devoted to housing, cataloguing, and guarding magical trinkets in every size, shape, and level of power, and that in-house collection is just the tip of the iceberg. I personally know he has several other secret locations filled with trinkets too.

The pen I'd retrieved for this job wasn't of any great value—only a level four at best—but Elric could use it to grant a favor to another mystic if he so chose, or to give as a gift to one of his employees who'd exceeded his expectations.

My house had its own collection of such presents from him, and I valued them as much for their magical qualities as for the symbolism of Elric's devotion to me.

I was equally as devoted. I'd worked for Elric as a recovery agent for at least the last seventy years. He liked to utilize me to recover trinkets that'd fallen into unbound hands as I seem to have a way with them, in that I don't look down at them as if they're second-class citizens compared to mystics. I believe that, while it's true that we'll outlive them, and we wield real magical abilities that defy physics and chemistry, and we exist in a secret world filled with power, money, treasure, prestige, and conflicts they know nothing about, we don't have to interact with them in a way that makes *them* feel like we believe we're superior to them.

I've personally discovered that treating the unbound with respect and dignity allows me to do my job more efficiently. I've always brought Elric back the prize while leaving the unbound to deal with whatever mess they've created, because, while I believe in treating them with respect, I also believe that sometimes they need to learn to leave things that don't belong to them alone. In fact, the lesson part is often the most important, because when it comes to magical trinkets in the hands of the unbound—the danger is real.

Sequoia appeared at the door again, leading in Nicolas. In an instant, the pen in Elric's hand disappeared.

"Nico," Elric said evenly.

Kallis was a stout man who somewhat resembled a bear, with big bushy eyebrows, a long nose, square face, and big round belly.

His eyes were perpetually squinting, causing their color to be something of a mystery.

I'd met him twice before, always in the company of Elric, who often took me as his escort on trips to Vostov's court.

Nico had been dispatched to Washington to smooth over a "misunderstanding" that involved one of Elric's spies and one of Vostov's assassins. It hadn't turned out well for either.

"Elric," Nico said, lowering himself as much as his belly would allow into something resembling a bow. "I'm sorry to disturb you," he began, his accent thick with a somewhat undefinable European accent. "After our meeting last evening, I ventured back to my hotel suite only to discover a most treasured trinket had been stolen."

"A Pandora," Elric said flatly.

Nico nodded gravely. "Yes. The Promise."

I suppressed a gasp. For any of the Pandoras to go missing was quite serious, but the Promise was a deceptively deadly trinket.

All the Pandoras resembled boxes, but the Promise was the smallest of the group. Shaped to resemble an ornately carved ring box, the Promise held only the certainty of death inside. Once opened, whoever gazed upon the glittering emerald ring inside would be bound to die by their own hand in the manner they feared the most. It was an assassin's weapon, and the fact that it'd been stolen was of great concern.

Elric folded his arms across his chest again and gazed at Nicodemus with a bored expression. "How is this *my* problem?" he asked.

The diplomat lowered his chin slightly, in a show of deference. "Normally, I wouldn't bother you with such trivial matters, however, the trinket appears to be in the hands of someone in your governance—"

"How do you know that?" Elric interrupted.

Kallis cocked his head slightly and there was a sinister cast to the hint of a smile he wore. "It is the only logical conclusion. You and your lovely wife do employ the very best thieves on the continent, after all."

"It could've been a rogue," Elric offered. "Not one of mine, of course . . ."

"Of course . . ."

". . . but perhaps Petra's minions are at work."

Kallis's gaze dropped to the carpet. "I've just come from her court. There was another matter I needed to see to there and she insists the thief wasn't one of hers, either."

Mystics are expert liars; we must be if we want to survive our first hundred years. But I knew that no mystic would lie about stealing a Pandora. Not even Petra. The Pandoras are part of the End Games Pact, which is a spellbound agreement between the Seven that prohibits each or any member from lying about the whereabouts of *the* most dangerous trinkets ever created. There are a few hundred trinkets on the list—including all five of the remaining seven Pandoras in existence.

"What about the comeback spells?" I asked.

Kallis shook his head. "This thief is very, very good. He or she has obviously disarmed all my comeback spells. It is a feat, indeed. Until today, I had thought my comeback spells impenetrable."

Comeback spells are designed to prevent the permanent theft of a trinket—by invoking a comeback spell on a trinket that's been stolen, the trinket will return to the rightful owner.

Were the Promise in the hands of a thief from any of the courts, the comeback spells wrapped around it would've all but ensured its return unless the thief was of *exceptional* talent in stripping away all the spells protecting it from being stolen.

Even then, the scenario of a rogue mystic thief stealing it was unlikely because comeback spells take time to strip away from a trinket that valuable. The Promise would've been layered with at least a dozen comeback spells, and if Kallis had only been missing the Promise for less than a day, it wasn't physically possible to have been fully stripped by now. That's something that would've taken much longer, I thought, and a courage most mystics don't possess.

I happen to be exceptionally good at stripping comeback spells from trinkets, but I'd definitely hesitate attempting to strip a trinket like a Pandora, as, often, the comeback spell on a weaponized trinket could boobytrap it into killing the thief trying to strip it.

"Elric," Kallis said, "whoever stole the Promise must not use it. You know this. Far too many powerful mortals exist in this city. It would be like unleashing hell."

Elric's gaze drifted to me, his brow arched expectantly.

I sighed but nodded. There would be other birthdays and opportunities for a day of self-care.

Getting to my feet I motioned toward Kallis, then at the door. "Take me to where the Promise was stolen and I'll get started hunting it down."

Kallis bowed again to Elric, then turned to leave, while I followed but paused slightly as I passed Elric to reach out and squeeze his arm. He covered my hand with his own and that same magical spark that'd been with us since the night of my binding sent a tickle of current all along my skin.

Leaning in toward my ear he said, "Come see me later, Dovey. We can celebrate your birthday together. Properly."

A delicious heat accompanied the spark currently igniting my skin. "Later then," I whispered, kissing him on the cheek.

I followed behind Nicodemus's town car, being driven by his personal bodyguard.

One thing I couldn't quite figure out was how a trinket as deadly as the Promise ever managed to escape Kallis's possession.

He was a skilled and powerful mystic—he'd have to be to be so high up in Vostov's court—so how the trinket had been stolen was almost as important as who had taken it and where it might be now.

We arrived at the Four Seasons Hotel, and I grudgingly gave up my keys to the valet rather than parking and making the diplomat wait, as I doubted he would.

After heading inside and taking in the grand lobby, we rode the elevator up to the Royal Suite. I waited patiently for Kallis to unlock the room—and by that I don't mean using his key card. If he'd failed to magically secure the room before the Promise went missing, he wasn't going to leave that to chance again. Anyone crossing the threshold uninvited would be dead within seconds.

Which is why, when he at last unlocked the door using his key card, and held the door open for me, I waved him through first.

Better safe than sizzled, I thought.

We entered the suite, and I took in the space, judging it to be nearly fourteen hundred square feet, which was an enormous amount of room in downtown D.C.

The nightly rate would certainly reflect that, but mystics like Kallis were rarely concerned with unbound money. At a level, powerful mystics high in the courts had all sorts of trinkets to collect wealth and make themselves supremely comfortable.

And that was perhaps the most curious thing to me: If Nicodemus had access to cash like he so obviously did, then why would a thief—any thief—take the personal risk of stealing the Promise when there would've been other, far more profitable trinkets at play?

Unless, of course, profiting wasn't the point.

Which meant that using the trinket to cause some destruction was.

And that was bad news for Elric and every other area mystic.

We work hard to escape the notice of the unbound. We like to blend in, so to speak, and not call attention to ourselves because we make up a relatively tiny proportion of the world's population, and if word got out that there were a group of individuals who possessed real magical powers which could often be transferred to everyday objects, there'd be chaos as the unbound sought out mystics to bind them, and that would most assuredly upset the balance of power, which was something Elric and the other members of the Seven kept tight control over.

"First," I said to Kallis, after we entered the room, "show me what the Promise looks like."

Although I'd certainly heard of all the Pandoras, I'd only seen the holograms of the two kept by Elric and Petra, namely Pandora's Prelude—a black velvet box holding a dagger, and Pandora's Perish—a red velvet box holding a crown.

Kallis moved to the sofa and plopped down heavily. He then turned one hand up and waved his other hand over it. In an instant the hologram of a blue velvet box decorated with bands of gold and small pearls filled his palm.

I nodded. "And inside?"

Kallis again waved his hand and the hologram box opened, revealing a beautiful gold band with an inlaid square emerald and two diamond baguettes flanking the center stone.

"Does the ring need to come out of the box before the spell is launched?"

"No," Kallis said. "To my knowledge, no one has ever removed the ring. Simply opening it is enough to ignite the spell."

"How many times has it been opened?" I asked, wondering if Kallis would tell me.

"A few," he said vaguely, and I smirked.

Trinkets lose a bit of power every time they're used; however, a series of trinkets as strong as the Pandoras would take hundreds of uses to diminish in power. Another reason they're on the End Games list.

I scanned the room, looking for anything that might catch my eye in the way of a clue. "How is it activated?"

"When the box is opened, revealing the ring, it casts its magic."

"Which is . . ." I knew the answer, but I wanted to hear it from Kallis.

"The Promise will fulfill the target's greatest fear. Whatever manner of death the target fears the most, is how that target will die. Once set in motion, the event cannot be deviated from."

I moved around the suite, simply taking it all in. "Pandora's Promise sounds less like an assassin's assistant and more like a torture device."

He shrugged. "It is both. Which is why it's employed very sparingly."

I glanced over at him, casting a doubtful expression. None of the Seven were known for their generosity or kindness. They'd come to their power through violence, betrayal, and treachery, and they'd stayed in their positions of power by being willing to employ further violence, betrayal, and treachery.

Vostov might have an alliance with Elric, but that didn't make them friends. Still, Vostov wouldn't dare draw fire from Elric by unleashing one of the Pandoras in his territory. That would start a conflict Vostov might not survive. I didn't know the circumstances for the Promise being in Kallis's possession, but Vostov was a known braggart and show-off. Perhaps entrusting Kallis with it on this trip was nothing more than an ego trip.

There was another possibility, however, and that was that Vostov—through Kallis—had intended to murder another court's visiting diplomat during the summit, throwing suspicion for the murder onto Elric and Petra. That would've been quite the gamble as blowback would've been both swift and severe, but I had to at least entertain the theory as I didn't trust Kallis as far as I could throw him.

Still, one thing was certain, and that was that Kallis couldn't return home without it, or it'd be his head on the chopping block.

Of course, if forced to return without the trinket, he'd no doubt blame the theft on Elric, if only to attempt to save his own skin. I doubted it'd work, but it would invite trouble between Vostov and Elric that neither of them needed, so retrieving the Promise was a serious mission. Failure wasn't an option.

"Who knew you had the trinket?" I asked after taking a tour of the suite.

"Only my assistant."

"Not Vostov?"

Kallis's face reddened. "Of course he knew. My liege is aware of all the more powerful trinkets in his court."

"Could he have had one of his thieves steal it from you?"

Kallis sighed heavily and considered me with barely veiled annoyance. "You mean, could Louis have sent a thief to take the trinket and use it as an excuse to have me executed?"

I folded my arms, eyeing him skeptically. "You tell me."

"I am not out of favor within my court, Miss Van Dalen. I'll remind you that I was sent here by my liege on a diplomatic mission. Louis would never entrust me for such a thing if I was out of favor."

"That's a fair point," I conceded. "Take me through the events that led up to you realizing the trinket had been stolen."

"Last evening, I attended a meeting for guests of the summit—"

"Which summit was it again?" I interrupted. I wasn't so involved with Erlic's court politics that I followed all the meetings and alliances happening amongst the various courts.

"The NAWEAEE Counter-Detection Summit."

"Ah," I said, like I knew all about it, when, really, I hadn't even paid attention to the local news. I suspected, however, that the summit was a gathering of the North American, Western, and Eastern European court diplomats on tactics and efforts to avoid being discovered by the unbound.

If I was correct with the acronym, it was certainly an important summit to shore up the commitment to conceal the mystic community from our unbound neighbors. And, while I mostly kept out of politics, I *had* heard rumors that there was a growing faction of mystics in Europe that weren't quite as committed to keeping themselves under the radar as the mystics in other territories.

From what I understood, it wasn't a serious problem . . . yet, but Elric hosting a summit here, where the community *firmly* believed in keeping knowledge of our magical powers from our unbound neighbors, was a strong indication that he took the happenings in Europe quite seriously.

Kallis continued his explanation of events from the evening before. "When I came back here to the suite, I noticed immediately that the guard I had stationed at the door was missing."

"Missing?"

"Yes. Henry has been with me for a few hundred years. A faithful employee, someone I trusted completely."

"And he was missing?"

"Yes."

"Have you since found him?"

Kallis sighed, clearly not liking my interrogation skills. "In a way, yes, I did find him."

"What does that mean, 'in a way' you found him."

"I found pieces of him."

I blanched. "Uh . . . which . . . pieces?"

"A hand. A foot. His shoulder."

I didn't want to ask the next obvious question, but I felt I had to. "Where did you find these pieces?"

"In the pen of one of Petra's pets."

I blinked at Kallis and he stared levelly back at me. I inhaled a deep breath to resettle myself before continuing. "I'm listening, Mr. Kallis. Please tell me what happened."

"As I said, Henry was not at his post, and this was a source of great alarm for me. When I approached the hotel room door, all my wards were in place, so at first I did not suspect that much was amiss except perhaps Henry had discovered some handsome American and was out spending some time with him."

I nodded, hoping this was going to lead somewhere other than Henry's romantic exploits.

"This morning, when Henry was still not here, I sent a page to try to find him. A bit later the page came back. He had discovered that last evening while most of the diplomats were at the summit, Henry had arrived at Petra's court and begged to be let into the Drazilla's pen."

"The *Drazilla's* pen?" I knew about the Drazilla. Part dragon, part creature that looked like Godzilla, but it was ten times as deadly, preferring the skin of its prey over the meat.

"Yes. Naturally, Petra's guards were only too happy to accommodate, and Henry was fed to the beast."

I shuddered. Henry had *not* died a merciful death. Or a quick one. "Poor man."

"Indeed. When I learned that Henry had asked to be fed to the Drazilla, I immediately suspected the work of the Promise, because you see, Henry's older brother once worked for Petra as her beastmaster, until the day when he went hunting for the Drazilla and then Henry's brother was no more."

"Let me guess, Henry's worst fear was being fed to the Drazilla."

"Precisely."

I shuddered again. I couldn't help it. This case was already making this my least favorite birthday on record and hearing about what happened to poor Henry was a major buzzkill. Pinching the bridge of my nose I asked, "So then what happened?"

"Well, then I immediately went to my trinket box, and lo and behold, the Promise was missing."

Kallis pointed to an ebony and gold-leaf humidor on the

coffee table. He reached for it, pulling it to his lap before muttering something softly and waving his hand above the lid. There was a clicking sound, and the lid of the humidor lifted, exposing an array of trinkets, from a sterling-silver cigarette lighter, to a solid-gold saltshaker, to a large men's ring with the head of a gold and onyx-inlaid panther on it.

The ring looked familiar, but I couldn't remember where or if I'd seen it before. Looking over the cache, I said, "What else did the thief make off with?"

"Nothing. He took only the Promise."

My brow furrowed. I had no idea what the power of some of the other trinkets was, but to only make off with the Promise meant that it was the thief's target all along.

"What's the highest-level trinket in there?" I asked, waving to the humidor.

Without hesitation, Kallis lifted the ring out of the box and put it on. "This," he said. And right in front of my eyes some of the streaks of gray in Kallis's bushy beard turned brown again, and there was a more youthful appearance to his countenance.

He then took off the ring and placed it back in the humidor, saying, "The ring is a trinket created specifically for me by Georges Maubossin."

My brow rose. "The *merlin*, Maubossin?"

"The very one," he said with a hint of pride.

Georges Maubossin was that very rare breed of mystic whose significant powers could be channeled into objects—almost always something made of precious metal—that took these objects up several levels to some of the most powerful trinkets within our world.

In other words, almost all mystics are capable of channeling power into an object to create a trinket, but most of us—the *vast* majority, in fact—can only channel enough power into a trinket to bring it to a level three or four on a scale that went up to fifteen.

Even Elric—arguably the most powerful mystic on the continent, and perhaps even in the world—could only channel enough magic into an object to bring it to a level seven or possibly an eight. That's impressive for a mystic, believe me, but merlins are in a category all on their own.

To channel energy—which is, at its simplest level, what all mystics do—we have a keen awareness of our own electromagnetic current, and this keen sense allows us to gather and direct that current into both objects and into spoken words of a certain iambic pentameter (spells).

Trinkets act like battery packs for the electromagnetic energy that we pour into them. In other words, trinkets allow us to store up and save our own energy for a later day or take additional energy from an object created by another mystic to redirect, restore, or even strengthen our own.

Merlins, however, are almost another species entirely. This class of mystic doesn't funnel their own energy into a trinket to make it powerful; they channel the electromagnetic current *around them* into a trinket. The energy they utilize is harnessed in tiny quantities from every living, breathing plant, animal, or human within at least a quarter-mile radius of their position, leaving those organisms virtually unchanged because each individual thing only contributes a tiny fraction of its energy.

Throughout our history there have been only a few dozen merlins (beginning with the first, Merlin from King Arthur's court), and their existence is often perilous because they're so sought after that they can become a slave to their trade. Most go into hiding after amassing huge fortunes, simply to escape the constant demand on their powers.

"What's its level?" I asked Kallis about the ring that had turned him suddenly more youthful.

Kallis smiled slyly. "A nine."

My brow rose in surprise. "So, this thief steals the Promise and leaves a level-nine ring behind?"

Kallis sighed and nodded. "My ring is newly minted, so it's possible that the thief didn't know how valuable the cache in the humidor was."

I doubted that, but I wasn't going to quibble over a valuable trinket being left behind.

"What about your attaché?" I asked.

"My attaché?"

"Yes, Mr. Kallis. The spy you invariably brought with you when you came to Elric and Petra's court."

Kallis's complexion flushed with anger. "That is a fiendish accusation!"

I yawned. No diplomat showed up in another territory without bringing along a spy of his own. Or two. Or twelve.

I moved over to a wingback chair and sat down, leaning into the cushion and lazily crossing my legs. With a bobbing foot I said, "Can we please dispense with the semantics, and may I speak to the member of your entourage that you left behind when you went to the summit but wasn't specifically assigned to guard your hotel suite?"

Kallis's lips pressed together in a thin line. To admit he had more in his entourage than it appeared, he'd be openly confessing to bringing along a spy, and copping to something like that in Elric's territory was dangerous business indeed.

"I'll keep whatever you disclose about this mystic to myself," I said, before holding up my pinkie and adding, "Pinkie swear."

Kallis's complexion reddened. I'd just angered and insulted him with the pinkie swear, but I didn't see how I had much choice.

There were no apparent clues in the hotel suite to point me in a direction, so I needed to speak to a witness who might've seen or heard something, and the best candidate for a witness to the theft was going to be Kallis's spy.

"The assistant to my assistant was in-house at the time of the theft, Miss Van Dalen, but I've already spoken to him, and he knows nothing."

I thought it a bit quaint that Kallis had used the words "spoken to" when we both knew he'd very likely tortured the poor man both as punishment for dropping his guard and to procure information.

"Still . . ." I said, letting the word hang for a moment before continuing. "I want to be thorough in my investigation. Speaking to your assistant's assistant is rather imperative."

Kallis worked his jaw for a bit. "I can arrange for a meeting in a few days," he said at last, which told me that he'd likely tortured the man to death. There would be no follow-up interview.

I sighed and got up from the sofa to walk toward the humidor. Pointing to it I asked, "May I?"

He eyed me warily but nodded. Lifting the lid, I peered inside and took note of a few of the other trinkets hidden within, namely a silver-and-pearl tie clip; a set of onyx cufflinks; a solid-gold Roman aureus with Emperor Augustus's likeness; a platinum sapphire-and-emerald broach in the shape of a dragonfly; and a gold-and-diamond Bulgari key ring, sans keys.

The odd mix of items wasn't necessarily what caught my attention; it was the magic wafting upward from the box that had my senses tingling. Frankly, the intense pulse of magic coming from the humidor was to be expected for someone of Kallis's age, experience, and title.

Still, I eyed the diplomat skeptically. "You're telling me that this thief managed to get past your guard, your attaché, *and* your wards, then into this room both completely unheeded and undetected and he only made off with *one* trinket, Mr. Kallis? One trinket when he could've taken all of these?"

Kallis's face reddened, and I realized that I'd embarrassed and insulted him yet again. He pulled a large breath of air in through his nose and said, "Perhaps that was intentional."

"What does that mean?"

"Perhaps it was a directive from another mystic . . . another *powerful* mystic to steal only Pandora's Promise and leave the other trinkets behind."

"But that doesn't make sense," I insisted. "No professional thief would resist the temptation to remove at least *something* else."

Kallis's flushed face became even redder. "And yet," he said crisply, "here we are, Miss Van Dalen, with only Pandora's Promise missing while the others have been left behind."

"None of the comeback spells have worked?" He'd said as much earlier but I wanted to make sure.

"No."

There were so many holes in Kallis's story that it was getting harder and harder to believe anything had been removed from his humidor at all. I was beginning to wonder if he'd invented the story of the Promise being stolen. Perhaps it was still in Vostov's court on the other side of the pond.

But then there was the story of Henry being fed to the Drazilla, and that made no sense at all, either. I just couldn't see the logic behind creating such an elaborate ruse.

Moving away from the humidor, I took a seat back in the wingchair, collecting my thoughts before I spoke again. "Sir," I said after a long moment of reflection. "I mean no disrespect, however, if the thief had taken all of your trinkets or even some of your trinkets, I might've been able to put together a suspect list of the professional thieves I know to be in attendance for the summit."

Kallis eyed me with raised brows. "You keep lists of the thieves from the other courts?"

"Of course we do. Elric Ostergaard is nothing if not solicitous but cautious."

Kallis scowled. Reaching into his suit coat's interior pocket, he pulled out a piece of folded paper, which he handed to me.

I took it and opened the folds, revealing a list of familiar names—including four who were employed at SPL Inc.

I smirked, but then I pointed out the names of the thieves that Elric employed and said, "None of Elric's employees could've been responsible for the theft."

"How do you know that?"

"Because Elric would hand them over to Jacquelyn in a heartbeat, and trust me, they'd be *wishing* they were about to be fed to the Drazilla."

Jacquelyn was Elric's professional assassin, and one of his most trusted advisors. I liked her in spite of the fact that she was rather bloodthirsty.

Jacquelyn also had an array of pet dragons (yes, they exist) and she occasionally offered the beasts something they considered a fine delicacy . . . a traitorous mystic.

Kallis held his hand out for the list, and I gave it back to him. "If it is discovered that anyone in your court had something to do with this theft, Miss Van Dalen, it wouldn't go over well with the other courts. Diplomats and their trinkets are off-limits by the rules of the Prussian conventions."

Much like the Geneva conventions of the unbound world, the Prussian conventions had been established at the end of the Mystic Wars to create order, build trust, and bind alliances. Every one of the Seven had agreed to the rules—thus binding them to the promises within the conventions. If Elric knowingly employed a thief to steal from the property of a diplomat, he'd be in breach of a convention, and that wasn't something his magic—even as powerful as he was—would ever allow. Contractual signatures were as binding as any binder's spell, which meant that he could no more break that oath than he could give away all of his magical powers. It was simply unthinkable.

"I will remind you, Mr. Kallis, that Elric signed the original conventions decree *and* all of its amendments. He's incapable of breaking any of those rules."

"But the mystics under him aren't," Kallis insisted.

"True, but no mystic under Elric's employ would *ever* dare to defy him. They'd be held . . . accountable. And made an example of. It couldn't have been anyone from his court. It simply couldn't."

"Then it was someone from another court," Kallis said.

I nodded. It was the only logical conclusion. But why they wanted only Pandora's Promise was a mystery. What would it gain them?

Eyeing Kallis thoughtfully I asked, "What did you use Pandora's Promise for?"

"What do you mean?" he asked coyly.

"I mean that the trinket was an assassin's tool, and you acquired it—I'm assuming—to fulfill that purpose, so why did Vostov entrust that particular trinket to you in the first place?"

Kallis surprised me with an honest answer. "I've had the trinket for nearly two centuries. I've only used it in the most extreme instances where the Court of Vostov was threatened."

"When was that?"

"Specifically?"

"Yes. Specifically."

"1901, 1919, 1938, and 1943."

My brow furrowed. Ticking the dates off on my fingers, I repeated them with their probable context. "1901 during the Boxer Rebellion, 1919 during the German Revolution, 1938 during the Spanish Civil War, and 1943 during World War Two?"

"Correct."

"Those were all conflicts from the unbound world."

"Yes," he said, without further explanation.

And then it dawned on me. "Pandora's Promise wasn't used on mystics," I said softly. "You used it against the unbound."

"As I said, I only employed the Promise when the Court of Vostov was threatened."

I knew that the Court of Vostov, once one of the weakest courts, had risen in power over the last century, but I hadn't known how. Only now did I see the connection.

It was an unspoken rule that mystics didn't get involved in the politics of the mortal world. It was far too risky for our kind to draw the attention of the unbound, so we generally stayed out of their politics.

Wars were a slightly different story, but not by much. Most mystics simply went into hiding, which wasn't a hard thing to do. A good cloaking spell could keep one out of the prying eyes of the unbound for dozens of years if need be.

So to hear that Kallis and the Court of Vostov had been involved in the shifting of power among mortals during several high-stakes conflicts to gain their own growing advantage was somewhat shocking. Perhaps given our nature it wasn't entirely so, but Elric wouldn't like to hear how Vostov had done it. Then again, when I thought about it, there was little Elric *didn't* know, so he'd likely voiced his disapproval but hadn't acted to prevent it.

"How dangerous is Pandora's Promise to a mystic?" I asked.

"If one of our kind is unsuspecting, then it's quite dangerous," the foreign diplomat said. "One would need to be aware that the trinket was at hand and avoid looking inside the box."

A lightbulb went off in my mind and I pointed to the humidor. "Which is why you thought your trinket box was safe. If a thief was looking inside it for goodies, he'd definitely want to take a peek inside the ring box. Which means that instead of coming back here from the dinner to a stolen trinket, you would've found yourself a dead mystic."

"Exactly," Kallis said. "The Promise *was* the ward of protection for the other trinkets in the humidor."

"So, who knew you brought the Promise here?"

Kallis shook his head. "No one," he said simply. "I told no one."

"Not even Vostov?" He'd already answered this but I wanted to make sure he was sticking to his story.

"Of course Vostov, but no one else."

"I still don't understand why you brought it here."

"I did not intentionally or unintentionally bring it along, Miss Van Dalen. It is simply a trinket I keep with me at all times."

"And now that it's missing, it poses a significant threat. You have to tell the other summit attending diplomats that it's missing."

"No," he said curtly.

"Mr. Kallis, if one of them ends up dead, *you'll* be blamed."

"I doubt that," Kallis said with a soft chuckle.

"What do you mean you doubt that?"

"We're in Elric and Petra's territory. Do you believe anyone would think the Court of Vostov would be so bold as to assassinate another court's diplomat within the protected territory of Elric and Petra? Risk incurring their wrath? No. It would be madness, and no one would believe it. But they *would* believe that Elric or Petra had done it in a display of power."

I frowned, processing the fact that everything Kallis had just said was true. If it was discovered that a powerful trinket like Pandora's Promise was responsible for another visiting mystic's murder—especially one from a rival court—no one would believe that the Court of Vostov was involved. They'd blame Elric and/or Petra. And that, I believed, was the *real* reason Kallis had brought the Promise to these shores. He'd intended to assassinate someone with it, he just didn't get the chance before it was stolen.

Staring hard at Kallis, because I knew my choices were limited, I said, "I'll find your trinket, Mr. Kallis, but then I'm handing it over to Elric, and he can decide whether or not to return it to you."

Kallis's eyes widened and then his expression darkened. "No! You cannot! It belongs to the Court of Vostov. It must be returned to me!"

I got up to leave, and as I passed him, I looked him dead in the eye. "Take it up with the Court of Ostergaard."

CHAPTER 3

I made it back to SPL Inc. just before six p.m. after conducting numerous other interviews with a few of the unbound hotel staff including housekeeping and the front clerks, eventually finding that no one had seen anything suspicious the night before.

I even looked through security video, but because there were several mystic diplomats staying in the hotel, all of the video footage was unviewable.

We're a secret bunch and we wouldn't trust the unbound to have video evidence of the odd employment of a trinket or two within the walls and halls of the hotel.

In other words, it was a day spent producing no leads or even a direction to go in. Elric wasn't going to like that progress report, but I owed it to him to tell him what I was up against. We might need to wait for an obvious sign that the Promise had been used before I could drum up a lead to follow.

"Hello, Sequoia," I said after stepping into the lobby.

She smiled at me in a way that seemed gleeful, and then she held up a silver ballpoint pen and depressed the clicker. In an instant she disappeared.

"Whoa!" I said, laughing.

She reappeared and that grin was even wider. Holding up the pen again, she said, "A new trinket for the coffers."

"Did Elric give that to you?"

"No," she said, disconsolately. "But he is letting me play with it for a bit. Oh! And I have money for you."

Sequoia dug around in her drawer and lifted out a thick envelope, which she handed to me.

"The brunette made it through?"

"She did indeed," she said, playing with the golden feather charm around her neck. "No one was more surprised than me, though. I'd have bet my falcon feather that she'd never leave the building on her own power."

"Well, good for her," I said, happily thumbing through the cash. Looking up again I said, "Is he in?"

Sequoia nodded. "He's got plans for dinner with the other members of the summit, but he doesn't have to leave for another fifteen minutes. I'll tell him you're—"

"Tortelduif," Elric said from just behind me.

"—here," Sequoia finished, with another big smile. Then she held up the pen as if to taunt her boss and clicked the stopper.

I laughed and turned to Elric, who seemed less amused by Sequoia's antics. He held up his hand, whispered a few words, and she was suddenly outlined by a glittering shimmer. "Take that to the trinket room, Sequoia."

"Awww," she complained, but then we watched her glittering form walk off toward the elevator and the trinket storage room one floor down.

"You're back," he said, pulling me close.

I put my hands on his shoulders. "You know I can never resist an excuse to see you."

He lifted a finger to tuck a lock of hair behind my ear. "You have news."

"I do."

"Come," he said, taking my hand. "We'll speak in my office."

I laced my fingers through his when I felt his hand stiffen, and his gaze traveled to the elevators, where Sequoia's glittering form still stood waiting for the boxcar. The bell dinged indicating the elevator had arrived and when they parted, standing there was Petra, looking radiant in a gown of glittery white, embossed with thousands of pearls and wearing a tiara of diamonds and rubies.

She took one look at Sequoia's glittering outline and snarled. Sequoia clicked the pen, appeared in full form, and bowed to Petra in a display of deference that I'd never give her.

As if sensing me in the area, Petra's gaze immediately found mine, and as it did so, my stomach muscles clenched, but it wasn't just my reaction. Hissing out a breath, I bent double. The pain was so sudden that it completely caught me by surprise.

"My pet," Elric said smoothly to her while never letting go of my hand. "Play nice."

I looked up at Elric, pleadingly when the pain didn't ease up.

His passive expression evaporated, and he stepped purposely in front of me to stare down his wife. "Do not goad me here in my court, my pet. There will be consequences."

Petra's smile was reptilian, but she released me from the spell and the pain in my stomach vanished, but it left behind a residual nausea that made me consider bolting for the ladies' room.

Closing my eyes, I focused my energy and was able to quell most of the nausea. I then stood up tall, flipped my hair out of my face, and stared defiantly back at Elric's wife.

I wasn't jealous of her in the slightest—Elric detested her—but there was no such thing as divorce in the mystic world because a promise made by two mystics, holding hands during their wedding vows, was a bond that could only be broken in death.

And, since reducing the power couple down to one would most definitely invite a challenge from one of the other five courts, they worked hard to protect each other while openly displaying their disdain.

Elric couldn't assassinate his wife, but he'd kill someone close to her in a heartbeat. And, while Petra had very, very few mystics that were close to her, it was said that she had a particular fondness for her new lieutenant, Finn the Flayer.

Who sounded *charming.*

In turn, Petra couldn't assassinate Elric, but she'd been working on plans to have me murdered since the early days of my binding.

The constant threat she posed made my life a rather . . . delicate dance of being close to Elric while staying out of her sightline, and the less she saw of me the better.

"There are rumors," she said, turning fully to him with the hint of a snarl.

"And they are?" he asked in a bored tone.

"A trinket was stolen. From one of the visiting diplomats."

Elric still held firmly to my hand while also continuing to shield me from Petra's view. He was six feet five inches, and she was five feet four—in heels—so it wasn't that difficult.

Still, I held very still, and waited for their tête-à-tête to wrap up.

"I'm aware of the rumors," he said evasively.

"And?" she snapped, resting her hand on her hip.

"And nothing. I'm dealing with it."

Petra wasn't having it. "This could turn into something much bigger than mere rumors and a stolen trinket, Elric. Kallis is one of Vostov's most trusted advisors. The fact that his trinket was stolen in your territory makes us look petty and ineffectual. At the very least it's an insult that we'd allow this sort of thing to occur in our court. If it gets back to Vostov, or if the other courts learn of it, we could be challenged."

"I told you, I'm dealing with it," he repeated, without a single hint of the irritation that I knew he must be feeling.

"So, it was one of yours, then," Petra said, less question than statement.

Elric chuckled. "Certainly not. I was thinking it was someone from *your* court, Petra. Perhaps that new lieutenant of yours. What's his name again? Fitz the Filleter?"

Petra was silent for a long, tense moment, which I spent holding my breath lest the burst of laughter I was desperate to hold back came out.

"I wouldn't be so quick to dismiss my lieutenant, *husband*. His skills are nearly a match for yours."

Elric puffed out a dismissive breath of air. "You've stated your case, *wife*. I've told you I'm handling it. There's nothing left to discuss."

"Again, you're too quick to dismiss the strategic next move."

"And that is?"

"We need to go to the dinner tonight presenting a united front. My car is waiting for us downstairs."

It was Elric's turn to take a long moment to contemplate Petra's statement. "Fine. Go to your car, Petra, and wait for me. I'll be along soon."

When I heard the clicking of her heels on the marble floor as she retraced her steps to the elevator, I squeezed Elric's hand and he turned to stare down at me. "Duty calls."

"It does." I put on a brave front, smiling up at him, but I felt so let down. It was my birthday and he wasn't even going to spend more than a few minutes with me.

"Duty calls for both of us," he said next, and I knew what he meant. It was now a more urgent matter to recover the Promise and put the rumors to rest.

"Understood. I'll get back on the case immediately."

He kissed me, then held me at arm's length and with a rare smile he said, "Tomorrow will be soon enough for that, Tortelduif. Tonight, enjoy your birthday."

I leaned against his chest and wrapped my arms around him, giving him a brief hug before leaving him via the back stairwell, in order to avoid any further encounters with Petra.

My first stop after leaving SPL was back home to feed Bits.

Bits, my hedgehog, was a gift from Elric, given to me in the summer of '43 . . . 1843 to be exact. I'm not sure why Elric chose the sweet little picklepuss for me; perhaps he had a feeling I'd take to the little guy immediately, which of course I had.

Keeping Bits alive all these years hasn't been too difficult. Elric had enchanted him, which is a feat all on its own.

Mystics are certainly capable of enchanting their pets—I know of a horse that's seven hundred years old, and a couple of cats that're perhaps older than that—but as a rule, we do it only rarely. If anyone knew that Elric had enchanted a hedgehog for no other purpose than to keep me company all these long years, it could throw into question his ruthless reputation, so I mostly kept Bits's origin story a secret.

When I walked through the door I found him on the counter, nibbling his way through a container of Cheerios. How he'd gotten on the counter or managed to open the airsealed container was a bit of a mystery. Bits had all sorts of odd quirks to him that are a result of his enchantment.

"Hello, Itty-Bitty," I cooed as I came forward to stroke his quills. Bits immediately rolled onto his back, exposing his soft underbelly while still eating his Cheerios.

I laughed and stroked his pinkish fur, adding a tickle, and he let out a little squeak, then he rolled back onto his paws and continued making his way through my Cheerios inventory.

"So what should I wear to dinner tonight, Bits?" I asked.

He set a Cheerio down and waddled forward into my palm as if he knew his expertise was needed.

Cradling him, I carried him upstairs to the master bedroom which I'd decorated in shades of ivory, bone, and white, with lots of furry textures, twinkling lights, candles, and minimal other accents to create the perfect hygge sanctuary.

Setting Bits down on the plush, white, lambskin fur throw that draped the edge of my bed, I went to my closet and began to riffle through my wardrobe. A little prickle at my foot let me know Bits had come in to help.

I looked down at him and set my hands on my hips. "Okay, you pick the outfit then, little minx. What should I wear to my birthday dinner?"

Most mystics are quite material creatures, and I'm no exception. It's all because we're conditioned to focus on trinkets and objects of value, and this extends to all other material objects we covet or crave.

Even before my binding, fashion was my obsession, and it's only become more intense through the years. But I tend to look at dressing myself less like an extension of who I am, and more as a means of communication.

Fashion, at its heart, is poetry. It's a way of flirting with the world without needing to say a word, and every day I engage with countless others in conversations simply by walking down a busy street filled with pedestrians or entering a shop or other public venue.

I love the magnificently nuanced language of fashion, and my wardrobe reflects it.

Bits has always seemed to understand this, and I've often wondered if Elric didn't specifically enchant the little guy with that particular trait simply to please me.

As I watched him waddle over to the far left of the closet, which was arranged by color, I once again delighted in this quirky side to his personality.

Abruptly, Bits stopped waddling and got up on his hind legs, sniffing the air above him. I looked to where he'd paused and saw that he'd chosen a silver-blue silk blouse that brought out the color in my blue eyes. "Good choice," I told him.

Bits then waddled back toward the right side of the closet and took up the same pose under a pair of ivory dress pants which clung to my thighs but flared out below the knee. "Love it," I said, reaching for the slacks.

Bits set off again, moving to the back of the closet where my shoe collection was neatly stacked. He stopped in front of a shoebox labeled MANOLO-BUCKLE PUMPS-BLUE.

"Excellent choice, Bitty!" The shoes were a favorite of mine, exquisitely made of cobalt-blue suede with matching buckle along the top of the foot, a slingback strap, and a kitten heel.

Bits seemed to feel good about his choices too, because he yawned, then curled himself into a ball where he'd no doubt fall asleep in seconds.

Lifting him very gently off the floor, I took him to the plush burrowing bed where he liked to sleep, which was next to my own bed. As I settled him in the folds, I observed that he now looked like a ball of cactus. Nothing of his face, ears, or soft underbelly was exposed. He'd be asleep for hours.

After showering and getting dressed, I reached for some jewelry without asking for Bits's help. Observing in the full-length mirror that I looked a bit like the beach on a summer's day, I continued the theme with some large pearl earrings, a thick pearl choker, a pearl-studded cuff bracelet, and a dome pearl cocktail ring surrounded by diamonds that'd been a gift to myself a few decades back.

Topping the entire look off with a silver-blue pashmina draped over one shoulder, I ran a manicured fingernail across Bits's round prickled body one last time and headed off.

At exactly seven thirty I arrived at my destination and parked in the driveway of an adorable cottage in the section of Alexandria called Old Town.

After knocking on the door, I waited a bit for the door to be answered, and when it wasn't I tried the handle and the door opened wide. "Hello?" I called from the front stoop. "Ursula?"

There was a shuffling sound from inside and I poked my head in to find one of my dearest friends rapidly wrapping herself in a robe, her skin wet and her platinum-blond hair twisted up in a knot on top of her head.

Ursula Göransdotter is one of the few mystics that I could trust besides Elric. Mystics are a scheming lot by nature, and most of us are always looking for an angle to exploit, but Ursula's different. She holds no love for court politics, even though her allegiance to Elric's court is unshakable, and she's almost never looking to advance herself by surrounding herself with underlings.

She's independent, opinionated, strong, and feminine in manner, appearance, and style. I simply adore her.

A drop-dead gorgeous, Brigitte Bardot lookalike, she's the epitome of seduction, which was appropriate given her talent for creating some of the most powerful love potions ever concocted. Other than that, she's not especially powerful, except in one key area that has been of so much importance to Elric that he keeps her on the payroll—at a handsome monthly allotment—for that one sole purpose.

"Dovey!" she said, seeing me in the doorway. "Come in, come in!"

I laughed as she skipped to me and wrapped me in a hug. "Hello, friend!"

Stepping back, she pushed at the lump of hair atop her head. "I'm so sorry, I'm running late. I spent far too much time today crafting a potion for one of the visiting diplomats."

"Oh?" I asked. "Which one?"

She smiled in that way that told me she wouldn't name names, but she'd give me a hint. "He prefers the gentle nature of a Nairobi princess."

I burst out laughing. It was common knowledge that Ram Agastaya, from the court of Mostafa, was absolutely infatuated with Elric's assistant, Sequoia.

Trouble was, he'd never been able to get more than an up-down look—filled with disdain—from her.

"How many love potions does that make so far for Ram?"

Ursula chortled, squeezing my arm. "Seven, but who's counting?" She added an airy wave and said, "Sequoia always sees him coming. He hasn't been able to fully capture her attentions yet, but he definitely gets points for trying."

As potent as Ursula's love potions were, they could never overcome a mystic's will. Ursula believed in love, romance, attraction . . . not the ability to take advantage of another. Anyone who consumed her potions was still firmly connected to reality and their own faculties. The potions simply allowed the object to see the suitor in their very best light, and if romance bloomed, then it bloomed willingly.

"Has he ever thought about pursuing her sister?" I asked. Sequoia had an identical twin sister, who was far more congenial to open displays of affection.

Ursula sighed. "I've tried to tell him, but he likes who he likes. Anyway, come in! I'm almost ready. I opened a bottle of wine and I'm letting it breathe. Make yourself at home and I'll be out momentarily."

I smiled at her departing form and moved toward the kitchen.

Ursula's cottage is decorated in a French parlor fashion, with plenty of vintage furniture and accents from Paris, circa the 1920s.

She'd lived in Paris off and on over the years—it was her favorite city—and you might think that someone with her beauty and her preoccupation with love would be a bit flaky or vapid, but Ursula is one of the smartest mystics I know.

She speaks well over fifty languages fluently, and she's a

scholar of European literature from the early tenth century to the current age.

Her home smells like gardenias and old books—which she has *plenty* of, and it's not unusual to find a huge stack of volumes near her favorite parlor chair, which she'll be reading all at the same time.

It's rumored that Elric is responsible for her binding as well as mine, but she's never admitted that to me, as I've never admitted my binder's identity to her. Still, her affection for him extends well beyond fealty. She absolutely abhors Petra, mostly because, in a fit of jealousy, Petra once killed one of Ursula's lovers.

Which is when she became very useful to Elric for a unique talent that my friend has mastered, and that is to lower or raise any mystic's or unbound's IQ. She can do it slowly or quickly, and I've seen her do it both ways firsthand.

Over the last decade, Ursula has been slowly lowering Petra's IQ one tiny point at a time. It's barely noticeable to those of us who've been patiently watching for signs that Petra's mental acuity is slowing down, and if Petra ever found out, she'd order Ursula fed to one of the many monsters she keeps in the bowels of the massive stronghold west of the city where she holds court.

I doubted Elric would allow Ursula to lower Petra's IQ much more than it is now, which meant she was still a very sharp and shrewd woman, but she'd almost always been able to outsmart her husband in centuries past, and now, often, she lost the game of wits to him.

Pouring myself a glass of Opus One, I took a moment to savor the smooth red wine's black currant and blackberry undertones, mixed with floral hints of lavender and lilac, and the tannins that lingered on the palate making savoring the wine even more delicious.

Ursula really knows her wines.

I moved over to the stove where something delicious simmered. In a jar next to the stove sat a small pot with a brown powder. Lifting it, I smelled notes of espresso and pepper. My gaze traveled to a plate with two beautiful cuts of filet mignon, pressed with the rub in the jar, now ready for the broiler. Roasting in one of the two double ovens were fondant potatoes, while roasted carrots topped with goat cheese, walnut, and balsamic glaze sat on the counter.

"Ursula, you spoil me," I whispered, taking another whiff of the espresso which would smother the filet mignon in a fireworks of flavors.

With a contented sigh I moved back into the living room and sat down on the feather-filled cushions of Ursula's wonderfully soft sofa and reached for the remote control, flipping on the TV while I waited for my host.

The local news was on, and the lead story immediately got my attention.

The news camera was transmitting images of a smoldering ruin of what, according to the chyron at the bottom of the screen, had been an art gallery owned by a prominent citizen named Augustus Ariti, a Greek national who hailed from the prominent and powerful Ariti family in Greece.

The reporter on scene was telling the anchor that it appeared Augustus had died in the fire, which the reporter noted was a tragically sad coincidence. In an interview Augustus had given to that same reporter when the gallery had first opened, he had mentioned how he'd been badly burned by a candle that'd caught his trousers on fire when he was a child, and he lived in fear of it ever since.

"I remember you interviewing him about that experience," said the anchor to the reporter, her face a mask of alarm and confusion. "He told you he still had nightmares from when he was a little boy."

"Yes," said the reporter. It was clear she was shaken by the terrible news. "I can't imagine how this could happen to Mr. Ariti."

The anchor thanked the reporter and swiveled back to face the camera, wrapping up the story to note who Augustus was survived by.

"Oh, goodness," said Ursula as she came up next to me. "That looks dreadful."

I got to my feet and turned to face her. "You're going to hate me."

She cocked her head curiously. "I could never, ever hate you, Dovey. You are terminally forgivable."

Placing my hands on her arms which were now ensconced in a light lavender angora sweater, I said, "I'm afraid I need to go."

Ursula's eyes widened. "Go? But you just got here!"

I closed my eyes and nodded, feeling such guilt because she'd gone to so much trouble. "A trinket was stolen last night from one of the visiting diplomats—"

"Which one?"

I opened my eyes and said, "Nicodemus Kallis. The trinket was one of the Pandoras."

Ursula gasped. "No!"

"Yes."

"Which one?"

"The Promise."

"That's the ring box, correct?"

I nodded. "And you may also remember, the Promise brings about the death of the subject in the manner in which that subject fears the most."

My friend tapped her lip with her finger. "I remember."

Ursula has a vast knowledge of the most famous trinkets on earth since she reads just about everything associated with the mystic world.

"The Promise being in some rogue person's hands is a dangerous proposition, Dovey."

"I'm aware. Which is why I need to get down to that gallery."

Ursula pointed toward the television, understanding dawning. "You think it did that?"

"I do."

"Was the victim unbound?"

"I believe so, but I'll need to confirm it."

"Do you think he was targeted?"

"Yes. Most likely, yes."

Ursula shook her head and blew out a breath. "Dovey, that could be really bad. You know how the courts won't abide using magic in such a public way. It'll draw attention. Attention we don't need."

"Agreed, and, again, it's why I have to go."

My friend frowned. "I'm coming with you."

"What?"

"I'm coming with you. Give me just a moment to tuck away our dinner—we can eat it later—and then we can go to the gallery. Or what's left of it. Maybe we'll even find the remnants of the trinket."

I nodded, but felt that that'd be far too easy, so I wasn't about to get my hopes up.

"I'll help you put away—"

"No, stay put," she said over her shoulder as she headed to the kitchen. "Finish your wine. I'll drive."

"Okay, I'll wait. But hurry, Ursula. This could get tricky for Elric. Quickly."

And the sinking feeling in the pit of my stomach seemed to confirm that the tricky times were just beginning.

Chapter 4

Ursula drove us to the gallery's location, which, when we got close, wasn't hard to spot. Fire trucks and news vans were cluttering the street, which was also roped off by caution tape and uniformed police.

"I'll have to park here," Ursula said, pulling over to the curb about two blocks away.

We got out and began to walk toward the smoldering ruins, but when we got close to the police line, one of them held up his hand and said, "You can't come any closer, ladies."

Ursula beamed her gorgeous smile at him. "We wouldn't think of it, Officer. I just wanted to offer you some water." Reaching into her handbag she extracted a clear bottle of water which she offered to the man. "Thank you for your service, sir."

He took the bottle eagerly . . . perhaps a bit too eagerly.

After unscrewing the cap, he took a tentative sip, his eyes widening, then he took a big gulp. "Wow," he said, holding the bottle aloft. "This water tastes so good! I didn't know I was that thirsty."

Ursula nodded. "You looked quite parched."

The officer downed the entire contents of the bottle, allowing himself a big sigh after he'd polished it off. Handing the plastic bottle back to Ursula he said, "Thank you. That was just what I needed." He then beamed a smile at us.

Ursula pointed to the caution tape. "We'd like to pass through here now."

"Of course!" he said, lifting the tape for us to duck under. "I'll wait here until you get back," he added while we bent to go under the tape and began to walk forward.

Ursula glanced over her shoulder, artfully allowing her sweater to fall away and expose the bare skin of her shoulder. "Thank you, Officer. We'll be a little while, but we'll be back."

I shook my head as we continued forward. "Do you always pack a love potion?"

"Of course I do. I wouldn't dream of leaving home without one." She then winked and added, "Or two."

I chuckled, looked down at the inlaid pearl bracelet I was wearing on my right wrist, and pushed a little bit of my essence into it, to activate the charm. Then I looped an arm through Ursula's, and we maneuvered together around the thinning cluster of first responders. The firemen were winding up their hoses, a few police were driving away, and even the news crews were wrapping it up.

No one seemed to notice us—which meant the bracelet was doing its job. And while it didn't make us invisible, it did subject the unbound who observed us not to think anything of our presence.

"That's a nice little trinket, Dovey," Ursula said, tapping the bracelet.

I grinned. "It comes in handy."

My work often takes me into unbound territory, and the bracelet allows me to canvas an area without anyone taking note.

Arriving at the still smoldering ruin, I let go of Ursula's arm and we stepped carefully over the debris littering the sidewalk to the very edge of what was left of the gallery.

Heat was still wafting off the embers and ash filling the hull that'd once been Ariti's gallery. There wasn't anything left, really, save the burned-out hull. Part of the roof had collapsed but half of it remained, and through one of the large, now open windows we could see a lone fireman, walking through the ash and rubble spraying any burning ember he could find with fire retardant.

He didn't even look up when we stepped close. "Are we going to shuffle through all that?" Ursula asked, her mouth curving down in a frown.

I sighed. Neither one of us was dressed for such a task, and I had no trinkets handy that would help keep the still hot embers from burning and ruining my shoes, not to mention what it'd do to my skin.

"Do you see anything of note?" I asked her, looking through the window.

"No. I have a few trinkets back home we could try to sift through this mess, but Dovey, it's too hot tonight to pick through."

I sighed again. "All right. Let's go back and scan the crowd. Maybe there's a mystic among the unbound one of us will recognize and we'll have our thief."

"Good plan," Ursula said.

When we got close to the officer again, Ursula lifted her hand to wave at him and catch his attention.

His whole face lit up when he saw her, and he chivalrously lifted the tape for us to scoot under again. "I was waiting for you," he said eagerly.

Ursula lifted his palm and patted the back of his hand. "I know, dear. Can you tell us if there's been anyone lurking about in the crowd that seems suspicious to you?"

The officer scanned the crowd and pointed to someone behind us on my left. "That guy," he said. "He tried to get through, but I stopped him. He said he was FBI, but he's got no badge, so I told him to beat it."

I turned to look and saw a figure weaving his way through the crowd. Letting go of Ursula's arm, I hurried after him, but he was a wily one. As I pushed my way through the crowd, I made no headway in my efforts to reach him, and once I was through the thickest part of the gathered crowd, I found myself on an empty street, with the suspicious character nowhere to be seen.

I growled low in my throat. He'd evaded me, which wasn't an easy thing to do, but then, I was absent my usual bag of trinkets that perhaps would've made the job a little easier.

Ursula caught up with me and asked, "Did you see him?"

"No. And I never caught a good view of him either."

"Mystic?" she asked next.

I looked around at the empty street and raised my palms. "I don't know. Perhaps."

Ursula took up my arm again. "Well, it's getting late, Dovey, and I'm hungry. Let's go back for your birthday dinner, and if you want my help with this tomorrow, I'll come back here with you."

"Thank you," I said, feeling a bit ashamed to be ditching my investigation in favor of eating some birthday dinner, but Ursula was right. There wasn't much I could do until the embers had all burned out and daylight was at hand. And now that I'd lost sight of the suspicious character the cop had pointed out, what else could I do until morning?

"Okay, let's go," I told her. "But not too much wine for me. I'll need to have my wits about me tomorrow."

"You've got a deal," she said, and we left the scene.

The next morning, I was up well before dawn. I'd barely slept through the night because I was anxious to get started on my investigation, and I worried about the political fallout if I couldn't quickly recover the Promise for Kallis.

The Court of Vostov was one of Elric's strongest allies, so recovering it quickly was essential, and I didn't plan on letting Elric down.

After taking a good spin on my Peloton, I showered and changed into clothes suitable for rummaging through ash and debris, donning knee-high riding boots, black leggings, a soft denim blouse, and matching denim jacket.

Grabbing a pair of rubber gloves on my way out the door, I paused to gently stroke Bits as he lay completely rolled up in a spiny ball and dropped a few pieces of banana in his dish by the snuggle he was sleeping in.

After driving back to the gallery, I parked Luna in front of the burned-out husk of the gallery then moved toward the front door, which had been partially boarded up. As I'd anticipated this, I pulled out my trusty Swiss Army knife trinket and, using the blade, tapped lightly on the nails along the rim of the board. They came slowly out of their holes, plopping neatly into my palm, and once they were all out, it was an easy matter of lifting the board away from the wall and setting it aside.

I then pulled out a pair of plastic coverings to slip over my boots before stepping carefully into the interior of what was left of the gallery, and, because dawn was only now breaking, I switched on a flashlight and aimed the beam all around.

Water still dripped from the charred remnant of the part of the roof that was still intact and there were puddles of ash and water everywhere. I stepped carefully, but it was impossible to avoid stepping in the black muck, making me thankful that I had the plastic coverings to spare my expensive riding boots.

From what I could tell, however, the gallery had been designed as one large square. The left side of the building was more charred than the right, and there was a spot not far from the door where the fire had obviously burned the hottest due to a large hole in the wall that exposed the outside and the fact that the roof over that section of the gallery had collapsed, leaving charred timber and roof tiles scattered about.

I moved carefully over to the area, and I could see that the wood floor had burned almost completely away to reveal the concrete slab which was charred in the macabre outline of a body.

Next to it was an eight-by-six-inch rectangle that had covered a section of the floor, protecting the slab underneath from being charred. My guess was that was where Augustus had set the gas can he'd used as an accelerant.

As I stared at the square a shudder went through me. It was an unimaginable death, beyond cruel, and it made me wish that the Promise had been destroyed along with the gallery, but as I shuffled the debris around with my feet and used my gloved hands to sift through the wreckage near where Ariti had died, I couldn't find anything that resembled the small box. Intuitively, I knew it wasn't here.

Whoever had used it to murder Augustus had held on to it after exposing the man to it. And that sent another shudder up my spine. I had no doubt that it would be used again.

But the question in front of me seemed to be why was it used on Ariti in the first place. When I'd gotten home the night before, I'd done a small bit of research into the victim. Augustus Ariti was, by all accounts, quite mortal. I could find no trace of bound magic within his history, which again begged the question of why a mystic would use such powerful magical means to kill a mortal. It wasn't like they were hard to kill. A simple level three or four trinket could take out an unbound and leave no trace of them, or clue as to who had done it.

Deepening the mystery was why the thief had taken such risk to acquire the Promise only to use it on someone who would've been easy for anyone of the thief's level of skill, to kill.

The murder felt quite personal, and if I couldn't find clues within the ash and ruin, my next best bet was to investigate Ariti's background and try to discover any mystical connection to him. The personal nature of the crime suggested he knew his murderer—so how did an unbound become the acquaintance of a mystic willing to go to such lengths to kill him?

"You can't be here," a gravel-laden voice said.

I jumped and twirled around, ready to defend myself by any magical means necessary. Standing close by was an impossibly gorgeous man. He stood well over six feet tall with copper-brown hair, closely trimmed facial hair covering his lip and chin, light gray eyes, long lashes, a noble nose, and a set of the most delicious lips I'd ever seen on a man.

His build was broad and muscled, tapering to a narrow waist and long legs. Best of all, he was dressed in a way that suggested he knew how to put himself together.

With his white dress shirt, camel-suede blazer, a fringe silk scarf of a lighter color looped loosely around his neck, and light-colored khaki trousers that hugged his lower half and tapered down to the cognac-colored suede Italian loafers—sans socks—I thought him more suited for a runway than a crime scene.

Still, I hadn't loved the tone he'd greeted me with, and I saw no badge or official logo to suggest he was with law enforcement.

Crossing my arms, I regarded him skeptically. "Late for a photo shoot?"

His stern expression shifted to surprise, so I lifted an index finger in an up-down motion. When he looked down at himself, I swear he blushed ever so slightly. "On my way to brunch," he muttered as he reached into his back pocket, which caused me to take up a defensive stance.

He noticed and paused for a moment. "I'm getting my badge."

I didn't relax my posture until he'd pulled out a leather wallet and flipped it open, revealing his FBI credentials.

My initial thought was, *Uh oh*, and I wondered if this was the man from the night before who'd eluded me when he'd made his way away from me through the crowd.

Elric frowned on interactions with the unbound's law enforcement. It was an unwritten rule that we were to keep well away from their notice—*especially* the notice of the FBI.

Certainly, we could create spells and use trinkets to thwart trouble, however, Elric was a powerful enough figure in the world to attract attention simply by existing. He didn't need the attention of the unbound's primary official investigative unit to complicate things.

"Special Agent Barlow," my unbound companion said. "FBI."

I relaxed my stance and adopted a smile. "Special Agent," I said with a nod. Pointing to myself I added, "Dovey Van Dalen. Private investigator."

Agent Barlow squinted skeptically at me. I didn't think he was buying it.

Pulling my purse off my shoulder I asked, "Would you allow me to retrieve my P.I. license for you?"

Barlow's skeptical squint shifted to my monogramed Louis Vuitton carryall. He beckoned it with two fingers. "Allow me," he said.

It was my turn to blush. My bag was filled with nothing but my wallet, lip gloss, and trinkets. They were all inactive until I pushed my essence into them, which meant he wouldn't be finding anything that resembled a P.I. license among the items.

Hugging my handbag under one arm I said, "I'd prefer not."

If he forced the issue, I'd have no choice but to hand over my purse, but I wasn't about to do it readily. I had no idea what he might be willing to "confiscate" and some of the trinkets in my purse were quite valuable.

When his brow lowered, I added, "I've got a few unmentionables with me, and I'd prefer to simply retrieve my license and show you that I'm here legitimately, rather than have you paw through my personal items."

The corner of his mouth quirked. "Paw?"

My gaze traveled to his hands, which were clearly clean and well manicured. Nothing about this gentleman resembled a personality suited to the FBI. Or, at least, my impression of the men and women of the agency.

I sighed and pulled open my purse, ignoring his renewed guarded stance. Curling my hand around a small cosmetic mirror, I pushed a little essence into it before withdrawing it and flipping it open for Agent Barlow to inspect.

The makeup mirror has come in quite handy over the years . . . I like to drive fast, and the unbound's preoccupation with traffic laws and speed limits is often a nuisance, so I've been pulled over more than a few times, and the compact mirror has given every unbound police officer prepared to write me a ticket the impression that I'm a surgeon, speeding to the hospital for a medical emergency, or whatever other identity and circumstance might get me out of a ticket.

The mirror simply reflects what I want it to, and the unbound who stare at it once it's active see exactly what they expect to see in the form of credentials. It's certainly a handy little trinket.

Agent Barlow studied the mirror for longer than he should've, his eyes roving over it as if he were looking for a flaw. I wasn't worried. The compact had been studied intently by more than him over the past few decades, and it'd never failed me.

At last, he lifted his gaze back to me. "As a licensed P.I., you should know better than to cross crime scene tape and enter a boarded-up building."

"It wasn't boarded up when I got here." Lying to the unbound came naturally to me.

"Still, you're disturbing evidence."

I wanted to laugh. Looking pointedly from the plastic coverings on my boots to his bare Italian loafers, I said, "I didn't realize Del Toro made sterile loafers."

Barlow again looked down at himself and that slight quirk to the right side of his lips tugged up in amusement. "As I said, I'm on my way to brunch. I got assigned to this case late last night, was in the neighborhood and wanted to swing by to have a look when I saw you trampling all over my crime scene."

I mimicked his amused expression. "Trampling?"

"Like an elephant," he said, his expression quite amused.

I couldn't help it, I laughed. "Disturbing a little ash is hardly compromising your crime scene, Special Agent Barlow. I'm sure your sly detecting skills will overcome any disturbance that I or a slight breeze might make."

It was his turn to chuckle. "Still, Ms. Van Dalen, you can't be here. I need you to exit the premises."

I tossed my hands up casually and said, "Fine, fine. I'm leaving."

Barlow waited for me to walk in front of him toward the exit before following me. When we gained the sidewalk, I noticed what appeared to be a brand-new Range Rover Evoque in Tribeca blue with a Corinthian bronze contrasting roof and trim.

I knew it because it'd been a consideration when I was picking out a birthday present for myself before purchasing Luna, and while his car wasn't prohibitively expensive for a federal agent, it still presented a sleek and eye-catching silhouette that suited Barlow to a T.

"Nice," I said, pausing in front of the vehicle.

"Thanks," he said studying me with a curious expression before lifting his chin toward Luna. "I'll return the compliment. She's a beauty."

For a moment, Barlow's gaze darted to me, then back to Luna, and I couldn't quite determine if he meant me or the car.

"If I didn't know better, I'd say you were a bit flirtatious, Agent Barlow."

That quirk came back to the edge of his lips. "I'm a lot flirtatious, Ms. Van Dalen. It helps with the job."

I wanted to groan, but not in annoyance. I was beginning to like this man, which probably meant trouble. Scratch that, it definitely meant trouble. "Well, I'll leave you to it."

Turning away toward my car again, I heard Agent Barlow say, "Ms. Van Dalen, can I ask what you were doing investigating my crime scene?"

Glancing over my shoulder, I said, "Investigating your crime scene."

The quirk to his lips gave way to a full grin. "Well, that clears *that* up."

"Happy to help."

"I'm serious, though. Who hired you to investigate?"

I thought about offering him up something like, "That's privileged information," or, "I'm not at liberty to say," but I decided on something that might serve me better should Agent Barlow and I bump into each other again as I investigated Ariti's murder on my own.

So I smiled politely and said, "The family."

He cocked his head curiously. "You know the Aritis?"

"Only professionally."

"Which family member hired you?"

"I'm not at liberty to say at this time, Agent Barlow."

He leaned against the hood of his car, taking up a casual stance by crossing his legs and arms. It was when he crossed his arms together that I saw he wore an Audemars Piguet rose gold watch with a blue watch face. I recognized it because Elric had procured the same make and model a few years ago as a prized trinket to add to his collection, and he'd been wearing it yesterday when we'd met up.

I found the watch especially beautiful, and Elric's enchanted trinket could literally stop time while allowing Elric and anyone else in the room to move easily and freely as the rest of the world lay frozen between one second and the next. Its value was exponentially greater than the unbound's version, but even an unenchanted Piguet would run in the hundreds of thousands of dollars, making Agent Barlow all the more intriguing a puzzle, because while the car might be affordable on a fed's salary, that watch definitely *wasn't*.

If Barlow noticed that I'd taken note of his timepiece, he didn't let on when he asked me, "Any leads so far in your investigation?"

"Not yet. But then I've only been at it a few hours longer than you."

"If you come across material evidence, Ms. Van Dalen, you're obligated to turn it over to investigators."

"Investigators like you, I assume?"

He grinned again, and I felt a slight blush touch my cheeks. The man was far too charming and beautiful for my own good. And yet, I wasn't scurrying away or giving him the cold shoulder.

"Exactly," he said, answering my question. He then uncrossed his arms and reached into his back pocket to pull out his billfold. Lifting a card from the inside, he leaned out to hand it to me, and I took it. "Call me if you have anything of interest for me."

I nodded but didn't verbally commit, wondering what Elric would think if he came across Barlow's card on my person. The world's most powerful mystic would never harm me, of that I was certain, but Elric was fully capable of making an unbound disappear, never to be heard from again. In fact, for him that'd be child's play.

Reaching into my handbag, I opened my own business card case and tucked Barlow's inside, squeezing the lid closed to make sure the clasp was secure. The card case was a trinket that could only be opened by me, and it hid the written words of some of the more powerful enchantments I'd procured over the years, yet, oddly, it'd never held a business card of mine or anyone else's. Until now.

"I'll let you get to your brunch, Agent Barlow," I said in farewell, turning fully away and moving to Luna.

As I pulled the door open and began to get in, I heard him say, "Drive safe, Dovey Van Dalen."

Chapter 5

I spent the rest of the morning at headquarters researching any mystic connections to the Ariti family—finding none—and some additional time researching all the Pandoras still in existence. Out of the seven originally created, only five were left, each owned by a separate court. Somewhere in Elric's inventory sat Pandora's Prelude, which was perhaps the most powerful (deadly) of all the Pandoras as it had literally been responsible for the downfall of the entire Breghammer court back in 1547.

I finally made my way over to Ursula's around lunchtime and found her in the middle of a purge. Not the kind of purge that the unbound might undertake, mind you. No, this was a magical trinket purge and it's a ritual that most of us practice at least once a year.

There's a limit to how many uses a trinket can have. Eventually, all trinkets lose their "juice" so to speak, but not all at once. They typically lose their power over a period of time, diminishing level by level. Most trinkets are good for at least a hundred employments or more before they become rather useless. Merlin-made trinkets are perhaps the exception in that they only lose a tiny fraction of their power after each use, and most merlin trinkets can last several hundred years, even with a good deal of application.

As old as Ursula is—at least one millennium—she's not especially powerful, so she resists putting much of her energy into the creating of trinkets, preferring to trade a good potion or the translation of an archaic text of spells for one.

Which is perhaps why Ursula's magic-wielding ability is somewhat limited. She'd much prefer to read books about the history of spells—or books in general—than train herself to become more powerful. Normally this might make a mystic vulnerable as our kind can be cutthroat and cruel, but Ursula is genuinely well-liked and well respected within the community and her potions are revered for their quality, taste, and no next-day hangover.

I've never actually sampled her love potion wares, of course (there's been no need), but I've heard from many a satisfied customer that Ursula's potions have delivered an exceptional experience for all involved.

I found my friend at her home, sitting amongst a cluster of cups, quills, jewelry, knickknacks, and various odd other objects, testing each one before placing it in one of two boxes.

"Is it purge day already?" I asked, taking a pillow from a nearby chair to join her sitting akimbo on the floor of her living room.

She handed me a round crystal paperweight. "No, that's next month, but I thought I'd get a jump on it."

I held the paperweight in my palm and pushed a little of my essence into it. It glowed a beautiful blue for a moment, then hummed warmly in my hand. "What does this do?"

Ursula looked at me and said, "I find you incredibly annoying, Dovey."

My jaw dropped at the hurtful insult from one of my dearest friends until the paperweight glowed bright red.

I looked to it, then back to Ursula, who was grinning.

I grinned back. "Lie detector?"

She nodded. "One of my favorites. But lately it's been misfiring. Sometimes it glows brown instead of the red, yellow, or the green it's enchanted to display. As the red is for a lie, the green is for the truth, and yellow is for half of each, I've yet to figure out what the brown color's for."

"Hmmm, would you like me to tinker with it?" I'm often able to bank some of my essence into a trinket to give it a longer life.

"Would you?"

"Of course." I put the trinket into my handbag then surveyed the others on the floor. "Anything else here worth salvaging?"

Ursula sighed and selected a white mug with a gold rim. "This is giving me some problems."

"Beautiful cup," I said after she handed it to me. "What's the issue?"

"It's become too enchanted if you can believe it. I've been offering it to clients needing love potions packed with a bit more punch, and the cup seems to have absorbed some of that punch. It's only supposed to be enchanted to hold the spell long enough for the subject to drink the potion, but I offered one of my clients some plain water in it the other day and he chased me round the living room before I could convince him to drink an antidote."

I laughed. The idea of one of Ursula's clients chasing her around her living room while she frantically threw together the ingredients for an antidote was hilarious. "I'll see what I can do," I told her, setting the mug near my handbag.

Ursula placed a hand on my arm. "*Bedankt*," she said, thanking me.

"*Graag gedaan*," I replied with a smile.

Getting to her feet and offering me a hand to help me up, she said, "Let's get some lunch, Dovey. And you can tell me all about the progress you've made on your case."

I took her hand and eyed her curiously as I stood up. "How'd you know I'd made any progress?"

She chuckled. "Why else would you be here with that glint in your eye?"

I rolled my eyes. "Come on, mystic. I'll treat."

We arrived at a favorite eatery of ours in Old Town a short while later and were seated at the best table in the house, thanks to a little trinket key chain that Ursula employed whenever she was looking for a good parking spot or a good table at a restaurant.

"I love this place," she said as we sat down and opened our menus.

"I know," I told her, adding a wink. Ursula was perhaps the most romantic person I'd ever met; she loved to be wined and dined.

"So, tell me," she said, her eyes still firmly on the menu. "What have you learned so far?"

"Not much. I went to the crime scene this morning and couldn't find any trace of the Promise, but I did find what I think is the source of the fire."

"Which is?"

"I believe Augustus used an accelerant. There's what I suspect is the outline of a gas can next to where his body was found."

Ursula gave a shudder. "To know what was coming and be unable to stop yourself . . . What a horrible way to die."

I sighed and set the menu down. "Agreed."

"Any sign that Augustus was bound?"

I shook my head. "I did some background on him last night and again this morning. As far as I can tell, he was unbound. He lived too much out in the open to be one of us."

As a hard and fast rule, once we become spellbound, mystics tend to disappear from the circle of family and friends who might catch on to our magical ways. Most mystics move to other countries and adopt new identities to keep the secret of our binding away from curious eyes. It's always safer that way, given how nefarious some of our kind can be. Making a newly bound mystic your personal slave by threatening their family of unbounds is one way to climb the power ranks.

"Just to be sure, I checked all the census rolls at SPL, no Aritis on them." Elric kept track of all the mystics in his territory, both those who worked for him and those who didn't.

"How frustrating," Ursula said, her gaze lifting from the menu to settle on something over my shoulder.

"Definitely. Complicating things is that there does seem to be an FBI agent assigned to the case."

Ursula's expression lifted a bit, as if she were gazing at a work of art. "The unbound are easy enough to work around," she said, continuing to look over my shoulder.

Curious, I turned in my chair to see what had captured her attention and met the gaze of someone looking back at us.

And it wasn't any "someone." It was Special Agent Barlow.

"Helloooo, gorgeous," Ursula whispered. "Have I got a love potion for you!"

I turned back to her, startled to see Barlow in the restaurant so soon after leaving him at the crime scene this morning. Had he followed me?

The idea both excited and annoyed me.

Which was curious.

And troubling.

Mostly troubling.

Ursula leaned in, a sly expression on her face. "Do you know him?"

"We've met," I said curtly.

I felt a presence close to my chair before I heard him speak. "Ms. Van Dalen," he said in that rich, gravel baritone.

Ursula was still pressed forward over the table. She lifted her chin and extended her hand. "Ursula Göransdotter."

Barlow extended his own hand over my shoulder and shook Ursula's with a polite smile, no doubt taken by my friend's beauty. "Special Agent Grant Barlow."

"Charmed," she said, and her smile showed it.

Without invitation, Barlow pulled out one of the empty chairs at our table and sat down. "Are you two colleagues?" he asked, pointing back and forth at the two of us.

"Of a sort," Ursula answered, an excited twinkle in her eye at the boldness of the unbound sitting with us. "You must be the FBI agent assigned to the Augustus Ariti murder."

Barlow swiveled his gaze from Ursula to me. "Murder?" he repeated. "Jumping the gun a little, aren't we, Private Investigator Van Dalen?"

My own gaze shifted to Ursula, and I hoped she could see the subtle warning in my eyes. "Suspicious death."

He nodded but didn't offer anything more.

"What're you doing here, Agent Barlow?" I finally asked, not caring that I sounded rude.

He spread his hands wide. "Getting lunch. Same as you, I bet."

My brow furrowed. "Weren't you on your way to brunch when last we met?"

There was an annoying quirk to his lips when he answered, "Brunch got canceled last minute, so I've moved on to lunch."

"Are you ready to—oh!" our server said after she stepped up to the table. "I didn't realize my two-top had turned into a three-top. Can I get you a menu, sir?"

Barlow smiled at her practically oozing charm. "Hi, Tracy," he said, reading her name tag. "What do you recommend?"

Tracy blushed. "Ummm, the chicken marsala and the chicken piccata are popular."

Barlow nodded like he agreed. "I've had both, but today I think I'll have the Waldorf chicken salad."

I grimaced. That was the dish I'd been planning to order.

Ursula's gaze shot to me, and a sly smile tugged at the corners of her mouth. "That's Dovey's favorite! Put her down for a plate of that, Tracy, and I'll have the sole."

Tracy scribbled furiously on her order pad. "Anything to drink?"

"Iced tea," the three of said in unison, causing Ursula and Barlow to laugh, but I wasn't feeling so humorous right now.

The second Tracy left our table I focused my full attention on Agent Barlow. "Did you follow me here?" The prospect that he'd followed me to SPL and then again to Ursula's and here was unnerving at best.

His brow creased with what appeared to be genuine confusion. "No. Did you follow *me* here?"

"Definitely not," I said, irritated at the heat I could feel on my cheeks.

Ursula's eyes were eagerly pivoting back and forth between me and the agent and I wanted to swat the table to get her to stop.

"I figured when I saw you here that you must work for Eleni Katapotis."

I opened my mouth, but hesitated for a moment because, although the name sounded familiar, I was so flustered that I couldn't remember where I'd heard it. "Why would you think that?"

He hitched a thumb over his shoulder toward the street. "She lives in the building across the street."

Trying to cover myself I said, "Yes, I know, but why would you simply assume that I'm working for her?"

He hitched his thumb over his shoulder again and repeated more slowly, "Because she lives in the building across the street."

I glared at him.

He grinned.

Infuriating.

"I figured you'd already filled Eleni in about your excursion to her brother's crime scene," he said.

"Ah," I said, putting it all together. That's right. Eleni Katapotis, formerly Eleni Ariti. It was a simple coincidence that we'd picked this restaurant near where Augustus's sister lived.

While I tried to deal with being flustered, Ursula was busy looking her new friend over like she recognized him but couldn't quite place him. "You know who you look like?" she asked.

"Who do I look like, Ursula?"

"A gentleman I once knew. Amias Barlow. You two could be brothers."

Agent Barlow cocked his head curiously. "Amias was my grandfather. He lived in Yorkshire, England."

"Yes," Ursula said with a sly grin. "I know."

Barlow studied her, his expression now confused. "He died thirty years ago. Did you know him as a child?"

"Yes," she said.

From the interior of my handbag came a red glow, and I realized the paperweight I'd taken from her was exposing her lie.

"What is that?" Barlow asked, looking down and momentarily distracted.

"Oh, it's just a silly little gadget I bought for my nephew," I said quickly, reaching to my handbag to close it up tight. Before I could snap the clasp, the paperweight glowed even brighter. "It's got a mind of its own," I added with a small laugh.

"Here we are," Tracy said, setting down our iced teas and offering a much-needed interruption to the moment. "Your food should be right out."

"Thank you, Tracy," Barlow said, adding a warm smile. She blushed and hurried away. After she'd gone, he turned back to Ursula. "Did you live in the UK as a child?"

"My family lived all over Europe," she replied, being purposely evasive.

"That makes sense. I was trying to place your accent and I

can't say that I can, other than it's lovely and you should never lose it."

Ursula tossed her head back and laughed. "I couldn't if I wanted to!"

Barlow turned to me. "You've got an interesting accent too, Ms. Van Dalen. Where do you hail from?"

"Amsterdam."

His brows arched. "One of my favorite cities. Were you born there?"

"I was." *Two hundred years ago.*

"What part?"

I smiled sweetly. The section of Amsterdam where I'd been born had been built over three times now. "Betondorp."

"I know it well," he said.

Not as well as you think you do, I thought. "How nice."

"Where are you from, Agent Barlow?" Ursula asked.

"I'm a local. Norfolk."

Ursula rested her elbow on the table, placed her chin in her hand, and practically purred at him. "How quaint."

Barlow laughed. "I've never heard it described as quaint, but it was a great place to grow up."

"How did you manage to find your way into the FBI?" she asked next, while I glared at her when Barlow wasn't looking.

"My dad was a G-man," he said proudly. "Worked for the CIA for thirty years. He retired when he got sick. Cancer."

"Oh, no," Ursula said, adding a pout. "I hope he's better now?"

"I'd like to think so," Barlow said, a sadness creeping into his eyes. "He passed away five years ago, and he suffered greatly for two years before that. He'd always wanted me to follow in his footsteps, and it's hard to turn down a request from your dying dad, so here I am, but with a different agency."

Ursula offered him an understanding smile. "I'm sure he's quite proud of you."

Barlow inhaled deeply and let out a sigh. "I'd like to hope so. He was a great man. I miss him."

"I can only imagine. But you still have your mother, correct?"

He shook his head. "No. My mom died when I was little. Drunk driver hit her on the way home from her night shift. She was a pediatric surgeon at Memorial Hospital."

"Oh, how sad for you."

He nodded adding a shrug. "I barely remember her. Your folks still alive?" he asked her next.

"No," she said bluntly. "They've crossed the veil too."

"It's hard being an orphan, right?"

"You get used to it," she told him.

Of course, she'd had well over nine hundred years to get used to it, but she wasn't wrong. I'd heard about my father and brothers passing away well over a hundred years ago. The pain had been somewhat blunted in that I hadn't seen any of them since my eighteenth birthday, but I still understood how odd it was to remain youthful while everyone connected to you gets old and dies.

Our food arrived and we all tucked in. I didn't say much during lunch, allowing Ursula and Barlow to supply most of the conversation. I'm a good listener and people don't realize they give up as much about themselves as they do during a pleasant conversation with a relative stranger. Ursula is a practiced conversationalist, at times able to elicit even the most private of details. In her past, this skill made her a very effective spy and Elric employed her services liberally until one particularly close call when Ursula had nearly been executed for spying on one of Elric's European rivals.

Through the course of their conversation, I learned that Barlow did his undergrad at UVA and got his master's in criminal justice at George Washington University.

He'd been at the FBI for eight years, liked the work but the hours were tough, and, most importantly given the gleeful expression on Ursula's face when he answered her question about his romantic partner situation, Barlow was single, but open to possibilities—whatever *that* meant.

"I'm sure you'll find someone soon," Ursula purred.

"That's the hope," he replied.

Tracy came to remove our plates and ask if there was anything else we'd like, and after declining and requesting the bill, Barlow and I each reached for our wallets.

"Allow me," he said smoothly once I'd extracted my wallet from my handbag.

"That's very nice of you, Agent Barlow—"

"Grant. Call me Grant."

"—but I promised Ursula I'd treat her to lunch."

"Next time," Ursula said as if this was now a thing the three of us did. We got together for lunch like old friends.

Barlow shrugged and laid down a one-hundred-dollar bill. "Tell Tracy to keep the change then." With that he got to his feet, kissed Ursula on the cheek, gave me a two-finger salute, and walked toward the exit.

"Wow," Ursula said once he was out of earshot. "Dovey! You were holding out on me!"

I avoided eye contact as Tracy arrived to deposit the bill. I handed her my credit card and Barlow's cash and said, "Put two lunches on my card and the third lunch you may take out of the cash and keep the change."

Tracy's jaw dropped. "Are you kidding?"

I put my hand over hers, holding the tray with the bill, my card, and the cash, and said, "No, dear. You were lovely and you deserve it."

She practically hopped away with excitement. "Sweet girl," I said.

Ursula tapped my wrist to get my attention. "Spill it," she said.

"What am I spilling?"

"Details, Dovey! Details!"

"I have no idea what you're talking about."

Ursula groaned but waited until I had signed my name to the bottom of the receipt and handed the copies to Tracy before getting to her feet with me to speak further. Ticking off points on her fingers she said, "He's gorgeous, obviously into you, single, and he's looking for that someone special. How did you not come bursting through my door earlier leading with *that*!"

"Because," I began, splaying my own fingers to tick items off to her, "He's pretty, but I have Elric. He's obviously *not* into me, more into *you,* and he might be single but he's *mortal*, Ursula. You know it never works out mixing our kind with the unbound."

Ursula waved that thought away like a pesky fly. "Oh, pish. I had a perfectly lovely relationship with that boy's grandfather, and I assure you he was quite mortal, although I did consider binding him simply because he was so much fun, and I *adored* him."

"What happened?" I asked, genuinely curious.

Ursula sighed. "He began to get older, and I didn't age a day and he suspected something else might be afoot, so he began spying on me. I always knew when he was somewhere close—he nearly religiously wore the cufflinks trinket I'd given him—and in the end I did it to spare him the pain of losing his youth to me. He'd never married, you see, and he was head of a vast fortune. I knew his mother was losing patience with her only son, throwing away his youth and prospects for marriage and children on a mysterious woman of questionable background who refused to marry him. So, I broke his heart, set him free, and he married within a year and had a son within a year after that."

I led the way through the crowded restaurant to the exit.

"Wouldn't Agent Barlow be shocked to learn you knew his grandfather intimately?" I giggled. It tickled me that the unbound had no idea of the adventures the mystics around them took as everyday occurrences. We didn't read about history so much as lived it, and it was a thrilling thing to think about how rich our lives were because of our longevity.

"Well, at least I now have one mystery solved," I told her.

"What's that?"

"Agent Barlow is obviously a man of means—his attire, that Piguet he wears."

"Leave it to you to notice the finer things," Ursula teased.

I smiled because it was true that I was an absolute snob for the finer things in life. It's not something I'm ashamed of. Mystics are by nature collectors of beautiful things, so I'd be fighting my nature not to take note of some of the more extravagant luxury brands and labels. I appreciated craftsmanship and good craftsmanship almost always came with a price.

I was rounding the front fender of Luna when I noticed Agent Barlow's Range Rover parked across the street. Pausing for a moment, I turned back to Ursula, who was waiting for me to unlock Luna's doors, and said, "If Ariti's sister lives right there, maybe I should go up and talk to her?"

"Isn't that where Grant was headed?" she asked, that sly smile returning to tug at her lips.

I sighed. She wasn't going to let up on this. "Probably. And if he's talking with her, I'll need to follow suit. Let's wait in the car until he comes out and then we'll go up and see if she's willing to have another chat."

We got into Luna and I started the engine to get some air flowing and allow the radio to turn on, and no sooner had I done that than there was a scream from a woman standing quite close to the car. It startled both of us, but then I noticed that the woman in front of my car wasn't alarmed at us. Her attention was pointed skyward. No sooner had I craned my neck to look up than something slammed into the top of Barlow's SUV, sending windshield glass flying and setting off the car's alarms.

In front of us the woman screamed again and again, horrified by what she'd just witnessed. Ursula and I jumped out of the car and while she went to console the traumatized woman, I dashed across the street to see what—or who—had fallen onto the agent's car.

Out of the corner of my eye as I dashed across the street, I saw cars coming to a full stop as people took note of what'd just happened and got out of their own cars. Still, I was the first to reach the SUV, and all I could see dangling over the top of the car was a thin, delicate arm, with a trail of blood slowly snaking its way down to the wrist and dripping to the pavement.

A man came up next to me, his phone in his shaking hand as he attempted to dial 911. "Oh my God," he whispered. "Oh, my God!"

I stepped in front of him to shield him from the grisly sight. "Take a breath and speak to the operator," I told him. Pointing to the large numbers painted on the awning of the apartment building, I added, "That's the address. Send them here."

He nodded dully and put the phone to his ear, turning away to speak to the 911 dispatcher. Meanwhile, a crowd began to hover near Barlow's SUV, and Ursula shooed away one or two trying to film the grisly scene while I focused my attention on finding the agent who was nowhere in sight.

"I'm going inside to look for him," I called over the murmuring crowd to Ursula.

"To look for who?"

"Barlow."

"How can you be sure he's inside?"

I pointed to the SUV. "That's his car."

Ursula made an *O* with her lips and widened her eyes.

I nodded, because what else could be said?

Moving through the gathering crowd, I pushed my way toward the front door, only to have it pulled violently open, which caused me to bump right into the man himself. "What happened?!" he exclaimed, looking from me to his car and back again.

"I don't know. But it's bad, Grant."

I didn't overthink the fact that I'd called him by his first name. The gravity of the situation simply necessitated it.

Pointing to his now ruined vehicle, I added, "My guess is that someone either fell or jumped from their terrace and landed on your Range Rover."

Barlow reached out to grip my arm as if he needed to steady himself before he let go, blanked his expression, and walked into the crowd while reaching for his badge and calling for everyone to step aside. I was torn about whether to stay nearby or take Ursula home, and she solved that dilemma for me when she appeared at my side and said, "Dovey! The victim is Eleni Katapotis!"

My eyes widened and my attention turned back toward the lobby doors. Without even responding to Ursula, I dashed through them to the inside of the lobby, searching the crowd for anyone who might look like a mystic. By now, more people had learned what'd happened outside, and there were about a dozen people all hurrying toward the exit. I scanned each face but saw no one who held that certain je ne sais quoi that most mystics carry, and no one in the crowd looked very sinister or smug about what'd just happened to Eleni Katapotis.

Still, the fact that I didn't see anyone in the lobby that might fit the profile of a murderer didn't mean they weren't still in the building. Rushing forward, I reached the elevators and stood near them, watching closely as people arrived at the first floor and moved out of the boxcars.

No one who exited seemed overly suspicious to me.

Flipping open my phone, I tapped at it for a few moments, waited briefly for my search to bear fruit, then headed inside the boxcar myself, pressing the button for fifteen—the penthouse where Eleni Katapotis lived.

Had lived.

The button didn't light up the first or second time I pressed it, which meant that to gain access to that floor you likely needed a key card or code to enter.

I studied the control panel and found a slot for a key card. After digging around in my handbag, I took out my wallet and removed what looked like a platinum Amex credit card but was really a trinket.

Inserting it into the card slot, I pushed a small bit of my essence into the card before once again pressing the button for the fifteenth floor which, to my relief, lit up.

The boxcar lifted off the ground floor and I waited while it climbed up the building, watching the floors tick by steadily.

At last, it crawled to a stop, and with a slight bump it settled on of the fifteenth floor. The doors parted and I stepped into a short hallway that went both right and left. At the end of each hallway was a penthouse suite. I focused in the direction of the one facing the front of the building, where stood a set of mahogany double doors with a big brass knocker at eye level.

One of the doors was open.

Gathering my essence, I formed two balls of energy within my downward-facing palms, ready to hurl them at any hint of a threat. I walked quietly along the hallway toward the open door, aware that the elevator had dinged when it'd reached the top floor, which would've likely alerted anyone still alive inside Eleni's apartment.

Moving to the right, I hugged the wall of the short hallway with my back and eased myself along so that I could peek at an angle inside the apartment.

A breeze touched my cheeks and ruffled the blouse I was wearing, indicating that either a window or a door was open inside the apartment. Inching along while feeling the pulse of my essence swirling in my palms, I stopped just in front of the right door to peek inside the open left, my arms and legs filled with tension, ready for battle.

The Promise was a powerful trinket, and if it was turned on me, I knew I'd have to fight hard to keep its effect from taking hold.

After hovering in the hallway for about a minute and roving my gaze over the narrow strip of interior front hall that I could see from my angled position, I decided to ease myself over to the cracked open door and get a better peek at what lay beyond.

The sound of approaching sirens reached my ears, drowning out any other sounds that might be coming from inside Eleni's apartment, so I made the decision to slip inside the opening without touching the door.

My essence was still gathered in my palms, and I was still ready for a fight, but nothing approached or jumped out at me once I'd entered the penthouse.

In front of me and to the right was a kitchen island with six upholstered barstools perfectly positioned four or five inches apart.

To my left was the door to what was likely the guest lavatory, and next to that was an exquisite, abstract oil painting in hues of pink, brown, and light green, which had to be at least forty inches wide by sixty inches high.

Straight in front of me on the opposite wall was an open sliding glass door leading out to the terrace. A bit of white silk, caught in one of the notches of the railing that rimmed the terrace, fluttered in the breeze.

Shifting to the left, I hugged that wall until I came up flush against the living room, which was a massive space filled with mid-century modern inspired furnishings, all in light cream, wood, and chrome finishes.

I noted that there wasn't any pop of color in the space—no

vibrantly colored throw pillows or rugs, which was obviously on purpose to shift one's gaze to the walls, which were lined with more stunning works of art—mostly abstract—in every shade imaginable, and to the white porcelain figurines placed expertly on every horizontal surface.

The effect was quite becoming; the space felt like a gentle cross between a living space and a gallery, and I liked it.

Eleni Katapotis seemed to collect and enjoy art as much as her brother had.

Shifting away from my spot between the kitchen and the living room, I moved to a hallway off the kitchen and discovered what appeared to be two guest rooms and the master bedroom, which was decorated in more creamy tones but absent the chrome.

A massive portrait of a lovely looking woman with long black hair, deep onyx eyes, a Grecian nose, and thin but perky lips hung centered over the ivory wooden headboard.

I'd seen a photo of Eleni when I was quickly hunting for her apartment number downstairs, and the subject of the painting was an excellent depiction of her. Within the painting she was adorned in a velvet blue gown that puddled around her seated form while she draped a hand over the arm of the love seat where she sat. The artist had taken pains with her expression, which captured a look of confident poise. Eleni seemed to wholly accept that she cut a stunning figure, and I wondered what she would've been like in person if we'd ever met.

"Freeze," someone behind me commanded.

I stiffened and the balls of energy still dancing in my palms collapsed inward to concentrate their energy. Smaller orbs of energy are easier to throw and tend to be more accurate.

But then I realized that I knew that voice, and I recalled my essence back into my palms, winking out the orbs in an instant.

"Or what?" I asked into the tense silence that followed. "You'll shoot me?"

"What're you doing up here?" he snapped, all pretense of congeniality absent from his tone.

I pivoted slowly around, keeping my hands turned up and wide to show him that I wasn't going to be reaching for a weapon. "Same as you, Agent Barlow. I'm investigating."

"Breaking and entering is more like it."

I studied him for a moment, noting his sweat-soaked brow and the tension holding his shoulders tight. He held a gun in his right hand, but it wasn't pointed at me, and his index finger was resting on the barrel, away from the trigger.

It was the first time I'd seen him break from his cool, almost cavalier demeanor, and it made me wonder which persona was more real.

"The front door was open," I said. "I knocked, and when no one answered, I came in."

"That's an interesting story," he said, hardly convinced. "Especially since I left here less than five minutes ago, and the door was locked. Not to mention that the only way up here is either with the aid of building management, or your own key card."

My mind raced through a list of responses that wouldn't get me caught in a lie. If I told him that building management had let me up here, he'd no doubt check to make sure they had, which could land me in hot water when they denied it. I could say that all I did was press the button for the fifteenth floor and it'd simply taken me here—which he wouldn't believe and would again land me in hot water. Or I could offer him a version of the truth.

"I have a key card," I said, lifting the elbow where my handbag dangled.

His brow furrowed, but he gave a slight nod allowing me to show him the key card.

Keeping my actions slow and precise, I reached into my bag and tugged open my wallet, retrieving the trinket card I'd used to get up to the fifteenth floor. Pushing my essence into the trinket, I altered its appearance to make it a blank white card.

Lifting it out, I showed it to him, but his expression remained skeptical. "How'd you get that?"

"Ms. Katapotis gave it to me when she hired me."

I wanted to confirm Barlow's suspicions that she had hired me, which would not only give me cause to be here right now, but also cause to carry on the investigation should the agent and I bump into each other again . . . and in a rather shocking twist, I realized that I hoped that we would.

"Show me," he said, motioning with his gun-wielding right hand over to the door leading to the hallway.

"Of course," I said, moving past him out into the hallway, then around the corner to the front door, which was pulled open wider than when I'd left it.

Moving through the door, I walked toward the elevator and pressed the button, waiting silently in front of it while Barlow stood at my back.

Finally, the bell above the elevator pinged and the doors parted, revealing a crowded boxcar of law enforcement, who seemed as surprised to see us as we were to see them.

Stepping to the side, I motioned them off first, noting that Barlow's attention was now divided between me and the detectives and uniformed police gathering around him, demanding information.

I moved into the now empty boxcar, turned, and waved at Barlow as the doors closed, blocking him from view.

Once the doors closed, I immediately pressed the button for the fourteenth floor, and the elevator descended one floor down before opening to a long hallway with a series of apartment doors on the right and the left. Before exiting I hit the button for every floor down, thinking Barlow wouldn't stand a chance at chasing after me if the elevator took five full minutes to head back up to the penthouse floor.

Heading out of the elevator with a bit of a smirk, I turned toward the left end of the hallway, trotted to the door leading to the stairs and I was about to press through it when I paused to hold still as a statue.

Closing my eyes, I could feel a strong trace of powerful magic in the air. Extending my arms out to better sense the energy, I retraced my steps slowly, feeling the trace all along the hallway. Pausing at the elevator doors, I wondered if the mystic wielding Pandora's Promise had done a version of the same thing I had, only using the stairs to head down one floor before getting on the elevator to exit the building. after Eleni had thrown herself off the terrace. The trace of magic suggested that's exactly what he'd done.

I moved back down the hallway and stared at the closed doors of the elevator, wondering if the killer had walked right by me when I'd stood in front of the exiting passengers, roving the crowd for any signs of suspicion.

But then, as if on a whisper of air, I felt the subtle trace of magic farther off to the right—past the elevator doors.

Furrowing my brow, I pivoted and took a step or two down the corridor, and it surprised me when I felt I could detect the traces of magic carrying on past the elevator toward the opposite end of the long hallway.

Reaching into my trusty handbag, I pulled out a spool of white thread. A trinket I'd gotten off the black market a few years ago.

Holding the tip of the thread in one hand, I pressed some essence into the spool with the other and tossed it on the floor.

It bounced when it landed and began to roll down the hallway, speeding toward the door at the end.

Still holding on to the thread, I ran after it, unworried about the excess thread getting tangled—the spool would wind up the thread on its own as I approached.

Reaching the end of the hallway, I paused where the spool

was bumping against the door like a tiny anxious dog, needing to go out. After opening the door and allowing the spool to zip through, I followed.

The spool spun over to the first stair and began to bounce down. I followed as quickly as I could. We wound down fourteen flights and by the time I reached the bottom landing, my legs were aching, and my breath was coming in huffs.

The spool, however, didn't need to catch its wind. It simply bumped impatiently against the door leading to the outside. Pushing open that door, I squinted in the bright sunlight, blinking hard to get my eyes to adjust so that I didn't lose the spool.

Seeing it roll into a parking lot next to the apartment building, I followed it to a now empty parking spot, in the mostly full lot.

Turning away from the spool, I looked up and down the street, not seeing any suspicious car peel away, and I was just turning back to the spool when a car pulled into the spot and drove right over it.

"No!" I cried, hearing a crunch.

The driver looked at me and held up his palms in a "What?" gesture.

Ignoring him, I tugged on the thread, and it snapped off, my magical trinket destroyed.

"Oh, drat my luck!"

The man in the car got out. "Miss? Is something wrong?"

I sighed. "No. I'm fine. It's . . . fine."

I left him looking at me curiously and walked away. It wasn't his fault, I knew, but that trinket had been a handy one for picking up traces of magic.

Needing a distraction, I looked around the area, hoping for a camera attached to either the apartment building or somewhere in the lot that might've captured the car the murderer drove.

My eyes finally spotted a security camera on a pole at the opposite end of the lot, and I walked to it to look up, seeing that it was pointed straight down to the machine that gave out the parking passes after collecting the required fare.

There were no security cameras trained on the lot itself.

Sighing in frustration, I walked back toward the stairwell door, pulling on the handle which had locked behind me. Leaving it, I thought of something and began to walk around the back of the building to the parking lot on the opposite side, and just as I suspected, there were three security cameras pointed at various angles all around the lot.

"There you are!" I heard a voice call. Spinning around, I saw Ursula hurrying toward me.

I winced at the sight of her, aware that I'd simply disappeared without any kind of explanation.

"Hi," I said as she neared. "Ursula, I'm so sorry that I darted off. I wanted to try and catch the thief."

"You mean murderer," she corrected, then waved her hand. "I knew that's what happened. I wasn't worried about where you'd gone, just worried I'd miss you in the throng gathered in front of the building."

"Still?" I asked. It'd been at least twenty minutes since Eleni had fallen onto Barlow's Range Rover. I would've figured the first responders would've taken her away by now.

"Oh yes. There's still quite a crowd. I just came from there and they've covered her with a sheet, but there're still plenty of police, news reporters, and bystanders gawking away."

"Vultures." Thinking of the regal nature of the portrait up in the penthouse, I was quite certain Eleni Katapotis would've hated the macabre spectacle her tragic death was creating.

"I take it you didn't catch the murderer-slash-thief?" Ursula asked.

I shook my head. "No. I did trace their path, however."

"They were back here?"

I shook my head again and pointed to the other side of the building. "There's a parking lot on that side with only one security camera pointed at the ticket vending machine. I think the mystic who's doing this did their reconnaissance and chose that lot and that entrance to make their way up to the fourteenth floor where they then entered the far end of the hallway to cross the building to the stairwell leading to the penthouse."

"Eleni's terrace was on this side of the building, eh?" Ursula asked.

"It was."

"How did they get into the building?"

I offered her a flat smile. "Has any unbound lock ever kept you out of a private space?"

She grinned. "Not yet, and likely not ever. The unbound have no idea how easy their locks are to pick with our magic."

"Exactly. Still, it is interesting that the mystic seems to have taken pains to avoid the security cameras."

Ursula grinned. Calling forth a small ball of energy in the center of her palm, she made a slight tossing motion toward the security camera facing us and I watched as the ball spiraled tightly up to the camera, disappearing on impact. A second later there was a slight *pop!* and a tiny sliver of smoke wafted out from the camera's lens.

"Child's play," she sang, placing her hands on her hips and puffing out her chest in mock triumph.

I laughed, then sobered quickly, mindful that I was still on an investigation to retrieve a powerful trinket killing some members of a wealthy and powerful unbound family. "Come on," I motioned to her. "Let's get you back to your place so I can continue this investigation."

She tucked in beside me as we headed down the pavement toward the street where I'd parked. "What's your next move?"

"I need to do some research into the Ariti family tree. I need to know why Augustus and his sister Eleni were targeted. What is it about this unbound family that has this mystic risking so much by stealing such a valuable trinket to use against them?"

"Are you sure they're all unbound?" she asked as we gained the street, still crowded with gawkers and police. "I know you researched Augustus, but maybe there's a family member who's bound but not well known?"

I glanced over at the spot where Eleni had met her death, seeing that her body had been taken away, and Agent Barlow's ruined Range Rover was hoisted up on a tow truck, ready to be hauled away, while the agent himself stood next to the truck, speaking to another man in a black suit with thinning gray hair, a large nose, and an underbite, giving off a strong vibe of authority and irritation with his arms crossed and a slight curl to his lip. The difference between the attractiveness of the two men was striking. Or maybe it was simply Barlow who was striking.

"I'm not sure about anything at the moment, Ursula," I admitted, secretly meaning more than about the Aritis.

Ursula swiveled her head to look toward Barlow and what was likely a superior agent. She laughed softly and shook her head. She understood *exactly* what I meant.

CHAPTER 6

I reached home about an hour later, stopping for groceries on the way back to my place. My mind was occupied with an array of random thoughts. . . .

Who in the mystic world would target the Ariti family with a powerful trinket, but fail to use mystic methods to cover his tracks?

What's the connection between Eleni's murder and Augustus's other than the fact that they're from the same family?

What's the name of that hypnotic cologne that Barlow wears?

What other family members might be involved?

Okay, so that third thought wasn't exactly relevant to my investigation, but the synapses were firing, and I was less in control of their electric pathways than I'd like to admit.

After feeding Bits a big fat cricket and some banana, I powered up my laptop and got to work, starting with everything I could locate online about Augustus and Eleni.

During my perusal of the information available online, I began to formulate a profile of Augustus that made me a little sad that I'd never met him. He was a lover of art, obviously, but he also saw art as a way to bridge the wide chasms that existed between various socioeconomic classes.

He didn't simply sell works by artists who were popular or

trending; he often showcased works by complete unknowns, and most of them from the inner-city youth programs that he was especially invested in. Augustus was a generous philanthropist and had given millions of dollars to inner-city youth programs that were willing to support art classes for anyone who wanted to attend. And through his support, several young artists were starting to catch the notice of some influential art dealers in New York, L.A., San Francisco, Chicago, Boston, Houston, and D.C.

In interviews that I read, Augustus was also humble and gracious, and it didn't appear to be an act. The man was genuinely altruistic and believed that art was an expression of the inner soul as much as a reflection of the current consciousness of the larger collective.

To my mind, there was no doubt that someone was targeting the family, but why start with Augustus? Nothing contained in the articles that I read led me to believe his personality was caustic or could drive someone to murder him. Especially given the method for that murder. Why go to all the trouble of stealing Pandora's Promise to murder an unbound and make Augustus's death particularly horrifying?

I believed he'd been chosen first for a reason, and I doubted that it was simply a matter of having easy access to him. The fact that Augustus worked in a gallery that would've allowed anyone off the street to walk in and have an interaction with him didn't feel like it was the only motivation for targeting him first.

The Ariti family was an interesting one. Their fortune came from packaged medicaments—they owned dozens of plants in Greece that manufactured pharmaceuticals for many of the largest drug companies in the world, and while the Aritis didn't seem to own any laboratories dedicated to creating original medicines, they did have a substantial foothold in the manufacturing of drugs worldwide.

They also owned massive farms in Greece where many of the plants that provided the raw materials for these drugs were produced. The family business had been started by three brothers back in the late 1960s, and, while none of the original three Ariti men were still alive, their children and grandchildren were still involved in the day-to-day operations.

Moving on to Augustus's sister was a bit more challenging. In years past, Eleni had been the social butterfly of the family, and was known for her great beauty. I found articles about her from twenty years ago where she spent the bulk of her time hobnobbing with some of the wealthiest young men and women in the world.

But shortly after marrying Konstantinos Katapotis, she all but disappeared from the society pages. And there wasn't much I could find out about Konstantinos other than he'd gone to work for the Aritis in the late nineties as part of their sales team and had steadily moved up the ladder to become head of international sales, based here in Virginia in 2012.

Eleni had filed for divorce after twenty-five years of marriage, and the divorce proceedings had been highly contentious with accusations of infidelity and domestic abuse coming from both sides. The divorce had finally been settled two years ago, and from what I could tell, Eleni had come out fairly unscathed due to an ironclad prenup.

I found it interesting, however, that Konstantinos had kept his job at headquarters, and, by what the few lines in an article describing the breakup could offer me, that the family hadn't gathered around to support Eleni like they had when they'd supported Augustus's brother, Ambrose, during his divorce right around the same time that Eleni's divorce had been finalized.

Ambrose's ex-wife, Gina, had been fired from her high-level position as senior V.P. of marketing and was forced to abide by a non-compete clause that prevented her from pursuing other similar employment within the state for five years. Ambrose had also taken great pains to drag Gina's reputation through the mud. He'd publicly accused her of having an affair with her assistant, a man half her age, and he'd also labeled her a drunk.

For me, that smelled like motive, but I still couldn't answer why going through all the trouble—and risk—of stealing, then using the Promise against the Aritis was worth it if Gina's ultimate goal was simply to knock off her ex-husband.

Plus, she would've had to have had knowledge not just of the Promise, but of mystic society itself, and I couldn't find any connection to anyone in her inner circle who sounded like they had those kinds of contacts. It just seemed implausible that she could be the one behind the murders.

I dismissed the idea that Gina was secretly bound. Surely, she would have to be to both know about and wield the power of the Promise, but I'd never seen her at Elric's headquarters, and she seemed too attractive for Petra's court.

Petra was a petty, envious, and deadly mystic, and Gina was a beautiful woman who wouldn't last a day in Petra's court.

Still, I might have to give some credence to the idea that Gina *could* be bound, perhaps even newly so. There were plenty of mystics in the area who floated under the radar. They tended to be on the lower end of the power scale, which again cast doubt about someone like that getting past Kallis's defenses and stealing the Promise without being detected.

Kallis wasn't well known to me, but as a diplomat in Vostov's court, he'd have to be a powerful mystic. There was no way to ascend a court's ladder if you couldn't hold your own in the magic-wielding department.

Therefore, whoever took the trinket was an adept thief. With a penchant for revenge against a family of unbound.

None of this made sense. It was a confounding case.

As I was making a list of people to interview the following day, my doorbell chimed. Bits, who'd been happily curled up in my lap, unrolled from his ball enough to look at me with one black eye, as if he were surprised that I might have a visitor.

He wasn't the only one.

"It's probably just a package," I told him, setting him on my desk while I got up and moved toward the door, glancing at my watch on the way. *A package at 9:00 p.m.?*

As I peeked through the peephole, my breath caught, and I pulled my gaze away for a moment trying to think of what to do.

"I know you're in there, Dovey Van Dalen," Agent Barlow called softly. "I saw you from the street through your window."

My gaze whipped to my left to see that I'd left the curtains open, which allowed anyone from the street to spot me sitting at my desk.

With a sigh I opened the door. "Good evening," I said, keeping the door mostly closed.

He smiled but it was obviously forced. Far from his perfectly styled image of this morning, the man looked practically disheveled.

As if he could read my mind, he ran a hand through his copper brown hair and said, "It's been a day."

My gaze moved to the street where I saw another Range Rover parked in front of my home, this one a bit larger and older that the one that he'd been driving this morning.

"Sorry about your car," I told him. The words felt awkward given the situation. His brand-new Range Rover had been totaled by a falling body, so I wasn't sure what words would've been appropriate to say, considering the circumstances.

"Yeah," he said, cupping the back of his neck and widening his eyes. "I spent a long hour on the phone with my auto insurance company. Try explaining that one to a claims adjuster."

I grimaced but didn't reply and the awkward silence that followed grew heavy with anticipation. "Can we talk?" he finally asked.

I studied him for a moment before responding. Even rumpled he looked good. In fact, he might've even looked better. And that wasn't a good idea for me, given my close association with a certain world's-most-powerful-mystic.

Besides, he was unbound. I'm bound. What could come of any interest in each other? Nothing but trouble.

The problem is that I like trouble. Sometimes, like that evening, I crave it, which is dangerous, and knowing that it's dangerous makes me crave it even more.

Taking a step back, I opened the door wider and waved him inside. "Come in."

He nodded in thanks and crossed the threshold, pausing for a moment to stand in front of the doorway and take in my sitting room.

"Nice," he said, with another nod of his head.

"Thank you," I replied, moving to close the door.

Barlow stepped forward and shrugged out of his suede jacket, moving over to the large leather chair by the fireplace to sit down.

"Can I get you some refreshment?" I asked.

"Whatever you've got on hand would be great," he said, making himself comfortable. The chair he'd chosen was a particular favorite of mine, purchased sixty years earlier from the estate of Winston Churchill, whom I'd met on more than one occasion. He and Elric had been acquaintances in the thirties, before the war.

I moved to the doorway leading to the kitchen, my mind racing to figure out what to serve the man. Heading to the fridge I pulled the door open and nearly sighed in relief when I spotted a bottle of white wine chilling, along with a head of brie, a block of cheddar, some grapes, an apple, and some prosciutto. And I knew I had some assorted nuts and chocolate-covered raisins in the pantry.

Gathering the ingredients for a charcuterie board, I quickly arranged fruit, cheese, meat, and nuts on a resin board I'd purchased at a farmer's market and carried it out with two glasses of white wine to the living room, only to find Barlow's head on his hand and his eyes closed.

I stood there for a moment to see if he was merely deep in thought, but as I watched the rhythm of his chest, I could see that he had in fact dozed off.

And as I stood there looking at him, I had the strangest urge to run my fingers through the tuft of hair that formed a slight widow's peak at the top of his forehead. Luckily, both of my hands were full, and common sense prevailed, so I turned on my heel and headed back into the kitchen, where I called out loudly, "Agent Barlow? Will white wine do?"

There was a grunt, then the clearing of a throat followed by, "I'd be fine with water, but whatever you're having would be great. Thank you."

I walked back to the doorway of the kitchen and held the charcuterie board aloft. "Snacks," I said, hoping he didn't suspect that I'd caught him mid-doze.

He blinked rapidly and stood up to hold out his hands for the board, which I handed to him then took my seat while he looked for a place to set it down.

"The ottoman," I said, pointing to the chocolate leather ottoman next to his chair.

He pulled it out to center it in between us, then carefully set down the board. The man was eyeing the charcuterie like he hadn't had a meal since lunch.

"This is really nice," he said, diving in. "You didn't have to go to all this trouble."

"No trouble," I said, swirling my wine and sitting back in the velvet wing chair to the side of him.

I waited for him to have a few bites before asking, "What brings you by, Agent Barlow?"

He blanched and put a finger to his lips, chewing quickly before answering. "Sorry. I guess I was hungrier than I thought. Obviously, I wanted to continue our discussion from this afternoon."

I cocked my head at him, noting the way his light gray eyes caught the soft glow from the nearby lamp, giving them an almost metallic appearance. The man had absolutely dazzling eyes. "What discussion was that?"

He popped another cracker and cheese into his mouth, chewing while offering me a slight grin, like "Isn't it cute, Dovey, that you want to play coy?"

"Eleni Katapotis," he said, as if the mere mention of her name would ring some bells.

"What about her?"

"What about her?" he repeated. "What do you mean, *what about her*?"

I shook my head slightly. "Agent Bar—"

"Gib," he interrupted.

"Excuse me?"

He sighed wearily. "Just call me Gib."

"Why would I do that?"

"Because you refused to call me Grant today at lunch, obviously preferring something more formal, and while I appreciate the respect that calling me by my title and last name offers, it feels a little impersonal at this point, don't you think? Calling me Gib would cut that down the middle."

A smile tugged at my lips and to cover it I ducked my chin and reached out for a slice of pear. "How is calling you Gib a compromise?"

"It's my initials," he said. "Grant Isaac Barlow."

There was no masking my smile now. "Gib," I said, softening. "Fine. I like it. I'm serious though, about wondering why you'd come here to ask me about Eleni Katapotis."

He studied me before shaking his head and muttering something I didn't quite catch.

"What was that?" I asked, leaning forward.

He sighed and stared at the area rug by his feet. "You're a beautiful woman, Dovey, and it's throwing me off my game."

I laughed. "Oh, I hardly believe that Agent—Gib."

He glanced up at me again and he wore a sly smile. "It's true. And I bet it's how you disarm people you're interviewing during your own investigations."

I didn't deny it, because there was no point. My mother was a celebrated beauty, and I looked enough like her to be her twin, so it's easy for me to admit that I'm pleasing to the eye, I always have been. And I take great care with my personal appearance, because it always seemed to be important to Elric. But right now, I was rather happy that my beauty was throwing Barlow off his game. I liked the way he looked at me, like he couldn't stop looking at me, and even though he was an unbound, I found myself wanting more of those looks.

He took a sip of wine and pulled the glass away to study it in the light. "This is nice," he said, as if he were surprised.

"Louis Jadot Chassagne-Montrachet," I told him.

He nodded and waved the glass at the charcuterie. "It's the perfect pairing."

"I'm glad you like it."

He took a few of the chocolate-covered raisins from the board, bouncing them in his hand before popping them one at a time into his mouth while he continued to study me, and I simply allowed the silence to play out. Helping him in his investigation was likely to get sticky for me, so I'd have to tread carefully here if I wanted to stay one step ahead of him.

"When did Eleni hire you?" he asked at last.

"Recently."

"Can you be more specific?"

"No. I really can't. My clients trust that, until subpoenaed, I keep my facts about their cases close to the chest."

He sighed. "All right, how about if I ask if she made you aware that she or her brother had received any death threats."

"You believe she was murdered?"

"This tactic of answering a question with a question isn't going to get me to go home any sooner, Dovey," he said softly.

A small shiver traveled up the nape of my neck and I felt a slight flush to my cheeks. The way he said my name was far too personal for my own good. "No," I said honestly. Eleni Katapotis hadn't shared anything with me. "She didn't make me aware of any threats. But more to the point, why do you think she was murdered?" I needed to know what kind of evidence Barlow had. The one thing I couldn't allow was for him to confiscate the Promise. It was far too dangerous a trinket to end up in an unbound's hands.

"I spoke with the other tenant on the penthouse floor. She knew Eleni well, and she told me that Eleni was terrified of heights. The only reason she occupied the penthouse suite was because she'd won the apartment in her divorce, and she'd known it had been previously used by her husband's lover."

I cocked my head at him. "She lived in a place that terrified her out of spite?"

He shrugged. "Seems that way. The point is that, according to her neighbor, Eleni never used the terrace. She'd said that she never even opened the sliding glass door, and when I looked, there was no furniture out on the terrace so that statement is probably true enough."

I nodded. "She was pushed, then." I wanted to point Barlow to a logical conclusion rather than to the elements of a magical trinket that had forced Eleni to take her own life.

"Seems that way. What I can't get over is that I was at her door probably at the moment she was being tossed over the balcony, and I didn't hear a thing. There were no sounds of a scuffle, or her scream, just silence."

I shrugged. "The killer could've drugged her or knocked her out right before you got to her door. If she was unconscious, then throwing her over the railing wouldn't be that difficult."

"You know, I considered that, but the penthouse had all those small porcelain sculptures on every surface available—"

"She collected Shio Kusaka's works," I said, remembering that I took note of the collection as well.

"Is that the artist who created all the figurines and sculpture?"

"Yes. She's quite famous. A truly gifted ceramic artist. If the pottery in Eleni's apartment was a collection of her originals, it'd be worth a fortune."

Barlow nodded. "That's what I figured. And there wasn't a single piece of broken pottery on the floor. If there'd been some kind of struggle, then I gotta believe Eleni would've put up a fight."

"She was drugged, then," I said, trying to poke holes anywhere I could.

He picked up a slice of apple, adding some cheddar to it, then held it aloft as he considered me. "How?" he asked simply before popping the snack into his mouth.

I shrugged. "Maybe the killer was someone that Eleni knew, and she let them in the door. To be a gracious host"—I paused to wave my hand toward the charcuterie board and wine—"perhaps she offered her guest some refreshment, and he or she slipped the drug into her drink when she wasn't looking."

Barlow squinted at me, and I refused to look away. "The kitchen was spotless, not a glass or a plate out of place."

"The killer cleaned up, disposing of any damning evidence."

"Do you know what we found in Eleni's refrigerator?"

"I haven't a clue."

"Nothing," he said.

I blinked. Had I heard him right? "I'm sorry?"

"Nothing," he repeated. "Not even a bottle of water. According to the doorman, Eleni ate every meal out, and she'd just returned from her lunch about ten minutes before I showed up at her door, and neither the doorman nor the manager remembers anyone asking for access to the penthouse prior to her death."

"Other than you," I said.

He nodded.

"Are you sure they're remembering correctly?"

He pointed at me. "That's where I had a few questions too."

"Meaning?"

"After combing through her apartment and finding literally nothing suspicious, I went back down to speak to the manager to ask him if he was sure he remembered her coming back into the building alone, and he said that he was certain because he'd been holding a package for Eleni, and he gave it to her before she went up to her penthouse."

Goose bumps lined my arms, so I made sure to sound as casual as I could when I asked, "What was in the package?"

"I don't know, Dovey. Do you?"

I blinked, then blinked again. "I'm sorry, are you *accusing* me?"

"I'm not," he said, holding up his palms to me. "I'm simply asking you if, before I found you in the penthouse—alone—did you happen to take a package from the penthouse with you when you left?"

"You watched me walk out the door," I reminded him. "I had nothing on me."

His gaze traveled over to the desk, and my handbag that was perched against it. He then looked from it to me meaningfully.

I sighed and got up to fetch my purse. Sitting back down, I began to unpack the contents into my lap, making sure that the three trinkets I had in there weren't activated in a way that would call attention to them. "I have nothing to hide," I lied, once I'd finished emptying the bag.

He nodded. "Thank you for showing me."

"You're welcome, and because you asked me, I'm assuming the package was missing from the contents of the apartment?"

"It was. I looked everywhere and found Eleni's mail on the counter, but no package."

"How big was it?" I asked next.

Barlow held his palm up to me again. "The manager said it'd fit in the palm of your hand."

"Ah," I said, but privately, my mind was racing. I knew *exactly* what'd been in that package, which meant that the killer had waited until Eleni threw herself off the balcony before entering the penthouse to retrieve the trinket. Getting past an unbound's locks would've been child's play for a mystic.

To busy myself, I put everything back into my purse and set it down next to me, while an awkward sort of silence developed between us.

Finally, Barlow glanced at his watch. "It's late." Standing, he added, "Thank you for the hors d'oeuvres and the wine, Dovey."

A small thrill went through me again. My God how I liked the way he said my name. As if we'd known each other far longer than simply today. "You're welcome, Gib."

He smiled at me in a way that wasn't simply friendly . . . there was something else there and that little thrill grew bigger.

To cover the blush I knew was touching my cheeks, I stood up as well and moved with him toward the door. "You're okay to drive home?" I asked as he paused in the doorway.

He glanced at his empty wineglass on the side table next to the chair he'd been sitting in. "One glass isn't going to impair me."

I smiled a little devilishly. "Of course it won't. What I meant was, are you okay to drive home after nodding off in my living room because you're so obviously exhausted."

He chuckled and it was his turn to blush. "You caught that, eh?"

"I did."

He raked his fingers across the top of his head, something I suspected he did only when he was thrown off his game or nervous. "It's been a *day.*"

"It has."

"Good night, Dovey," he said, looking me straight in the eye.

I was keenly aware of how close we were standing to each other, and that small divot on his upper lip that simply begged to be kissed. Inhaling a cleansing breath, I said, "Good night, Gib."

He waved over his shoulder as he trotted down my front steps, then over to his car, calling back, "I'll be seeing you."

I closed the door before he had a chance to look back, then leaned against it and let out a long sigh.

Bits, who'd been resting on the little bed on my desk, unrolled himself, sniffed the air, his small snout wiggling, and looked at me with a squeak, like he could smell the chemistry in the room.

"The man is trouble, Bits."

My hedgehog yawned and blinked his bleary eyes. I went to him and scooped him up, then moved over to the remnants of the charcuterie board and offered him a slice of pear. "I'm going to have to solve this case quickly. Inviting trouble like Special Agent Grant Isaac Barlow into my life isn't part of the plan."

But even as I said the words, I felt my spirits dampen. There was something incredibly intriguing about the man. A chemistry existed between us that was as powerful as the one between me and Elric, and that should've bothered me enough to want to keep Barlow well, well away. But as I carried Bits upstairs to bed, I couldn't let go of the hope that I'd see the federal agent again soon.

And I didn't know what to make of that other than tangling too much with Barlow would be its own Pandora's box of trouble.

Chapter 7

I woke late the next morning after a fitful night's sleep. Elric would want an update on my progress today, and I didn't know what I'd tell him. I certainly couldn't mention Special Agent Barlow. Elric would expect me to "handle" any unbound law enforcement's interest in the case. But I wasn't sure *how* to handle Gib. Other than at arm's length. For the good of both of us.

I'd kept Bits up well past his bedtime, so he was fast asleep while I hovered in the doorway of my closet choosing an outfit carefully. I needed to dress in a casual, approachable style. Something I've long observed about the unbound is that the more formal the attire, the less likely they are to open up and offer information, so I had to dress like a woman they'd *want* to talk to. Especially the men. That meant ensconcing myself in something slightly sex kittenish but with taste—a trickier balance than you might think.

After pulling together the look I was after, I dressed myself in white skinny jeans, a georgette-black, loose-fitting blouse, knee-high, black-leather, fold-over boots with a bit of brass at the top, and my favorite black Fendi Boston bag. Topping it all off, I left my hair long and slightly tousled, donned a set of large Fendi Jackie O. sunglasses, packed a few trinkets into my purse, then headed out to begin the day of interviews.

The first place I started was a coffee shop across the street from Eleni's office. In my online search I'd discovered that she was renting office space only a few blocks from where she lived, and the coffee shop logo imprinted on a to-go cup had appeared on her desk in more than one of her social media posts.

By the time I arrived at the coffee shop, the morning rush had thinned out considerably, and I only had to wait in line behind an elderly man with a cane who seemed to be trying to cheer up the barista behind the counter.

The barista, whose name tag read KIONI, did her best to hide her watery eyes, and offered the old man a smile, but it was clearly forced, and I felt for her. Satisfied that he got her to smile, the man quickly moved down the counter to await his order.

"Hi," I said when I got to the counter.

"Good morning," she said, struggling to keep that smile plastered onto her face. "What can I get for you?"

I eyed her sympathetically. "You having a tough day?"

She swallowed hard and shook her head. "I'm fine," she said. "What can I get for you?"

"I'd love a tall cup of coffee and one of those muffins," I said, pointing to the case next to us.

She nodded and punched my order into her register before saying, "That'll be twelve seventy-two. Would you like that muffin warmed?"

"I would, thank you."

I handed her a twenty and she metered out my change, then turned to get my coffee and muffin while I shoved a twenty into her tip jar.

Coming back with my coffee, she noticed the twenty and said, "Oh! Thank you!"

I took the coffee and offered her a smile. "I can't make your day better than simply offering you a generous tip and my sincere condolences."

Her eyes sprang even wider than they had when she'd noticed the twenty. "How do you . . . ?"

"You have that look like you've lost someone important to you. And I know how hard it can be to work on days when you'd rather be home giving yourself some self-care."

Her eyes misted and she wiped at them, obviously embarrassed. "I don't know why I'm so emotional."

I suspected I knew, but simply stood there, allowing her the moment to gather herself. She cleared her throat and turned away from me to get the tongs and put a muffin in the steamer.

When she turned back, I said, "We're almost never prepared to lose the people who're important to us."

Her jaw opened and she nodded again. "She was a regular customer here," she said, lowering her voice almost conspiratorially. "She died yesterday."

"I'm so, so sorry, Kioni."

She nodded for a third time, something I noticed she did when she was trying to compose herself. "I even waited on her yesterday."

"Oh, my dear . . . that must be so hard to carry with you today."

A tear leaked out of her eye and ran down her cheeks. This time she didn't bat it away. "She was always so nice to me. Six weeks ago I broke up with my fiancé—I caught him cheating with one of my best friends and Eleni—that was her name—made a point of stopping by on her way home right around closing time to just hang out and talk to me. All my friends wanted to focus on what a scumbag my ex was, which was keeping me in a really dark place, but Eleni . . . she kept turning the conversation back to what I wanted to do next."

I sipped at my coffee, listening to Kioni, and knew that I could probably interview a dozen of Eleni's close friends and none of them would give me a clearer image of her character than this barista. This was Eleni being kind simply for the sake of being kind.

"What *did* you want to do next?" I asked.

Another tear slid down her cheeks. "I want to fly planes."

My brow shot up. "You want to be a pilot?"

She nodded. "I know it sounds crazy, right?"

I barked out a laugh. "Crazy? No. It sounds *badass*!"

She laughed too, but quickly covered it with her hand. "Two weeks ago, I got a call here at the shop from the president of this flight school, and the guy says that I've just won a scholarship for their two-year flight school program. Everything's covered. Tuition, books, flying time. I looked them up online and the scholarship is worth *ninety thousand* dollars!"

She whispered that last part before turning toward the steamer to retrieve my muffin. After wrapping it in a paper bag and handing it to me she waited on two more customers before continuing our conversation. "I mean, can you even *believe* that?"

"How incredibly generous," I said, fully understanding why Kioni had been brought to tears by the knowledge that Eleni was dead.

"Right? I start on the first of next month! And typical Eleni, when she came in the next day for her coffee, I tried to thank her, and she wore this big old smile and pretended like she didn't know what I was talking about. She just kept telling me that a fairy godmother must have seen my potential and was making sure that I reach it."

"Wow, Kioni, this Eleni woman sounds amazing."

"She so was. God . . . I am going to *miss* that woman!"

I pinched a bit of muffin between my index finger and thumb, nibbling on it before I asked, "So what happened? How did Eleni die?"

Kioni shook her head sadly. "The news said it was a suicide.

That she heard about her brother dying in a fire the day before and that drove her to it, but I . . ."

"You . . . ?"

Kioni looked me in the eye and whispered, "I don't believe it."

"Why?"

"I waited on her yesterday," she said, her eyes unfocused as she recalled the memory. "She was really sad about her brother, but she didn't seem *suicide* sad, you know?"

"I do."

"And . . ."

"What?"

She took a deep breath in and leaned over the counter to whisper, "I think she was scared."

"Scared? Of what?"

Kioni shook her head as if she had knowledge of something that frightened her too. "Four days ago, while I was locking up the shop, I saw Eleni across the street—her office is right there." The barista paused to point out the front door at a building across the street. "And she was kind of being pushed into a town car by this mean-looking guy who had her by the elbow. I can't say that he was outright abusing her, but it looked like he was pushing her faster than she could go. I yelled at him to stop, and that's when I saw Eleni in the car look up at me and mouth, *I'm okay*. But she didn't look okay, you know?"

"Do you think he had something to do with her suicide?"

She shook her head and stared at the counter with that same faraway look in her eyes. "I don't know. But supposedly, she jumped from her penthouse apartment, and Eleni didn't like heights. I know that because when I told her that I wanted to be a pilot she made a big deal about how brave I was and told me she had to take a Xanax and a tranquilizer to even *think* about boarding a plane because she's so scared of heights."

"Ah, then jumping off the top floor of a building makes no logical sense."

"No," Kioni said, her eyes still wide. "It doesn't."

"Have you shared this with the police?" I was curious if she had spoken with anyone who might mention it to Barlow.

Kioni bit her lip. "No?" she said, like she was asking a question, but she quickly explained, "I haven't had good experiences with cops." My brow rose and she added, "I was at Lafayette Square in 2020 for the Black Lives Matter rally. I got pretty beat up by three LEOs. No way would I ever go up to one of *them* with something like this. They'd probably end up blaming *me*."

I tapped the lid of my coffee thoughtfully. "Kioni, I have a friend of a friend who's in law enforcement, and I believe he'll be familiar with this case. What if I tell him that I was the one who saw Eleni being strong-armed into the back of a limo just last week?"

"You'd do that?"

"Of course I would," I lied as I riffled through my purse and pulled out a pen and a small notepad. "Eleni seems like she was a wonderfully kind soul, and we women need to look out for each other. Tell me what this guy looked like."

Kioni stared at the countertop for a beat. "He was tall, I remember that. Eleni was just a little bitty thing. She was maybe five-foot-three or so, and he towered over her."

"If you had to guess his height, what would it be?"

"Maybe six-one or six-two. Could've even been taller."

"Got it," I said, scribbling. "And what was his hair color?"

"Black. Like, jet black. And a little wavy on top."

"Great. His complexion?"

"He was either really tan or he had dark skin."

"Was he Black? Middle Eastern? Indian?"

"Not quite that dark. Maybe Italian?"

"How about Greek?"

Kioni snapped her fingers and pointed at me. "That tracks."

"Great. What about any other features on his face?"

"He was wearing sunglasses—aviators, and he had a good-sized nose."

"Body type?"

She laughed mirthlessly. "He looked like he worked out a lot."

"A big guy."

"Oh, yeah."

"Perfect. Any facial hair?"

"No. Clean shaven."

"What about his clothes?"

Her lips flattened out and she stared at me for a moment before she said, "Expensive."

"You could tell?"

"Oh, yeah. He was in a suit that looked like it'd been made for him, and I'll bet you it was."

"What color was the suit?"

"Blue. Like a silver blue. And he wore a white button down under it."

"Did you see him walk?"

"Walk?"

"Yes, like if you saw him walk, maybe he had a distinctive gait?"

"Oh, yeah, I did see that. He walked around the car and glared at me while I just stood there and glared at him."

"Did he have a limp or any other discernible features to his gait?"

"He . . ." Her voice trailed off as she stared at the wall behind me. "He walked like he was looking for a fight."

I cocked my head at her. "What made you decide that?"

She shook her head. "I don't know. Just the way he kind of bounced on his toes a little and flexed his arms, all big man on campus like."

"I know exactly what you mean." I stowed my pen and ink-pad back inside my purse. "I'll let my friend know and he can investigate it if he wants to."

After saying my goodbyes to Kioni, I went back to my car and drove across the street, then around to the other side of the block, parking behind the building where Eleni had worked. Lucky me, there was a back entrance, and I went to all the trouble of moving my car because I didn't want Kioni to see me walk into the main entrance of the building and wonder what I might be up to.

Once inside, I headed toward the front of the building, managing to find a directory and saw that E. Katapotis Inc. was on the second floor.

Using the stairs to reach the second floor, I walked the length of the carpeted corridor until I came to her office. I looked to the crack at the bottom of the door, but there was no light coming from the other side. "Nobody's home," I whispered.

Reaching into my purse again, I retrieved a thin key, pushed a little bit of essence into it, and inserted it into the keyhole. Twisting the key brought a satisfactory *click* and the door unlocked. Pushing inward, I entered Eleni's office suite and quickly moved through the small lobby area to the one closed door at the back of the hallway off the lobby. I turned the handle, but it was locked too.

Frowning at the inconvenience of having to work my way through the unbound's locks, I inserted my key again and the door easily opened.

Closing it behind me once I entered, I flipped on the light switch and had a look around.

The space was somewhat spartan, and not nearly as neat as her apartment, which was good because it made my chances of finding something to follow up on a little better.

Beginning with Eleni's desk, I paused to unlock the three drawers and began riffling through them.

The drawers were mostly filled with various odds and ends: receipts of all kinds, notecards—some blank, some scribbled with doodles and others filled with random reminders—desk supplies, four sets of reading glasses, and a journal.

Lifting out the journal, I cracked it open and began to read.

Eleni's journal entries were an invaluable look into her private life, and from what I was able to quickly skim, she looked for ways to distribute kindness wherever she went.

I learned that Kioni wasn't the only recipient of Eleni's generosity; there were several others, and most of them were people she encountered in her everyday life.

There was a young librarian who dreamed of getting her PhD. Next to that entry was a page from a bank ledger showing that Eleni had opened a trust in the young woman's name, with the sum being large enough to pay tuition and books at a public or private university. Then there was the car mechanic who dreamed of opening his own shop, and next to it the name and contact info of a commercial real estate agent; no doubt Eleni either intended to or had purchased space for the mechanic.

And on and on it went. By my count, Eleni had helped at least a dozen people realize their dreams, and I took a moment to sit down at her desk and simply mourn her loss. She'd been a gift to the world, and someone from my world had taken her out in the cruelest way possible.

It upset me more than it normally would've. Mystics don't typically get emotional over the loss of an unbound. We know their lives are fragile and sometimes end far too easily. It makes us a bit jaded perhaps, and disconnects us from the daily struggles of genuinely good people. Sitting there, thinking about Eleni and Augustus, I felt a bit ashamed. Something I haven't felt in a long, long, *long* time.

"I'm going soft," I murmured. Clearing my throat, I flipped

to the last few entries in the journal and found just what I was looking for—sort of.

The entry from a week earlier read:

> *Summoned today by that infuriating man. God, I hate him! Discussed money, of course. He wants me to have less of it. I want him to die a terrible death. Pulled some cards and scared myself. His death is imminent. Pulled some more, and I'm done playing with them for a while. They're starting to creep me out!*

My brow furrowed at the entry. "Cards?" I muttered out loud. On a hunch I pulled open the desk drawer immediately above my lap and noticed a cloth covered bag with an envelope clasp. Lifting the bag out, I realized it had the heft and feel of a deck of cards. Opening it confirmed my suspicion, with one note: The cards weren't playing cards, it was a deck of tarot.

Curious, I flipped over the top card; it depicted a man, armed with a sword, surrounded by fire as if he were about to cut his way through the flames. The next card showed a woman falling from a tower.

One more card showed me a woman standing in a small lake, pouring a cup of water into it.

And then I turned over the next card and my breath caught again. "Whoa," I whispered, looking at a skeleton in a shroud, holding a scythe. "Death."

I sat back in Eleni's chair and furrowed my brow. There was something I'd either heard or read about certain unbounds who had a prophetic gift . . . but I couldn't pull it forward in my mind.

"What was that?" I said as I tapped my chin, trying to recall something that had to do with the gift of sight elevating an unbound's energy. Was that it? Again, I grasped at the gossamer thread of a thought, trying to pull it to the front of my mind, but the string seemed to snap and no matter how I focused I couldn't get it back again.

But that didn't mean that I didn't have a resource who could help me put the puzzle pieces together.

Placing the deck of tarot cards back in their cloth bag, I tucked them plus the journal into my purse and put everything else back in Eleni's desk just as I'd found it.

Then I left her office and made my way down the stairs. As I headed to the back door, I bumped right into Gib.

"Well, well, well," he said with a wide smile when we'd both recovered from the shock of knocking into each other. "Look who it is."

"Agent—Gib," I said curtly. This wasn't where I wanted him to find me. I probably looked suspicious as hell.

"Good morning," he said, standing firmly in my way.

I sighed heavily. "Good morning." I just knew he was going to make this a thing.

"Where're you coming from, I wonder?"

I stared him straight in the eye. "I have an office on the third floor."

We mystics are natural liars, given the fact that most of us lose our conscience somewhere around the fifty-year mark. I still held on to a bit of mine, but lying wasn't something I felt bad about.

"*You* have an office *here?*"

"Yes."

"In the same building as Eleni Katapotis?"

I adopted a quizzical look. "Eleni had an office in this building?"

Barlow looked like he itched to roll his eyes, but he decided to humor me. "Yeah, you didn't know?"

I shrugged. "I hadn't looked into it yet. But that explains the note I found slid under my door yesterday."

"What note?"

"The one where she hired me to look into the death of her brother."

He nodded like he remembered my telling him that Eleni and I hadn't met yet, and that she'd hired me via message. Still, his expression suggested that he was going to need proof.

"The message that you threw away," he said doubtfully.

I tapped him on the shoulder three times to emphasize my next three words. "That. Very. One."

He laughed but his eyes remained squinted, like he could ferret the truth out of me if only he looked hard enough.

"You know, I'd like to see this office," he said.

"Eleni's?" I asked, hoping to dodge what I knew was coming.

"Yes, and also yours. How about you accompany me upstairs to check out both?"

"Do you have a warrant?"

He barked out a laugh. "You want me to get a warrant simply to see your office?"

"Absolutely. My clients' privacy is of utmost concern to me. There's no telling what your curious eyes might discover that could land one of them in trouble. And I won't allow even the chance of that."

He crossed his arms and considered me with a look that said he knew I was full of it. "How about if I just escort you up to the third floor to see where your office is located, and pinkie promise not to set foot inside."

"You don't believe I work in this building?"

"Oh, I want to, but my brain is just *filled* with doubt." For emphasis he shook his hands by his head and widened his eyes.

I sighed again. I didn't really have time for this. "Fine," I said curtly. "Let me fish out my keys." Reaching inside my purse

I pushed a few things around before lifting out some loose change. Amongst the change was a very special silver dollar. Pushing some of my essence into the coin, I said, "Hold this, would you?"

Barlow held out his hand and I dumped the change into his outstretched palm then went back to fishing around in my purse again. After about ten seconds I looked up to find a far-away look in his eyes, entranced with the aid of the dollar.

"That's better," I whispered, taking back my spare change.

He continued to stand there, staring off into space while I adjusted the contents of my purse and then I moved to walk around him, pausing to whisper, "You never saw me here."

"I never saw you here," he muttered.

"You're on your way to Eleni's office."

"I'm on my way to Eleni's office."

"It's on the second floor."

Gib used his index finger to point upward. "It's on the second floor."

I smiled and was about to head to the exit when I paused to look him up and down and admire the view. Barlow was dressed in a crisp white dress shirt, unbuttoned to allow a little chest hair to show, and the sleeves were rolled up, displaying his lightly tanned skin. Over the shirt he wore a navy-blue vest, skinny dark blue jeans, and brandy-colored oxfords—sans socks.

The outfit was perfection on his well-muscled frame and lent him a dichotic air of casual intensity. He seemed to dress himself the same way I did, using his wardrobe as an extension of speech before he even opened his mouth.

Allowing one corner of my mouth to quirk, I whispered into his ear, "That look is sexy as hell on you."

"This look is sexy as hell on me."

I giggled, patted him on the shoulder, then walked to the door, pausing to look back and wait for the moment the spell let go. It only took a few moments before he shook his head, looked down at the phone in his hand, and began walking toward the stairs.

"That's a good boy," I whispered to his retreating form. "You'll forget we ever ran into each other."

Proceeding to my car, I set a course for Ursula's, arriving at her place at the exact same time as a solidly handsome man arriving in a bright yellow Mustang.

I recognized him immediately. "Dex," I said in greeting to the fellow mystic.

He nodded. "Dovey."

We fell into step with each other as we proceeded up to Ursula's door. "What brings you by?" I asked.

"The usual."

I pressed my lips together, suppressing a grin. Ursula was madly in love with Dex, and she'd tried every love potion she could craft to get him to feel the same way about her. For a mystic, Dex had about average magic-wielding abilities. However, the man could take a punch like no one else I knew. Only the strongest spells, trinkets, or potions could have any kind of effect on him, so the potions that Ursula typically plied him with worked only temporarily, much to her consternation.

And it wasn't that Dex was the "player" type, using Ursula to get a little action. The situation was apparently more complicated. Dex was part of a two-person thieving crew, and his counterpart was the woman he was completely devoted to.

From what Ursula told me, however, the other woman didn't feel the same way, and she'd put Dex solidly in the "just friends" category, which was a pity. Or maybe not. I couldn't quite decide what would ease the longing for my dear friend when it came to Dex.

I had to give him some credit, though, because the Aussie native was quite charming and built like a prize bodybuilder—tightly coiled muscle on top of tightly coiled muscle.

Additionally, as well as being tall and handsome, he was also sweet and thoughtful—at least according to Ursula. They had this on-again-off-again thing, and I tried not to butt in whenever she mused about whether they could have a future together. I knew Dex liked my dear friend, but I wasn't convinced he was that into her. Or ever would be.

A few steps from the porch, the front door opened, and Ursula stepped out wrapped in a dress she must've sewn herself into, holding a wineglass of purple liquid.

"So, she's not hiding the love potions this time, eh?"

Dex grinned. "We're in agreement on this one."

I allowed Dex to go first up the stairs, and he bent to give a quick kiss to Ursula before he took the glass from her and disappeared inside.

She waited for me only long enough to say, "Dovey, whatever brings you by, can it wait? That potion is strong but not long-lasting, and I want to enjoy every minute."

"How long is he sticking around for this time?"

"A day. Maybe two if I'm lucky," she said with a wicked grin.

I shook my head but offered her an understanding smile. "Call me when you come up for air."

"Promise!" she said, then turned quickly and headed inside.

After getting back in my car, I decided to stop by SPL headquarters to give Elric an update. It was a little past noon when I arrived and headed inside, moving to the elevators when Sequoia stepped out from one of them and said, "Oh, Dovey. Sorry, luv, he's not in."

"He's not?"

"No. He's gone to identify a body."

My brow shot up. "He's what?"

"Rasputin," she said, like I'd know what she meant. When I continued to look quizzically at her, she added, "You haven't heard?"

"No. Are you talking about Grigori Rasputin?" The mystic had been on the run for over a century, and he carried with him a very, *very* valuable trinket in the form of a Fabergé egg which granted the power of rejuvenation, even after all signs of life were gone.

There was a rumor that Grigori had woken up in the middle of his own autopsy when his coat was returned to the autopsy room and in its pocket was the highly valuable trinket.

"Yeah. He's finally bit the dust," Sequoia said.

"The egg gave its last offering?" The egg supposedly only had twelve offerings before it disintegrated, and Grigori had no doubt already used up at least four or five by the time he fled Russia.

Sequoia shook her head and there was a glint in her eyes. "No. If it really is Rasputin in the unbounds' morgue, then the egg has gone missing. Elric's got a thief on it, but my bet is that it's lost to the ages all over again."

"That would be unfortunate. Elric has always wanted that egg. Still, Sequoia, would you pass along to him that I'm making progress on the case, but it might take me another day or two to acquire the Promise?"

"I will, love. Count on it."

"Thanks. Where're you off to?"

Sequoia tilted her head slightly and said, "Lunch. With the boss out of the office, I figured it'd be safe to dine in an actual restaurant for a change."

"Your secret is safe with me," I assured her. We walked together out of the building and parted ways at the sidewalk.

As I walked toward my car, however, I couldn't help looking over my shoulder. I'd known Sequoia since she was first bound, well over seventy years ago, so I knew her before she'd developed the skills necessary to survive in the mystic world. I wasn't her mentor, but I'd helped her in the beginning, and something that I'd discovered was that, whenever she told a lie, she'd start it off by tilting her head ever so slightly. I'd never pointed that out to Sequoia, and it made me wonder what she was really up to.

Elric trusted her enough to keep her close to the vest, but there had always been something about her that had prevented me from fully trusting her, hence why I never told her that she had a noticeable tell.

For a moment I debated following her to see where she went, but I decided against it because if she caught me tailing her, she'd resent me for it, and as she was Elric's personal assistant, that wouldn't be in my better interests.

After getting back to the car, I pulled out Eleni's journal and flipped through the pages, trying to find any more references to the brute who'd forced her into the car.

Most of Eleni's days were occupied with family business, and it appeared that she was the recipient of a *very* handsome monthly stipend, which she tended to spend mostly on art and philanthropy.

"Why would someone want to kill you, Eleni?" I mumbled to myself while I thumbed through the pages and didn't find any other references that sounded like they fit the profile of the thug who'd strong-armed her.

And then I had another thought, mostly because of the way Eleni had phrased the events of that day. She'd pulled some cards and scared herself because she'd wanted the unnamed brute to die and had noted that his death was imminent.

Reaching for my purse again, I pulled out the tarot deck and turned over the same couple of cards from the top, laying them in my lap to look more closely. "Was it Augustus she found infuriating?" I wondered aloud.

And then I had another thought: What if Eleni had hired a mystic to murder Augustus, and maybe she hadn't been willing to pay the rest of the fee and the killer had used the Promise on her?

The scenario didn't feel like it fit, but I knew I had to investigate it anyway.

And there was another lead I wanted to track down as well, one I felt was more pressing than the other, so I pulled out of the parking space and headed toward the warehouse district.

CHAPTER 8

I arrived at Gert's Mystic Bar, which was opened to all bound and unbound, but far more mystics ventured here than our unbound cousins.

The place is owned by a mystic named Gert. I don't know her last name, in fact I don't even know if she *has* a last name, but the woman knows everyone who knows anyone within the mystic community. She's an unapologetic gossip, but if you ask for a straight answer, she'll give it to you. She holds almost no allegiance to anyone but herself, and never takes sides within the power conflicts of the town we all live in, cementing the fact that, for all intents and purposes, her watering hole is Switzerland.

"Hi Gert," I said, finding a seat at the bar.

"Dovey," she said, smiling in welcome. "What'll it be?"

"Surprise me," I told her with a small laugh. Gert had a knack for giving you what you needed over what you wanted. Many a time I'd ordered a glass of white wine, and she'd instead presented me with a chocolate martini, or a kiwi-infused gimlet.

On one particularly bad morning when I'd been frustrated by an entirely different case, I'd ordered coffee and she'd set a mug of rich hot chocolate with mounds of whipped cream and chocolate shavings in front of me.

It'd probably been the best cup of cocoa I'd ever had.

Today, after she presented me with a cup of milk and a chocolate chip cookie (Gert made the *best* chocolate chip cookies), she rested her elbows on the bar and batted her eyes at me. "What's up, Turtledove?"

I smirked because the only person besides Elric who calls me by that pet name is Gert. After taking a sip of milk to wash down the bite of cookie I just ate, I said, "I'm looking for a mystic who might've recently shown up in town."

"You'll have to be a bit more specific."

"Nicodemus Kallis is in town—"

"From Vostov's court?"

"Yes."

Gert made a face that revealed how little she cared to hear that news.

"Anyway," I said, "he brought with him one of the Pandoras."

Her eyebrows arched. "Which one?"

"The Promise."

Gert shuddered. "Elric knows this?"

"Of course."

"Then what does this have to do with a mysterious new mystic?"

"The Promise was stolen."

She snorted out a laugh and waved at me. "Get outta here."

"No, Gert," I said softly. "It's true."

Her eyebrows re-elevated. "Dovey, that's not good. That trinket's quite deadly."

"You don't know the half of it."

"So, tell me."

"Two unbounds have already been killed with it, and it's only been missing a few days."

The eyebrows crashed into confusion. "Unbounds? Who'd want to kill them?"

"I don't know, hence why I'm here inquiring about any new mystics being in town. Possibly for hire. Maybe even by an unbound."

"You think an unbound hired a mystic?"

"Possibly. I haven't been able to account for why a brother and sister from a prominent and wealthy family were targeted for assassination with a trinket as powerful as the Promise unless an unbound was somehow connected to the mystic world."

Gert puffed out a breath. "Small few of them in existence, that's for sure."

"I know it's a longshot, but I'm working a case where I don't have any clear leads and it's beginning to annoy me."

Gert nodded and folded her arms across her ample bosom. "The only mystic that I haven't recognized coming in here was a blonde, recently bound."

"How recently?"

"She might've just graduated from her mentorship."

While I knew even a very newly bound mystic could wield the magic of the Promise, I didn't know if anyone would hire someone so newly *minted*, so to speak.

"Any other details on her appearance? Was she with anyone?"

Gert puffed out another breath. "She was tall, thin, pretty-looking thing. And she was with Tick's girlfriend, if you can believe it."

My own brows arched. "Bree?" Bree was an unpleasant woman. She had an on-again-off-again relationship with Marco, Petra's son.

I'd met Marco a few times, and although he was a bit self-serving, I didn't find him to live up to his reported reputation of being an annoying little man. In fact, I'd enjoyed the brief conversations we'd had, and I'd always felt sorry for him to have been raised by such an evil woman. I'd heard that he'd once displeased his mother and she'd invoked his binding spell, letting him twitch and writhe for a day and a half, which had in fact killed him, but she'd then brought him back to life with one of her more powerful trinkets and made sure that he understood the next time he defied her, she wouldn't bring him back to life.

It was another reason I hated Petra. She was excessively cruel.

"How do I get in touch with Bree?" I asked. It wasn't much of a lead, but it might be something.

"You don't," Gert said.

I cocked my head at her but then said, "How about Marco?"

Gert shook her head and leaned forward conspiratorially. "Bree's dead and Marco's missing."

My jaw dropped. "What?"

"Happened the night before last. There was an explosion at Bree's place, which she didn't survive, and Marco was there at the time, but no one's found a trace of him since."

"Did he set the explosion?" Marco and Bree were always fighting. It wouldn't have surprised me if he'd decided to end it once and for all.

"Doubtful," Gert said. "Word on the street is that he was wounded bad enough he couldn't have made it out of the building on his own.

"Someone helped him."

"Seems like it."

"Maybe this new mystic? The blonde?"

Gert shrugged again. "Listen, I'll keep my ear to the ground if you tell Elric to send a few more SPL employees here for happy hour."

I slipped my hand inside my purse, finding the little trinket I had meant to give to Gert anyway, and brought it up with an open palm.

"Cute," she said, taking the little doggie Monopoly player's piece. "What does the trinket do?"

"Push some essence into it and anyone within ten feet of you will become very thirsty," I said with a wink.

Gert's face lit up. "I do love a thirsty crowd."

I set some cash on the bar to cover the milk, cookie, and a generous tip, then slid off the barstool, offering Gert my good-byes before heading out to Luna again where I took a moment to do a little internet sleuthing. When I had the address I needed, I headed first to the nearest flower shop, then to the other side of town.

I arrived at a tony row of brownstones only a half hour later, smiling to myself because the trip should have taken at least fifteen minutes longer, but I know more than a few good spells for turning red lights green, and making the unbounds in front of me switch lanes or speed up. It takes a bit more concentration, but it's worth shaving off an extra fifteen to twenty minutes for every commute across town.

After parking the car, I approached one of the brownstones, taking in the tiny front yard that was overflowing with spring flowers in the center of which was a four-foot-tall, partially oxidized copper statue in the shape of angel wings, folding inward.

I loved it. And somehow, looking at that lovely statue amid those beautiful flowers didn't seem to reconcile with my theory that Augustus could've been the brutish man whom Eleni was referring to in her journal. I simply doubted that someone who seemed to enjoy the elegance and beauty of fine art could be a brute. Plus, I remembered all his philanthropic good deeds, and the two versions of his personality simply didn't jibe.

Still, I owed it to myself to at least confirm it, so I headed up the steps and rang the doorbell. It was opened by a young woman wearing a glorious mane of long black hair, with breathtaking features and a body to kill for. She was wearing a cream velvet tracksuit and fuzzy black slippers. Her outfit managed to look more trendy than casual.

"Yes?" she asked.

"Hello," I said, offering her the bouquet of white lilies I'd selected from the flower shop. "My name is Dovey Van Dalen and I just heard about Augustus's passing. I know this is an intrusion, but I couldn't help myself. I wanted to offer my sincere condolences to his family."

She took the bouquet and offered me a sad smile. "Thanks, Dovey. Did you know him?"

"I did. He was in a few of my art classes."

"At Carnegie Mellon?"

I nodded. "Back in the day," I said, adding a wink.

"Wow, you don't look the same age as my uncle."

I gave a demure pat to my hair. "Why thank you. The right moisturizer helps."

She smiled genuinely and I took the opportunity to pretend that my phone had just vibrated and pulled open my purse to say, "Oh! Where is that phone?" Taking out the same handful of loose change that I'd handed Barlow, I offered it to the young woman and said, "Could you hold this for a second?"

She accepted it with her free hand, and I only had to wait a few moments before her look became vacant. "You want to invite me in," I said.

"Would you like to come in?"

"You'd like to offer me some coffee and have a little chat about your uncle and Eleni Katapotis."

"I'd like to offer you some coffee and we can chat about my uncle and Aunt Eleni."

"Yes, thank you," I said, taking back my change from her still outstretched palm. "Please lead the way."

We moved through a rather dark foyer, past a staircase on the right, a study on the left, and a closed door off the hallway that could've been a powder room, all the way to the back where the kitchen and living room were located.

The kitchen was a nice mix of espresso-colored wood tones

and a stunning resin countertop with great swirls of blue, gold, and black tones against a white backdrop.

Five different barstools were set up to the countertop, and beyond the kitchen area was a gorgeous living room, painted black with an ebony-colored velvet sectional, adorned with dark chocolate pillows in varying textures from leather to fur and an oversized cashmere throw in a rich dark umber. Above the seating area was an array of abstract paintings all designed by the same artist who painted black canvases with shiny copper logographs.

And in the center of the sable-colored coffee table was another partially oxidized copper statue of a pair of angelic wings taking the shape of a heart.

Again, I loved the entire setting.

"Beautiful home," I said, taking a seat at the counter while my host popped a pod into the coffee maker.

"It's my uncle's," the woman said, and I could tell the effects of my silver-dollar trinket were beginning to wear off.

"And your name is?" I asked.

"Hermia," she said. "Hermia Ariti."

"Ah, and you're the daughter of . . . ?"

"Ambrose Ariti," she said, her back still to me. And then she stood still for a moment and shook her head, and I knew that the trinket had fully released her from its spell, but she wouldn't remember being under its influence and she likely wouldn't think twice about the fact that I was in her uncle's kitchen.

"I'm also sorry about your aunt Eleni," I said gently.

She turned and there was a sour look on her face. "Uncle Augustus I'll mourn, but not my aunt."

I cocked my head at her. "Oh? You and your aunt didn't get along?"

"No," she said offering no further explanation.

And then I was back to wondering where the lines of bad

blood might lie within this family. "Well, your uncle usually spoke fondly of her. At least when we were in school together."

She placed a steaming mug of coffee in front of me. "Uncle Augie loved everybody. But Eleni earned her banishment. Believe me."

My brow rose in surprise. "Banishment? She was banished from the family?"

"Yep," Hermia said, again offering no further explanation.

I tapped my fingernails against the porcelain coffee cup. "Still, it's a tragedy what happened to both your uncle and aunt. And both deaths so close together."

Hermia shook her head. "I've had nightmares about what happened to my uncle. He was terrified of fire, you know."

"I remember," I said, as if he and I had discussed it at length in our youth.

"I just don't understand how it happened. Why didn't he get out? He was right in front of the exit! All he had to do was walk a few feet to the front door, and he would've been clear. Why would he stand there and die?"

"The smoke might've disoriented him," I said gently. "Or he was so quickly overpowered by it that he died before he even had a chance to run."

Hermia stared with wide, horrified eyes at the countertop as if her imagination could replay the scene of what'd happened in that art gallery.

I was glad she didn't know the truth, which was that Augustus was alive and conscious of what he was doing when he doused himself with gasoline and lit the match, and was just unable to stop himself. A shudder threatened to crawl up my spine, but I was able to suppress it.

Hermia sighed and lifted her own mug to sip the black liquid demurely. "Uncle Augie's wake is tomorrow night. Are you coming?"

"Of course," I said, and meant it. "What time and where again?"

"It's a closed casket, obviously," she said, shutting her eyes and shaking her head, clearly still haunted by the details of her uncle's passing. "But it starts at six and ends at nine, at the De Vol Funeral Home on Wisconsin."

"I'll find it. And, without meaning to upset you, do you know the details of Eleni's funeral arrangements?"

Hermia's eyes went flat, and she said, "Auntie committed suicide, so no funeral for her. We're strict Greek Orthodox in my family. She'll get cremated and laid to rest in an unmarked grave."

Again, I couldn't help my surprise. Eleni's journal was filled with good deeds and kind thoughts for others. What could she have possibly done to earn the rejection of her family so intensely?

I wanted to prod a little more, but I was worried that, now that the trinket's effect had worn off, Hermia might get suspicious if I pushed the sensitive topic, so I went back to focusing on Augustus.

"Do you live here too?" I asked, again making a point to look around and appreciate the surroundings.

Hermia sighed sadly. "No. I was born here but live in Italy now—anything to be away from so much of the family drama. I flew into town for the annual family meeting, but that's been postponed until my dad can figure out what effect Uncle Augie's and Aunt Eleni's estates are going to have on the distribution of monthly annuities to the rest of us. He's asked me to stick around for a while and, as I was already staying with Augie, he said to just hang out here until everything gets figured out."

"You stayed with your uncle over your parents?" I asked as innocently as I could.

"I'd stay in a lion's den over staying with my parents. It'd be safer."

I laughed lightly. "Are you an only child, Hermia?"

She sighed dramatically. "Yeah. And I probably fit the spoiled brat, daughter of rich parents stereotype, but in my defense, my parents are both narcissists and growing up in that house was not fun. I spent more time with Augie than I ever did with either of them. My uncle was more a father to me than my dad, that's for sure."

"Are your parents still together?" I knew the answer but wanted to hear her tell it.

"Nope. They split a couple of years ago, during the end of my senior year in college. Thank God I was at least out of the house by then. Mom's living in New York, working her way up yet another corporate ladder, and Dad's got a new wife, so he's clearly moved on."

Hermia's nose wrinkled at the mention of the new wife, so I said, "Not a fan of your dad's wife either, I gather."

Hermia leveled her eyes at me. "She's three years older than me, and all about the bling." For effect she held up her left hand and pointed to that ring finger.

"Ah," I said. "A wallet sniffer."

Hermia laughed. "That's one way to put it."

Noting that Hermia had tapped her left ring finger, I asked, "How long have they been married?"

One corner of Hermia's lips curled into a snide smile. "A week," she said, with a meaningful look. "Now that there are two less players on the distribution list, her timing for coming into the family fortune is impeccable, no?"

"Eerily so," I said.

Hermia puffed out a breath. "If I didn't know better, I'd say Daddy's new wife had a hand in my uncle's death, but he told me that the police have ruled out foul play, and that it was just an accident."

I nodded, noting that, as much as she disliked her father, at least he was trying to protect her from the truth that Augustus was the one who'd set himself and the gallery ablaze.

Still, the mention of her father being in a new relationship did set my warning bells ringing. Could she be the one who'd hired the mystic to get rid of the other family members? And was Hermia perhaps in danger?

The thought was unsettling. Standing up from the chair, I placed the cup in the sink just beyond where I'd been sitting and said, "Thank you for the coffee, Hermia. I should let you get back to your day."

She smiled but the sadness in her eyes remained. "Thank you for caring about my uncle."

Hermia walked me out and I waited until I was back in my car before lifting out my cell phone and the card with Gib's number.

"Hi," I said when he answered. "It's Dovey. I need to talk to you . . ."

Chapter 9

Gib arrived on time, which I always appreciate in a man. The rain that'd been threatening all day finally showed up just before four—which was when I made it to a local coffee shop called Bette's, which is just down the street from my place.

I knew Bette, she'd opened the coffee shop in the 1980s when she'd divorced her husband and had to support herself and her young son. The shop had done well, mostly because the woman knew how to make a great cup of coffee and a light, flaky pastry. Plus she was personable and kind, which I respect in an unbound.

Bette had passed away in 2010, which was ten years after I'd had to find a different coffee shop. We mystics age so slowly that our perpetual youth can start to attract a little too much inspection, and, since I hadn't aged a day in nearly twenty years, Bette had started to grow suspicious.

After her death I heard that the shop had been inherited by her son and his young wife, who was the one who ran the place now. She had no idea of my history with the neighborhood going back a hundred years or so, and I'd loved haunting the coffee shop again, especially after finding out that Stella—Bette's daughter-in-law—also knew her way around a great cup of coffee and a delicious pastry.

She'd managed to keep Bette's reputation intact, while simultaneously honoring her mother-in-law, and I also respect that in an unbound.

When Gib came through the door shaking off the rain, I was cuddled up in the corner of the shop, nearly the lone patron, sitting near the gas fireplace, nibbling on a cheese Danish.

The moment he spotted me, his eyes lit up, and I was glad that it was rather dim in the shop today, what with the lack of daylight streaming in through the windows. Otherwise, Agent Barlow might've seen me blush.

"Hey there," he said, pulling a chair out before tilting it on one leg to smoothly twirl it under his fingers before stopping it when it faced backward so that he could straddle it and look at me across the small table.

Damn, I do love a man who knows how to straddle a chair.

"Gib. Thank you for coming."

He smiled and it held a flirtatious quality that nearly made me break eye contact. "Wouldn't have missed it," he said, the loose gravel of his voice reverberating through the timber of his tone. Crossing his arms over the top of the chair he added, "What's up?"

I subtly held up a finger as Stella emerged at our table, producing a steaming cup of black coffee and a second cheese Danish. "I did the honor of ordering ahead for you," I told him.

His grin widened and he looked from me to Stella and said, "Nothing better than a coffee and cheese Danish combo. Thank you, ma'am."

It was her turn to blush, and she did a small, crossed-ankle curtsey before hurrying away. I tried to stifle a laugh, but it was impossible.

"What?" he asked, chuckling along with me.

I shook my head. "The effect you have on women must be a

burden. How *do* you manage to get through the day with all that great charm and good looks?"

His hesitant laugh turned full-bodied. "It's the clothes," he said, sweeping a hand down his torso. "This look is sexy as hell on me."

I ducked my chin and lifted my coffee cup, doing my level best not to burst out laughing again. My silver dollar trinket had made a definite imprint on him today.

Still, as he said that part out loud, he seemed to catch himself and he shook his head ruefully. "Wow. Don't I sound full of myself? Sorry. I don't know where that came from."

I do, I thought. But I certainly wasn't going to tell *him* that. "It's fine," I assured him. "That look definitely flatters you."

He shrugged. "Before joining the FBI I did some modeling."

"Where?"

Gib spooned some sugar into his coffee. "New York, Milan, Paris . . . the usual places."

I rested my chin on my hand, absolutely fascinated by this man who'd gone from a high-end modeling career into the FBI.

"Anyway," he continued, "I ended up buying a lot of the clothes I was photographed in, and from there I started to get my own sense of style. I like fashion both as an expression and as art."

I nodded with enthusiasm. "I feel the same way. I've often thought of fashion as its own language, and each of us on any given day are living breathing logograms."

He cocked his head, studying me curiously. "Huh. That's a fascinating way to look at it. I completely agree."

"Thank you," I said, feeling the blush touch my cheeks again.

Gib bit into his cheese Danish and moaned. "Wow!" he said, his mouth still full. "That's . . ." He paused to chew a little more, finishing with another "Wow."

I nodded toward the woman behind the counter. "Stella bakes them herself."

Holding up the Danish, he turned toward Stella, who was back behind the counter, periodically glancing over at us. "Delicious!" he told her, and Stella's face turned beet red, but her smile was ear to ear.

"Try the coffee," I told him, knowing he'd love that too.

Obliging me, he wiped his mouth, then lifted his coffee cup to blow on the steaming liquid before taking a sip. "Oh, wow," he said again. "That's smooth. I swear Americans have gotten so used to the tar they serve at most coffeehouses that they've lost the ability to *taste* a good, perfectly brewed cup of coffee."

"Exactly," I said, pointing to him.

Taking another longer sip, Gib swallowed and set down the cup. "So, why are we meeting today, Dovey Van Dalen?"

"How's your investigation going, Gib?"

He grinned at me. "Still answering questions with questions, eh?"

"I do what works," I replied with a smile.

He nodded. "I can respect that. In answer to your question, lots of dead ends so far. You?"

I tapped the table with my index finger, trying to decide if I should trust this man or not. "Have you spoken to any of the family members?"

"You mean the ones still alive?"

"Naturally."

"I have yet to speak to Ambrose. We had an appointment to meet yesterday, but then Eleni died and that threw the whole day into a tailspin. I have a message in to speak to Augustus's partner, but I haven't heard back from him yet. I'm due to bring Ambrose up to speed by the end of the day, but I don't have much in the way of leads. It's still early in the investigation, but if you have anything you'd like to share, I'm all ears."

"I spoke with Hermia Ariti—"

"Ambrose's daughter," he said with a knowing nod. He'd done his homework.

"Yes. She lives abroad but came home to visit and she was staying at Augustus's place when he died. She was close with her uncle but despised her aunt Eleni. According to her, the family had all but shut Eleni out."

"Why?"

"She didn't say."

"Hmmm, that's curious, don't you think?"

"It is, because I have it on good authority that Eleni was kind, thoughtful, quite generous, and very philanthropic. From everything that I've been able to gather about her personality, she was a lovely woman with a good heart, so I haven't a clue what the family found so objectionable about her that they'd turn her into a pariah.

"She's not even getting a proper burial. The Aritis are of a strong Greek Orthodox faith and they've decided to cremate and bury her without any form of a ceremony."

Gib's brow lowered. "That's harsh."

"Agreed."

Stella appeared at the table with a pot of coffee and another Danish. "Need a warmup?" she asked him like I wasn't even present.

"I'd love one," he said, even though he'd only taken a few sips of his. As if he was aware that there wasn't much room in the cup, he held up his index finger and slurped a few times to give her room for the fresh brew. After topping off his cup, she set down a blueberry cheese Danish and said, "This one's on the house."

He pressed his palms together and held them up to her. "Thank you, Stella. You're the best."

Stella inhaled a surprised breath, no doubt taken with the

fact that he knew her name without her wearing a name tag, and she did another ankle curtsey before hurrying away.

Gib watched her go, then turned back to me, thumbing toward her retreating form to say, "Nice lady."

"Indeed," I agreed. Stella really was.

Gib then did something surprising by reaching for the knife at the side of his plate and proceeding to cut the Danish in two, lifting half onto his empty plate and sliding the other half toward me.

It was a small thing, for sure, but it was meaningful in that most men I'd met—especially in this town—would've simply eaten the entire Danish themselves. But not Gib. He didn't even have to think about it. He was simply self-aware, and I found myself softening toward him again, which was dangerous, but I was having a hard time keeping my emotional distance. I couldn't help it. I liked him. I simply liked him.

"Thank you," I said, taking the pastry and cutting into it with my fork. I'd had every kind of Danish Bette's had ever created, but the blueberry was indeed a favorite.

"Oh my God," Gib moaned, biting into his half. Again, he turned toward Stella and offered her a thumbs-up. After swallowing he called across the room, "I'm going to need a dozen of those to go, Stella. You'll make me a hero with the guys back at the office."

For fun he offered her a double-arm bicep pump, and she laughed and laughed, then trotted off to start emptying the pastry cabinet.

Turning back to me, he grinned wide again, and I had to hold in another laugh when I saw the bit of blueberry on his upper lip. I motioned to my own lip, tapping it to let him know that he needed to wipe his, but his expression became a bit devilish when he said, "Oh, do I have something on my mouth?"

I laughed. "Yes, you do."

Gib wiped the other side of his mouth as if unable to figure out which side I meant. "Did I get it?"

I rolled my eyes, but I was still laughing. "No. Other side."

He wiped the same side again and said, "How about now. Is it gone?"

I pointed my gaze at the tabletop. "Yeah, you got it!" I refused to look at him and continue the game.

"Well, that's a relief. Wouldn't want to walk around with goop on my lip. Now, where were we?"

My gaze remained fixed on the table as I tried to keep from laughing. This was serious business after all. Taking a cleansing breath I said, "Augustus's wake is tomorrow night from six to nine at the De Vol Funeral Home on Wisconsin. I think we should go."

"Together?"

I lifted my gaze to tell him no and saw a giant blob of purple on his lip, the scoundrel! He'd added to the mess. And the laugh I'd been holding in burst out and my sides shook as he looked at me innocently before breaking out in a grin himself.

And we laughed like that for several moments before I sobered and took my own napkin to reach across and wipe off the distracting fruit filling. "You're irascible," I scolded.

"And you're beautiful," he said. My breath caught.

Our gazes locked and for a heartbeat I forgot who and where I was. The urge to lean forward and kiss the man was a spell all its own. I found myself blinking furiously against the chemical spark that seemed to ignite between us whenever Gib was nearby.

"I . . ." I began, but I couldn't seem to form words beyond that.

"You?" he said.

"I . . ." I tried again and just as I was about to add more the door opened with an incoming patron and my blood turned cold.

The energy in the shop immediately shifted, and I knew without even looking that Elric Ostergaard had just entered.

Across from me, Gib said, "Dovey? Are you all ri—" And that's as far as he got before he froze, as did everything and everyone else in the place.

Sitting back in my chair, I willed my heart to stop hammering away at the inside of my rib cage and looked up at the man I'd loved for nearly two hundred years.

"Tortelduif," he said softly, moving to stand at the side of our table.

"Hello, Elric." I was unable to add more.

Elric's expression was . . . confused? Angry? Suspicious? Jealous? For the first time in our entire relationship, I couldn't read what he was thinking.

And that scared me in a way that he'd never scared me before.

"Who's this?" he asked, his gaze sliding to Gib, who sat completely frozen, his mouth open mid-sentence. He had his right elbow resting on the table, his hand lazily relaxed which exposed his Audemars Piguet, the second hand notably stopped in its silent rotation around the dial.

My eyes darted to Elric's wrist and the nearly identical timepiece he wore there. He'd stopped time, which meant that he and I were now contained in a bubble that existed outside of time, and within which Elric could do anything he wanted to anyone in this room.

"He's an unbound," I said, looking up at him in a way that I hoped projected calm confidence.

"Yes. And . . . ?"

"And he's with the FBI. He's been assigned to the suspicious death of Augustus Ariti, and his sister, Eleni Katapotis."

"The gallery owner and the philanthropist," Elric said. It didn't surprise me that he knew the details of a case he'd assigned without receiving any formal update from me. Elric had spies everywhere, which didn't mean he'd been spying on me. Bette's was less than half a mile from my home, and Luna was hard to miss being parked out on the street. If Elric had come looking for me, I'd made myself easy to find.

"How is the case coming along, my dove?" he said, his voice the same soft, soothing sound I'd come to love and adore, but there was a hardness to his eyes that was impossible to miss. He'd never looked at me like that, and it shook me to the core.

"It's confounding, my love. It's possible that a mystic is using the Promise to kill the unbound members of a powerful family for reasons of their own, but it's also possible that an unbound has been able to hire a mystic to commit the deeds."

"What could an unbound offer a mystic valuable enough to take the risk of stealing the Promise?"

"I do not know," I admitted with a sigh. "But I've learned that there was bad blood between Eleni and the rest of her family, and perhaps she was the one who hired a mystic to kill her brother and when she didn't pay up, or when the mystic felt like Eleni was a loose end, he used the Promise on her."

"It still begs the question what Eleni could've had that was valuable enough to a mystic to hire him or her in the first place, doesn't it?"

"It does. It had to be something more than money, because what do we care about the unbound's useless paper currency? Trinkets are our currency of choice."

"Yes," Elric said, his gaze sliding to Gib for a second time.

"My running theory is that maybe Eleni had a powerful trinket all her own."

Elric's eyes sought mine again. "Go on."

"Well," I said, thinking this through on the spot and feeling the pressure of keeping Elric's attention long enough for him to be satisfied with my progress, then hopefully depart leaving everyone in the coffee shop alive. "Augustus and Eleni collected art and they both had large private collections. What if the mystic wasn't trying to kill off the family members so much as he or she was trying to hunt down a specific trinket that one of them had unwittingly come into possession of."

"Hmm," Elric said, tapping his chin thoughtfully. "If you're right, and the mystic used the trinket to steal another trinket, then I'll want to know what it was, *and* I'll want the Promise back in the hands of Kallis before he's scheduled to leave in three days."

"Of course," I said quickly, but inwardly I tensed. Could I locate the Promise in time? If my theory was right, and the mystic had acquired what he or she had been looking for, then had they already left town?

The killings seemed to have stopped, so maybe the murdering mystic had escaped to parts unknown.

Elric continued to look at me expectantly and I tried to offer him a genuine smile. It helped that we shared 182 years of history together, and for that entire length of time he'd been my whole world.

And when I offered him that smile, I saw his eyes soften, and he leaned forward to kiss me ever so gently before stroking my hair and standing tall again. Pointing to Gib without looking at him, he said, "Be careful with that one, Dovey. The unbound don't belong in our world."

"I know," I told him truthfully, and the realization was more disappointing than I expected.

With that, Elric turned on his heel and headed out of the coffee shop, and even before the door had fully closed, I heard Gib say, "—ight?"

I focused on him as if I hadn't skipped a beat. "Of course I'm all right. But I do have to leave for another appointment. I'll be in touch if I learn anything else."

Getting to my feet, I gathered my purse and keys and was about to leave when Gib's hand came to rest gently on my arm. "Was it something I said?"

I looked at him, ready to brush him off and distance myself from him, but as I stared at his beautiful face with those fathomless silver-gray eyes, I found myself softening. "No," I told him. "It wasn't. I . . . I just have to get on with my day. Let's meet at the funeral home tomorrow night around seven."

"Okay, sure," he said, releasing me, but when he did so, his watch slid off his wrist and hit the floor where it broke into several pieces like it'd been made of eggshells.

I sucked in a breath as I saw the watch crumble. That was Elric's doing.

"What the . . . ?" Gib said, staring at the broken timepiece like he couldn't believe his eyes.

Seeing an unexpected opportunity, I bent down, picked up all the pieces of his watch, and said, "I know someone who can repair this better than new, if you'll let me have it for a few days?"

Gib's mouth hung open, obviously still in shock. His eyes went from me to the pieces of the watch in my hand, back up to meet my gaze again.

"Good," I said, as if he'd already said yes. "Thanks for trusting me." With that I hurried out the door.

Many hours later I sat in my car, waiting patiently for a light to go on in the top-floor window of a three-story house belonging to a mystic I knew well, and quite adored.

Bits lay bundled in my lap, curled into a ball atop a cashmere beret I'd been fond of wearing until Bits became fonder of turning it into his traveling bed.

I often liked to take him with me on stakeouts like this. Even though he slept through most of these excursions, knowing he was with me helped take the loneliness out of the duty.

At last, at nearly quarter past one a.m. a light went on in the top floor of the three-story house. I brought Bits up to my chest to cuddle him and whispered, "I'll be back in a few minutes, my sweet picklepuss."

Setting him down again, I pivoted in my seat and got out of the car, closing the door as softly as I could.

Approaching the house, I avoided the front door and went around to the back. Once there I took out of the pocket of my large tote bag a pair of high heels with small steel plates affixed to the bottom. Stepping out of the shoes I was wearing, I carefully put the other pair on, then lifted my knee high right next to the house and whispered,

"*Where the air has met no stair,*

"*My heels to dance can take the chance,*

"*And climb the wall that's there.*"

Immediately I felt the area under my elevated heel gain purchase, and from there I climbed up the side of the building as if I were merely climbing a staircase, each footfall tapping against the invisible steps.

Once I reached the window with the light on in it, I tapped lightly three times, then paused, then another three times, with yet another pause, followed by four knocks separated by one beat.

The window creaked open and from inside I heard a man's voice say, "Dovey Van Dalen, it's been too long."

Bending low I eased myself in through the window to stand in the middle of a large room that was littered with the broken bits of thousands of trinkets stacked all over a series of tables that encircled the room.

I opened my arms wide. "Hello, Arlo, my friend."

The man across from me was a giant—literally. He easily stood seven feet tall in a hunched-over posture. My guess was that he'd been closer to seven feet, three or four inches tall when he was younger.

Over the centuries, his posture had become more and more hunched due to constantly bending over the trinkets he repaired or infused, which he was quite adept at. While not a true merlin in the sense that he couldn't harness immense quantities of electromagnetic current, he was still able to harness a great deal more than the average mystic which made him both a sought-after resource and someone who lived in fear.

Merlin mystics—even those that are close to that skill level—are never quite safe from other mystics seeking greater power, and Arlo knew he lived in a precarious middle ground that he was quite careful to tread.

He bent down awkwardly to hug me very gently before stepping back and asking, "What do you need?"

I pulled out the broken pieces of Gib's watch and said, "This watch, or what's left of it, repaired and infused."

Arlo held out his giant palm and I placed the pieces into it. His eyes flashed from it back up to me. "This isn't a trinket, Dovey."

I nodded. "It's not a trinket *yet*, Arlo."

He sighed and flipped the face of the watch over to inspect it. "A Piguet. Elric has one just like it. Does he want a duplicate?"

"No. This is for another friend of mine."

The bushy eyebrows hovering over Arlo's pale blue eyes arched. "Some friend."

I bit my lip. "He's an unbound."

One corner of Arlo's mouth lifted to a knowing smirk, and he shuffled over to a nearby stool to sit down and consider me. "What power would you like this infused with?"

I shifted my weight from foot to foot. What I was going to request wasn't an easy ask, and, if it got out that I'd asked Arlo to design a trinket with this specific function, it could look very bad for me. Still, it wasn't Gib's fault that I'd put him in danger. That weight landed squarely on my shoulders. "I need the trinket to give an unbound some protection."

"An unbound needs protecting? From whom?"

"Elric Ostergaard."

Arlo's brow shot up and he eyed me in alarm. "You want me to create a trinket that will give an unbound protection against *Elric*? Are you out of your mind, Dovey?"

I sighed. "I might be."

"What has this unbound done to warrant a need for such a trinket?"

"He had coffee with me."

"Did he refuse to pass the cream and sugar?"

I blew out a breath. "It's complicated."

"When isn't it?"

"I just need this man to have a little protection, Arlo. Just even enough so that he doesn't immediately fall dead should Elric snap his fingers."

"An unbound is no match for Elric's fatal power, Dovey. Most *mystics* aren't a match for that. In fact, I suspect there are less than half a dozen mystics in the world who could withstand a fatal curse from Elric, you and I included."

I stared at my shoes. I knew for a fact that Elric had witnessed the chemistry between Gib and me, and even knowing that Elric would never hurt me, I knew he wouldn't think twice about dispatching a rival for my attention. It didn't matter that Elric had plenty of other women he enjoyed keeping company with—it only mattered that he was my one and only.

"Why don't you spellbind this selfish keeper of cream and sugar?" Arlo asked. "That way he'd have at least some natural protection. Not enough to withstand Elric, but it'd be better than nothing."

I sighed heavily and looked skyward before focusing my gaze back on Arlo. "That thought had crossed my mind, but I don't think it's fair to bind an unwilling mortal."

"How do you know he'd be unwilling?"

I didn't waver answering. "Keeping him unbound helps me keep my distance. And I *need* to keep some distance, Arlo."

Understanding dawned in the mystic's expression. "You like him."

"I don't know. Maybe? The point is that I *can't* develop feelings for him. It'd be akin to killing him myself. Elric wouldn't stand for it."

"No. No he would not," Arlo agreed. "All right, Dovey. I'll fix you up a trinket. If Elric targets your unbound it might not make any difference, but it could buy you a little time to convince him to reverse the spell. That's all I can promise."

"Thank you!" I said on a breath of release.

"You're welcome. When would you like it?"

"By tomorrow night?" I crossed my fingers hoping he'd do the rush job for me.

He nodded. "I can accommodate that deadline."

"You're wonderful, Arlo. Thank you again. What did you want in return?"

I knew the trinket master wouldn't want money, he'd want something else, and I was hoping I could pay whatever his price was without too much fuss.

He didn't even take a moment to think about it. "There's a trinket I'd like back. It was taken from me a few months ago by a thief named Lavender."

I grimaced. "I know her."

"Good. It'll make it easier. The trinket is a hand lantern, circa the 1870s. It's small, only about twelve centimeters tall and the roof of it rotates to display either a green, yellow, or red glow from the candle inside."

"Weren't those used by the police to control traffic back in the day?" I asked. I remembered seeing them around town in the late 1800s. They'd been a precursor to the traffic light.

"They were."

"What's the trinket's purpose now?"

"The red light douses all other light within a controlled environment. The green light lets the light back in. And the yellow light gives me a youthful glow." He pursed his lips and fluffed his white hair for effect.

I laughed at his antics but then realized its true purpose. "You drove with it, didn't you?"

"I did," he said. "As you well know, I can't tolerate sunlight, and while I don't mind my nocturnal lifestyle, occasionally I do like to venture out during the daytime. That lantern allowed the whole interior of my car to remain dark even during the brightest days. I've been cooped up here every day since it's been gone, and I'd replace it on my own except that the trinket also has significant sentimental value. It was given to me by Mercedes Stark."

"*The* Mercedes Stark?" The mystic was a bit of a legend. She was an artist of magnificent talent and imbued most of her artwork—mostly sculptures—with her own essence, turning them into trinkets that the mystic world had come to covet. Like Arlo, she was also an albino and in recent years she'd become quite the recluse and hadn't produced a work of art in a long, long time.

"Yes, *the* Mercedes Stark," Arlo confirmed. "I've known her since she was newly mystic. She and I even had a tryst for a decade or two, so it's not enough for me to recreate a trinket that will do what that lantern can. I want *that* lantern, Dovey. It means something to me."

I reached out and laid a hand on the man's arm. "I'll bring it back to you, Arlo. I promise."

He softened and gave my hand a pat. "And I'll give you a fine trinket for your unbound."

I left Arlo to his work, making it back to my car, and once inside I let my forehead rest against the steering wheel. Lavender was a very good thief. She didn't work for either Petra or Elric, preferring to freelance. Because she was a free agent, she'd not only be hard to find, she'd be dangerous to deal with.

I also couldn't request the aid of anyone that worked for

SPL because that might raise some flags with Elric. He'd want to know why I was trying to find Lavender, and my binding spell made it impossible to lie to Elric Ostergaard.

Even then, most mystics wouldn't, either.

Still, pursuing Lavender was far too dangerous to go it alone.

Reaching for my phone I dialed a number. "Hey," I said. "It's me. I need your help, and I need it soon . . ."

CHAPTER 10

"This plan has so many flaws," Ursula grumbled in the late afternoon the following day.

My dear friend was sitting in a booth at Gert's place, waiting for Lavender to appear. Ursula had asked to meet with Lavender on the pretense that she needed to hire the mystic for a job and was willing to pay a decent price for it.

I was across the room in another booth, watching the door, and could hear Ursula perfectly given the thimble trinket I'd loaned her.

I didn't bother to verbally console her because the thimble only worked one way. Still I agreed. My plan had been cobbled together rather quickly as time was of the essence, but its flaws couldn't be helped now. We were in for a penny and a pound.

While we waited for the thief to appear, my gaze traveled to the bar where a group of boisterous SPL employees were eating and drinking, running up a large tab. Behind the bar, Gert glanced at me and winked, happy to have an increase in business for an otherwise slow day, which was precisely why she'd agreed to serve a drink that she wouldn't actually make to table number five, where Ursula currently sat, as soon as Lavender appeared.

Taking a sip of the cucumber-and-mint-infused lemonade

Gert had presented me with, I glanced at my phone to check the time, and just like I thought, Lavender was ten minutes late.

Like most mystics, Lavender came with a professional reputation, which was probably a C+ overall. She was known for being perpetually late, indifferent to urgent requests, sloppy, difficult to work with, and underhanded in most every way.

And because she was rarely on the up-and-up, she was a suspicious creature, which meant we'd need to play this very, very carefully.

Five minutes later, Lavender finally walked in. She scanned the bar with narrowed eyes, looking for any signs of trouble. I felt her gaze slide over me as I pretended to be on a phone call. At last Lavender acknowledged Ursula with a nod as my friend waved her over.

"Thank you for coming," I heard Ursula say when Lavender slid into the seat.

"You got a job for me?" the mystic replied, not even apologizing for being late.

"I do, but it's a bit tricky."

I looked over at Gert, who was already on her way to the booth where the pair sat.

"Lavender," Gert said when she arrived at the table. "Long time no see."

Lavender shrugged. "You know how it is, Gert. I'm a busy girl."

Gert thumbed over her shoulder toward the boisterous group at the bar. "Preachin' to the choir. What can I getcha?"

Lavender pursed her lips and surveyed the bottles that adorned the shelves above the bar and at that moment Ursula sipped loudly through the straw of her drink.

Lavender's attention pivoted to Ursula's cocktail. "What's that?" she asked, pointing to the glass.

Ursula shrugged. "Gert made it for me, and it's fantastic. I'll have another, Gert, if you don't mind."

Lavender nodded. "Bring one of those for me too. Makes it easy."

Gert smiled, then turned on her heel and went back to the bar while Ursula and Lavender continued their conversation.

"You were saying that the job is tricky?" Lavender asked.

"Yes. A trinket from my collection has gone missing, and I suspect I know who took it, but it'd be politically unwise to inquire about it. I'm hoping you can retrieve it without my having to make an accusation."

"Who do you think stole it?"

"Nicodemus Kallis."

Lavender's eyes widened. "From Vostov's court?"

"That's the one."

"Huh," she said. "Why would he steal your trinket?"

Ursula sighed as if she were ashamed to admit what she'd say next. "Nicodemus requested a love potion from me that didn't turn out as planned. The object of his affection came to her senses in the middle of dinner and caused quite the scene."

"Ouch," Lavender said.

Gert arrived at their table and set down two cocktails, both looking an identical shade of pinkish purple. "Here you are," she said with aplomb.

"Thanks, Gert," Ursula said, pulling her drink forward for a long sip.

Lavender nodded at Gert, then raised her glass. "Cheers."

Gert bowed and headed once again to the bar, winking at me when her back was to Lavender.

"Oh, that's good," Lavender said, holding her drink up to eye level to inspect it.

"It is, isn't it?" Ursula agreed. "I'm trying to parse out the ingredients. Gert has such a good palate, and I'm always looking to enhance the flavor of my love potions."

Lavender nodded and took another long sip while I crossed my fingers.

"So, Lavender," Ursula said casually. "Steal any good trinkets lately?"

The thief set down her now only half-full glass and cocked her head a bit. "Yes, actually. I lifted a silver heart off the neck of Lucinda Penult while she was at a club the other night, and I'm not even sure she knows what's happened to it yet. And let me tell you, that trinket's a *doozy*! I've been peeling off the comeback spells on it for the past two days, and I'm still only half convinced that it's going to stay put."

"What's it do?" Ursula asked, pushing Lavender's cocktail closer to her, encouraging another drink.

Lavender smiled and lifted the glass to her lips again, downing most of what was left in the glass. "It can pivot back time by three minutes, so if you say or do something you regret, as long as it was within the last three minutes, you can go back to that moment and give yourself a do-over."

"Wow. That's powerful!"

"I'm going to fence it later today. Wanna take a look?"

"Absolutely," my friend said, and that was my cue.

Getting up, I hustled over to Ursula's table and pushed myself into the booth, next to Lavender.

"Hey!" she protested, staring at me in alarm.

I took advantage of her surprise to snatch the heart locket from her hand. "Thanks for that," I told her, pocketing the trinket. "Now I'd like to know where Arlo's lantern is."

"I will never tell you that I've hidden it in my crypt."

I worked hard to suppress a grin. Lavender had no idea she was saying the quiet part out loud. While it's true that Ursula is one of the best love potion masters in our world, it's also true that she's equally good at concocting truth serums.

"Crypt?" I asked. "You have a crypt, Lavender?"

"Yep," she said proudly. "But I'll never tell you that it's at the Old Mill Road Cemetery. I got in a little deep with a group of unbound thieves a long time ago and I had to fake my death to avoid incarceration."

"The crypt is in your name?" I pressed.

"It's under the family name. My parents and little brother were buried there in the early 1900s."

"What's the family name?"

"MacGillivray."

"Excellent." Turning to Ursula who'd been watching our conversation, I said, "Keep her here at least an hour if you can."

"I'll do my best," she said, lifting her hand to motion to Gert, who nodded and put another prepared cocktail on a tray to begin walking it over. The next round wasn't more truth serum, it was a cure for insomnia.

On the off chance that Lavender had a strong constitution for sleep serums, I fled the bar.

I found the cemetery without too much trouble, but locating Lavender's family crypt took far too much time for my own comfort.

At last, however, I found the crypt in question, but getting through Lavender's protection spells was no easy task. When I was unable to get the iron gate protecting the crypt to unlock, I had to resort to magically tunneling a hole into the earthen wall of the crypt and crawling my way in.

"Ugh," I said when I stood tall inside the darkened enclosure. My black puff vest, navy-blue sweater, and jeans were caked in mud from head to toe.

Activating a votive candle trinket that created light with the snap of my fingers and floated in the air so I didn't have to hold it, I looked all around the small enclosure, noting the four caskets against the far wall while down at my feet was an absolute treasure trove of trinkets.

I wasn't especially interested in raiding Lavender's stash—no need to make her even more angry than she'd be with me once the potions wore off—but getting that lantern back for Arlo was critical. Gib's life might hang in the balance.

Pushing a few things around with my foot and not seeing the lantern, I finally retrieved yet another trinket from my pocket, a very small vial holding some very fine glittery sand. Uncorking the bottle I tossed the sand over the shin-level pile of trinkets, then lifted one hand to make a whirling motion and pushing some essence out through my fingertips while I spoke an enchantment.

"Hidden treasures now exposed,

"Show me Arlo's lantern,

"Before Lavender knows."

A small glowing light illuminated an area near one of the caskets. Moving over to the area, I picked through several trinkets until I located the source of the glow, which was the lantern. "There you are," I said, lifting it from the pile. Leaning against the casket behind me, I added, "That wasn't so bad."

The second those words were out of my mouth, a vibration rippled along the wood of the casket I was leaning against.

I gripped the lantern, freezing in place. The vibration paused and I very, very carefully shifted my weight away from the casket.

For a moment, nothing happened, and I eyed the tunnel I'd created with longing. I don't get creeped out easily—if you live as long as I have, not a whole lot scares you—but right now I was terrified. Something was in this crypt with me. Something that slithered.

"Hissssss," came a sound that snaked its way from just behind me and to my left.

And then trinkets began to move near my feet, as if they were floating on water while some sinister creature swirled beneath their depths.

There was no doubt in my mind that Lavender had set a serpent loose in the crypt to keep watch over her treasures.

Unlucky me, I had very little with me that could act as a defense weapon, and, while the area around my feet was cluttered with trinkets, I had no idea what any of them did, and no time to play with them to see if they could be used for protection.

But then I remembered the locket I'd taken from Lavender. Three minutes might be all I needed to get the heck outta here.

Slowly I began to ease one hand toward my pocket while otherwise holding perfectly still.

"Hissssss!" the serpent warned.

My hand stopped, hovering just over the opening of the pocket on my vest jacket. And then, as I watched with large, frightened eyes, there was a bubble of movement right in front of me and a snake with a head as large as a dinner plate rose up from the floor.

I gulped, staring at the thing as it materialized from the depths of the pile of trinkets.

It swayed in front of me, its tongue flicking out toward me two or three times, as if sampling how I might taste. I watched it closely and began to feel dizzy. In the back of my mind I realized that the snake's power wasn't just its size and perhaps poisonous bite, but also the power to hypnotize its prey.

Try as I might, I couldn't seem to close my eyes, and my gaze fixated on the snake as it reared its head back, readying the strike.

Sweat broke out across my brow. I knew I had maybe three to four seconds to live if I didn't do something, but I couldn't look away from the snake's powerful gaze.

Using what remained of my will, I pushed my hand toward my jacket pocket just as the snake opened its gaping maw to reveal three-inch fangs moving toward me, and in a split second between life and certain death my fingertip connected to the heart locket, receiving my essence in that same moment, and suddenly I was standing at the hole I'd created, in the pitch black of the crypt, the hand that'd held Arlo's lantern empty. I was statue still for nearly a minute before I realized that the serpent wasn't up and about. Taking out my trusty candle trinket, I lit it and then rushed over to the area where I'd found the lantern, digging through the pile trying to locate it, but in my panic I couldn't seem to find it.

The longer I searched for it the more frantic I became. In my haste, I realized that I'd grabbed onto Arlo's lantern, but threw it out of the way. Pivoting, I dove for the lantern where it landed, but it sank within the pile as the serpent slithered underneath, swirling the river of trinkets as it began to rear its enormous head.

Barely able to hold in a scream, I dove for the hole—anything to get away from the deadly serpent. Clawing my way up, I heard a loud hiss from just behind me and not even a second later I felt the beast's fangs dig into my ankle, easily snapping the bone. A pain like I have *never* felt ignited from the point of puncture, lighting up a fire that raced with frightening speed through my foot, up my leg, surrounding my hips, and heading for my heart.

Shoving my hand into my pocket, I clutched the heart locket, pushing my essence into it, and in the next instant I was standing once again at the base of the hole in the pitch dark of the crypt, with a racing heart, panting for air. The pain from the venomous strike had completely disappeared and I knew I was back to the beginning of the three-minute period between when I'd first entered the crypt and had awakened the serpent.

Slowly, slowly, slowly I eased my hand into the pocket of my vest and wrapped my palm around the heart locket. The metal felt weaker, and I knew that the trinket had already begun to lose some of its power.

Without pushing any of my essence into the locket, I began to think through a plan.

There was no telling when the serpent would rear its ugly head, but the longer I stood here, the better my chances were of recovering Arlo's lantern and making it out of here alive.

A plan began to form when I realized that I'd be where I was standing three minutes earlier, but everything else would remain as it was when I first entered the crypt.

Once I thought through the plan, I lit the votive but dimmed the light as much as I could while still being able to see. Holding perfectly still I listened and watched for any signs that the serpent had awakened, but the crypt remained undisturbed and unchanged.

Slowly, slowly, slowly, I inched my way forward, trying to make my movements as small as possible. One clink from the pile of trinkets covering my feet was all it might take to awaken the beast.

Sweat broke out along my forehead as I carefully waded through Lavender's stash, making my way toward the section where I knew Arlo's lantern lay hidden beneath the pile.

At long last I made it close enough to the area to stop in my tracks. Reaching into my pocket I pulled out the vial of sand. I brought the vial to my mouth and bit into the cork stopper, pulling it free of the vial. Then I held the vial of sand aloft, over the area where I knew the lantern to be, but I didn't tip it out just yet.

Instead, I began to count. I needed to get to 180 seconds, standing in this exact spot, ready to dump the sand so that I could snatch the lantern and make a break for it before the serpent woke up. If it kept biting me, eventually the locket's power would run out, and I'd be dead for sure.

As I held the locket in my other hand, I could already feel that it was becoming more fragile. I didn't know how many uses the heart locket had left in it, but I was hoping for at least one more.

Eighty-two, I mentally counted, closing my eyes to concentrate on trying to calm my breathing while I rattled off the seconds.

Just when I thought I could get myself under control, I felt the tiniest ripple of movement against my left boot.

Eighty-nine . . .

Another ripple of movement slid a trinket from the top of my boot down to lightly clatter against the others.

No, no, no! Not yet!

Another, stronger ripple of energy rustled the trinkets in the crypt and then even more began to jostle as the serpent awakened.

One hundred and four. One hundred and five . . . I'm never going to make it!

Panic sent my heartbeat skittering and I almost lost count. The rustle of trinkets paused for a moment, as if the serpent were waiting for a telltale sign that it wasn't alone in the crypt.

"Hisssssssssss!" it called.

As much as I tried to steel myself, I couldn't calm the fear and I began to tremble. Sweat broke out along my brow again and the back of my neck, the vial of sand in my hand threatening to slip free of my grasp as my hand shook with tremors.

One hundred and twenty-three. One hundred and twenty-four, I counted.

Opening my eyes, I focused on the votive candle, hovering close to my head. Without touching it, I pulled back my essence from it and doused the flame.

It was the last thing I wanted to do, but it was the safest thing to do in that moment. I was certain the serpent could see in the dark, but on the off chance it couldn't, I didn't need to tempt it with such a large target as my frame against the backdrop of the crypt.

One hundred and thirty-five. One hundred and thirty-six . . .

"Hissssssssssss!"

The serpent was on the move, rustling the trinkets as it slithered around the crypt. My breathing was rapid, shallow, and uncontrolled. Nothing I did could quell the terror of being in this pitch-black, underground crypt with a python that would like to swallow me whole.

One hundred and forty. One hundred and forty-one.

Over thirty more seconds to go.

An eternity.

Trinkets rattled more loudly now, the sound coming from all around me. And then something slithered against the back of my heels.

I shuddered, nearly dropping the vial of sand as sweat poured down my back and my whole body trembled.

One hundred and fifty-nine. One hundred and sixty!

In front of me there was a clatter of trinkets and, although I couldn't see the serpent, I knew that it was beginning to rise in front of me only a foot away.

"Hissssss!" it challenged.

In the next instant I felt something sticky bat my cheek. It took *everything* I had not to scream when I realized the serpent's tongue had brushed my skin.

One hundred and sixty-three! One hundred and sixty-four!

Sixteen more seconds. That's all I needed. I had to be right *here* when I activated the charm for a final time. I couldn't be anywhere else in the room because if I wasn't standing here when I activated the charm, then every step closer to this spot that I needed to take would alert the serpent to my arrival, and it'd kill me before I made it out of the crypt.

Even with this much of a lead on it, I had my doubts about whether I'd survive. Still, I knew I had to stall. Drawing on every single ounce of courage I had, I sent a pulse of essence at the votive, causing it to shine to its full capacity.

The votive lit up the crypt and out of the darkness emerged the head of the serpent two feet from my own. It recoiled slightly as I mentally sent the votive right between its eyes.

One hundred and seventy-three! One hundred and seventy-four!

The serpent shook its massive head, recovered itself, then opened its gaping maw to reveal those massive fangs. *"Hisssssssss!"*

One hundred and seventy-eight! One hundred and seventy-ni—!

The serpent shot forward, its jaw enveloping my head. I felt the pinch of its fang begin to pierce my temple . . .

Nooooooooooo! I mentally shouted, pushing my essence into the locket.

In the next moment I stood in the exact same spot, my vial of sand hovering over the space where I knew the lantern to be, the cork stopper still between my teeth. My count must have been slightly slower than real time. I didn't waste a second overthinking it; instead I tipped the vial over and whispered the incantation, and a burst of blue light erupted under the pile. I thrust my hand into the center of that light, pulling up the lantern.

Pivoting, I bolted for the hole, while at the other end of the crypt I heard a rattle of trinkets. But I wasn't slowing down or stopping.

Jumping up into the hole I squirmed and shimmied, using my forearms to crawl forward while I waited to feel the bite of the serpent at my feet. The locket was still clutched tightly in my hand, and it felt hot. Too hot. It might not last even one more use.

I slipped, slid, and grunted my way up through the tunnel, now hearing a crash of trinkets being tossed violently around behind me. A sound began to erupt from deep in my throat that was half terror and half determination.

At last, my elbows gained purchase on the grass and I kicked from behind, using every ounce of strength I had to get free of the hole.

Once my hips were clear, I pressed my fists into the grass and lifted my feet out from the hole, finally free but definitely still in danger.

Grabbing the lantern trinket where I'd momentarily dropped it to clear the hole, I crawled forward, and got my knees underneath me. Planting my toes, I pushed up and forward to get to my feet. I stumbled a few meters away from the hole, barely managing to stay upright when there was a small explosion of dirt behind me, pelting my back with clods of earth and grass.

The serpent was free of the crypt.

Laboring hard, my lungs heaving, I climbed a hill in front of me, knowing my car was on the opposite side.

"Hissssss!" The serpent sounded from no less than fifteen to twenty feet behind me. I had little doubt that it could move as quickly as I could—and very likely even faster.

Refusing to slow down I pushed every single step forward to be as fast as the last, and finally, *finally* I crested the hill, but behind me I could hear the great beast slithering with alarming speed behind me, the earth under my feet vibrating with the movement.

I dared not look over my shoulder, lest it pin me with its gaze. Instead, I launched myself off the steep hill, flying through the air, and landing halfway down it on the other side.

The maneuver likely saved my life as it opened up a greater lead between me and the serpent.

Fighting to keep my feet underneath me, I pinwheeled my arms out at my sides, still clutching both the lantern and the locket while I raced forward, headed to Luna.

With every step closer my sense of panic rose. I couldn't tell how close the serpent was to me, I only knew that it'd be gaining fast.

Pumping my arms and legs as hard as I physically could, I leapt over a gravestone, landing hard at a slight angle and twisting my knee.

Crying out in pain, I stumbled the next step, recovered, then stumbled again. The pain was excruciating, but if I stopped, or fell, I was a dead mystic.

Somehow I managed to keep running, but I cried out at every other step. Rounding the tree, I pounded forward the last few steps to the car and heard the slithering beast coming up behind me far too fast.

Tucking the lantern under my arm, I pulled out my key fob and pressed the unlock button. Luna beeped and I grabbed at the handle, but my palm was too sweaty, and it slipped off without opening the door. The beast was practically on top of me, I could feel its great bulk nearly at my back. Yanking the handle up again, I got the door open and dove inside, trying to pull the door closed after me, and if I hadn't had the door closed even partially, I would've died in the next second as the serpent slammed into the car door, shutting it and sending my torso into the passenger seat.

I lay across the front seats, the gearshift digging into my rib cage, while I trembled from head to toe. My breathing was ragged, my terror at its peak, but in the back of my mind, I knew I had to fight against freezing in place. I had no doubt that the serpent would figure out how to break the glass of a window or windshield and eat me alive.

Pushing off the passenger seat, I wriggled myself to sit up straight at the wheel, then pressed the start button and Luna came to life.

Another tremendous *WHUMP* hit the car door, and out of the corner of my eye I could just make out the shape of the serpent, looming up to pin me with its terrifying gaze.

Turning away from it, I reached for the gearshift, but I was still clutching the locket and my hand slipped off. Trembling so badly that I couldn't seem to get my limbs to cooperate, at last I managed to drop the charm into the cupholder and grip the gearshift firmly. Just as I began to throw Luna into drive the serpent slammed itself on top of my hood, its head coming straight at me.

Screaming in fear, I pushed up on the gearshift, shifting it into reverse, and punched the accelerator. Luna rocketed backward while I spun the wheel, sending the serpent flying off the hood and into a large headstone. It hit with such force that it demolished the marble grave marker, but I didn't wait around to see what other damage it might cause. Pulling the gearshift back into drive, I once again punched the accelerator and shot forward, squealing out of the graveyard at rocket speed.

I didn't slow down until I was several blocks away from the cemetery, and it took a lot longer than that to calm myself down enough to be able to safely navigate the streets. Even still, I trembled all the way to Arlo's house, and when I got there, I needed another fifteen minutes simply to stop shaking like a leaf.

Taking long sips of water from a water bottle I always kept in my car helped, but the adrenaline continued to course through me. While I sat there, I picked up the heart locket from the cupholder to look it over. It definitely felt more fragile between my fingers. I had little doubt that it was on its final uses.

I thought about asking Arlo to juice it up again, but I'd already asked him for the favor of creating a powerful trinket for Gib, which had nearly cost me my life. I shuddered to think what he'd want in return for a power infusion to the locket.

"Another time, then," I whispered, tucking the trinket into my vest pocket.

When I felt I could get out of the car and walk without stumbling, I made my way over to the back of Arlo's house, slipping into the magical heels again, but it took several tries to get the enchantment rhyme out of my mouth because I kept stuttering, unable to get my mouth and tongue to cooperate.

I finally crested the roofline and tapped on the windowpane. There was still a hint of daylight left, but I was hoping Arlo would take pity on me and let me in.

I heard a click and saw that the lock on the window had swiveled to the unlocked position. Hauling up the pane, I poked my head into the workshop, finding Arlo sitting on his stool, his arms crossed, waiting for me to enter.

"Hello, old friend," I said, my voice hoarse from the panic and the hard run to the car.

"Dovey," he said with a nod. Then he stood up, helping me through the window. Handing him the lantern, I said, "One precious, sentimental trinket, delivered as promised."

He took it and his own mouth quirked into a grin when he looked me up and down. I could only imagine that I looked like I'd been rolling in a muddy swamp. "Any trouble getting it away from Lavender?"

"None at all. Why do you ask?"

"No reason," he said, his smirk breaking out into a grin. He then moved over to the window, set the lantern on the sill, and twisted the top of the lamp, which put a red filter in front of the window. With a snap of his fingers the wick inside the lantern began to burn and Arlo pulled up the window shade, revealing total darkness outside.

I gasped, and went over to the open window to poke my head out. Dusk was approaching but we were nowhere near total nightfall just yet.

Pulling my head back inside again I said, "That is one nifty trinket. So glad I almost died retrieving it."

Arlo reached into the pocket of the apron he wore, bringing up Gib's watch. "Here. I think you'll like it."

I took the watch and held it in my hand. After giving it a little essence, I could feel it warm against my palm, and the surge in power was quite impressive. "Thank you."

"You're welcome."

I turned toward the window and hitched a thumb over my shoulder. "I hate to cut it short but I need to call Jacquelyn at SPL."

"Jacquelyn? Why? You need a dragon?"

"Maybe. If she's got one that enjoys snake for dinner, then definitely."

Arlo laughed. "So, the rumors are true?"

"What rumors?"

"Lavender was once a member of the circus. Her act involved snake taming."

"It's no wonder she quit the circus then, because there was nothing tame about that snake."

"Where did you leave it?"

"Loose. Which is a problem I've got to solve immediately. Lord knows we can't have that thing running around, gobbling up the unbound."

Arlo chuckled and helped me back out through the window. "Come visit me again, Dovey. Preferably after you've had a bath."

I surprised myself by laughing, the trauma from just a half hour ago finally abating, and I blew Arlo a kiss, then headed back to the car and home, where I'd only have about forty minutes to get ready for a wake that I was hoping would produce a lead.

On the way to my house, I called Jacquelyn, who assured me that she had a dragon in-house that considered serpent a delicacy.

CHAPTER 11

After getting home, I headed straight to the laundry room and dumped everything I was wearing into the wash. Grabbing the well-worn robe that I always keep in the laundry room for occasions like these, I padded out to the kitchen to make myself some calming tea and retrieve a hard-boiled egg from the fridge for Bits.

He took it greedily and offered me a series of squeaks that sounded very close to a squeaky dog toy.

Once I had the tea brewing, I took the steaming cup and myself up the stairs for a long, hot soak in the tub.

Finally emerging from the tub, I toweled off, blew-dry my long, wavy blond hair, and applied a little makeup. Next, I headed downstairs to retrieve Bits, who wore a hint of a smile and a round belly, with no sign of any leftover egg nearby.

Taking my beloved picklepuss upstairs, I set him down at the entrance to my closet. "Okay, Bits. It's showtime. I'm headed to a funeral tonight, which, an hour ago, could've been mine, but that story is for another day. Tonight, I'll need to look respectful, but not boring."

Bits stood on his hind legs, sniffing up at me for a moment before curling himself into a ball and rolling into the center of my closet. Once there he unrolled himself and looked right, then left, then to the front. Waddling to the left, he settled on a sleeveless black, one-piece satin pantsuit with a flare at the bottom of the legs, giving the pantsuit a billowing effect whenever I walked.

"Excellent choice, Bits. I approve."

Next he curled into a ball again and rolled over to where a cashmere indigo pashmina hung. "Yes," I said, moving forward to select the pantsuit and the pashmina. "Shoes?"

Bits waddled over to the right and paused in front of a simple pair of patent leather pumps with a flared four-inch heel, continuing the theme of the legs of the pantsuit perfectly. Comfortable and fashionable. "Love it. Thanks, Bits."

He made chuffing noises as he waddled out to the bedroom and after I got dressed, I found him curled up on the nightstand, snuggling into his favorite sleeping cozy.

I don't quite know how Bits gets to the places I sometimes find him. I've never actually seen him teleport, but it's the only explanation for some of the spots he's wandered out from. If he teleports, he does it when I'm not looking, but I'm rather convinced that's what's going on because I once saw him peeking out from the top shelf of my built-in bookcase.

Regardless, if the little whippersnapper is enjoying life, I'm not one to quibble about the places he gets into.

After putting a kiss on my index finger, I tapped him lightly on the head and whispered, "I'll be home soon, my little love."

I arrived at the funeral home at seven fifteen. Turning into the parking lot, which wound around the back of the building, I spotted Gib's older Range Rover and parked nearby. Hurrying inside, I paused in the vestibule to check where I should head next. There were two viewings currently underway: Augustus Ariti's and a woman named Betty Bettendorf.

"A.A. and B.B. funerals today," I mused. "Odd."

The sign at the entryway told me that the wake for Augustus was upstairs, which is where I went next. Cresting the landing,

I turned left and entered a large room with rows of chairs and a decent-sized crowd filling them. Across the room was Augustus's silver casket.

I sighed sadly for him and for his family. There are so many mystics well past five hundred years old that the frailty of the human condition is often lost on us.

Scanning the room, I was anxious to find Gib so that we could come up with a plan for who, amongst the mourners, to subtly interview.

I didn't see him at first, so I began weaving my way through the crowd, toward the front, nodding to everyone I passed. There seemed to be an awful lot of sadness in the room. It made me wonder who would've come to Eleni's wake if she hadn't been on the outs with her family.

After making my way through the crowd to the area near the casket, I paused again to have a look around, and I still didn't spot Gib. My concentration was broken by the sound of someone in a deep state of distress.

Leaning around the casket slightly, I spotted the source of the noise.

In a pair of chairs over on the opposite side from me was a man in a charcoal suit, with graying hair and a thin build. He sat hunched over with his head in his hands, his shoulders shaking from the sobs coming from what sounded like his very soul. Next to him sat Gib, attired perfectly in a black blazer, ebony silk shirt, black tapered jeans, and black patent leather shoes. Currently, he was bent forward with a soothing hand on the man's back. I could see that Gib was talking to the bereaved man, but I wasn't sure the other was listening.

The scene moved me. Deeply.

Edging closer to the pair, I could hear more of what was being said.

"I loved him, I loved him, I loved him!" the man sobbed, slapping at his forehead with clenched fists.

Gib squeezed his shoulder, letting him know he wasn't alone. "I get it, bro. I'm so sorry. I bet right now it seems like this pain will crush you for the rest of your life, but I've been there, and I can tell you that in a few months it starts to get a little easier to bear."

The bereaved man lifted his head out of his hands and looked up at Gib. "How do I make it through the next few months if I can't even make it through today?"

The heartbroken understanding in Gib's expression was enough to bring tears to my eyes. "That's the thing, Toby. You *are* making it through today. You're here, paying your respects within a room filled with people who loved Augustus, and you're not at home curled up in a ball on the floor. You've made it through the second hardest day of this loss—the first one being when you heard that Augustus was gone. You're up by two points, man. And if you got through the two most difficult days, then you can make it through tomorrow. And the day after that. And the next days, weeks, and months after that."

Toby wiped his wet cheeks with the sleeve of his blazer and looked toward the casket. His lip quivered and the devastation in his countenance was almost too much for me to bear. "I loved him," he said softly. "I'll always love him."

Gib sat back in his chair and crossed his arms in an *X* over his heart—a gesture of unity, and then his gaze darted toward me, as if he knew he was being watched. "Dovey," he said, and the way he said my name always seemed to send a thrill right through me.

I walked over to the pair and laid a hand on Toby's shoulder. "I'm so sorry for your loss."

He glanced up at me. "Thank you. Did you know Augustus?"

"Not as much as I would've liked to. He seemed like such a lovely man."

Toby swallowed hard and choked out a reply. "He was definitely that."

Reaching into my purse, I pulled out a brass button and held it out for him.

His brow furrowed. "What's that?"

"Hope," I told him, offering a sad smile. "The day I found it was the day I learned that someone close to me had passed away. I took it as a sign from them that they were okay, and that made me feel a little better. Since that time, it seems that, whenever I find myself missing them, that brass button almost magically appears. I've always taken it to mean that they know I miss them, and they're telling me I'll see them again, someday when I'm ready to cross that rainbow bridge."

Before his fingers could close around the button I activated the charm, which was a healing trinket capable of assisting the repair of trauma both physical and emotional.

It wouldn't completely take away Toby's pain, but it would ease his suffering in the next several days and weeks.

"It's warm," he said as he held it.

"You know what's funny? The day I found it, it felt warm to me too, which is why I thought it must've come from the spirit of the loved one I'd lost."

Toby nodded, and right in front of us, his watery eyes stopped leaking and the deep heartbreak in his gaze lessened. He took a deep, shuddering breath and held the button to his chest. "Thank you."

Gib reached into his pocket and extracted a business card. "I meant it when I said you can call me anytime if you just want to talk, Toby."

Toby nodded and took the card without looking at the information printed on it. He simply pocketed it and offered Gib a quivering lip as he fought to keep his composure.

Gib squeezed Toby's shoulder a final time, stood up, and

pointed to me. "Dovey and I should make the rounds. Are you okay here?"

Toby sniffled. "Yes. Thank you again, Grant."

I walked away from Toby with Gib. He led me to the left side of the room and stopped near a huddled group of mourners who resembled one another. Looking at them, I spotted Hermia, and realized that the group must be the Ariti family.

Hermia's gaze looked toward me, and I offered her a small wave. She left her family and came over to us.

"Hi, Dovey. You made it."

"I wouldn't have missed it." Motioning with my hand around the room which was quite crowded I added, "It must be of some comfort to know that Augustus was well loved."

"He really was. It's nice."

Pivoting to Gib I said, "This is a friend of mine, Grant Barlow."

Hermia nodded to him and took his outstretched hand when he offered it. "I'm so sorry for your loss," he told her.

Hermia's gaze roved hungrily over Gib, and I could tell she was just as attracted to him as I was. The beautiful young lady held on to his hand a little longer than she might've if he looked a little less like a movie star. "Nice to meet you."

I pointed subtly over to the group she'd just come from. "How is the rest of your family holding up?"

She sighed. "When we first got here, I thought they'd be civil to each other, but nothing's changed with any of them. Nothing will *ever* change with them."

I glanced over at the group. Having done my homework, I knew about Augustus, Eleni, and Ambrose, and now Hermia, but the rest of the people in the Ariti huddle were unknown to me.

"Who's who?" I asked, motioning toward them.

Hermia looked over her shoulder. "My dad is the tall man in the middle and his three cousins are standing to his right.

Evander, Lino, and Kyrie. They still live in Greece. The vultures."

Gib arched an eyebrow. "Not a fan of your extended family?"

"I'm not a fan of my family period. Well, except for my uncle."

The three of us looked toward the casket, spotting Toby leaning his head against it, with both palms pressed against the metal.

"Poor Toby," Hermia said softly. "Uncle Augie was his soulmate. He deserves to get a share in Augustus's estate, but there's no way that crowd"—Hermia thumbed to the group over her shoulder—"would ever even consider it."

I frowned. "That's a shame."

Hermia nodded and scowled at her family. "Not a single one of them even spoke to Toby to offer their condolences. He and my uncle had been together for seventeen years!"

Gib grunted. "That's cold. Toby's a sweet guy."

"You know him?"

"Only from tonight. He looked like he was having a hard time, so I sat with him for a bit. He loved your uncle very much."

Hermia dropped her chin and offered her thanks. Then she lifted her gaze and said, "I gave him a hug earlier, but I didn't have a chance to sit with him. I'll do that after I use the powder room. Do either of you know where the ladies' room is?"

I pointed to the exit. "It's right outside the door on the left. I saw it on my way upstairs."

After Hermia had gone, I turned my full attention to Gib. "You were very sweet to Toby."

Gib looked off to the side, as if he were embarrassed. "I'm a softie at heart."

"You told him you'd lost someone you loved too." I was genuinely curious to know the circumstances of that statement.

Gib cleared his throat and continued to avoid my eyes. "My wife."

I blinked. "Your wife? You're a widower?"

Gib sighed and finally turned his gaze back to me. "I am. Julia."

He didn't elaborate and it was easy to see that it still pained him. The flood of emotion that took visceral root to my insides was a surprise. I was both sympathetic and jealous. Something I hadn't felt in decades.

In the early days of my bound life beside Elric, I never had a reason to suspect he was with anyone but me, but as time wore on, he became more secretive and absent from our bed. I tried to tail him on occasion, but Elric wasn't the kind of mystic you could sneak up on. I'd lost him within minutes of trying to follow him each and every time.

Then, one day I slipped a trinket into his pocket—a Roman bronze coin that I'd enchanted—and when he didn't come home that night, I called the coin back using a comeback spell. The next morning, I held the coin as I left the house and used it as a sort of heat tracer. When I was on the track he'd taken the previous night, the coin would heat. If I took a wrong turn, it would grow cold.

It took well over an hour but at last I found the flat that he'd visited the night before. Waiting outside the building proved to be as frustrating as not being able to trail him.

After hours of waiting, I finally went home, but the next day I made the same journey only much earlier and I was rewarded for my intentions, if rewarded meant that I saw my beloved come out of the flat, holding a beautiful woman to his chest and the pair kissed like they were madly in love.

Devastated, I returned home, packed all my belongings, including all the jewels and trinkets Elric had ever given me, and I'd booked passage from France—where we were living at the time—to Spain.

After I'd settled there for several months and had been missing Elric terribly, he appeared one morning on my front step and kissed me as if nothing had happened between us. "Are you ready to come home, my dove?" he'd asked.

"Are you ready to be faithful to me?" I replied tartly.

I'll never forget the disappointment in his eyes as he stared down at me and what followed was a lecture that was both cruel and kind. Essentially, he told me that he loved me more than anyone he'd ever been with, but Elric wasn't my husband, nor would he ever be my husband.

The binding agreement that'd been made when he and Petra were married—and mind you they were married only an hour after they'd met each other—was an unbreakable enchantment. The only way either of them could ever marry another was if one of them died, and from what I'd heard in the mystic circles the endeavor to kill each other while still obeying the rules of the binding was a challenge that had started on their wedding night.

The pair loathed each other, but they were bonded by magic, so they were also bound to protect each other from everyone except each other.

And because they were both nearly equal in power, the ability to kill each other wasn't something either could manage without perhaps being mortally wounded themselves.

I realized in that moment in Spain when Elric was lecturing me that marrying him wasn't actually an end goal for me. I *liked* my freedom, and if I could simply get over the fact that my one true love had no intention of ever being faithful to me, then we might actually have a wonderful relationship.

The trouble was that I'd never fallen out of love with Elric, so *I'd* been the faithful one which was an arrangement he encouraged.

Over the years I'd stopped feeling hurt and jealous when I'd see him out with some beautiful blonde, mostly because his affection for me had never faltered. All the other women—save Petra—had come and gone, but not me. Never me.

"I'm so sorry, Gib. I had no idea you'd lost a wife."

He stiffened and crossed his arms. I could see that this wasn't a subject he had any intention of discussing so I let him off the hook.

"We're both here to do some covert interviewing, right?" I said into the awkward silence.

He relaxed his stance a bit. "We are. But first I want to ask if you've known Hermia longer than you've let on?"

I smiled and winked at him. "I met her for the first time yesterday when I went to Augustus's house. We had a lovely chat. She's a sweet woman."

He looked to the exit where Hermia had gone. "She seemed to know you longer than just a day."

"I can't help it if people think I'm easy to talk to, Gib."

He offered a small chuckle. "No. No, I guess you can't, Dovey. And I'm in agreement with them on that front. You are easy to talk to."

Gib lowered his voice to nearly whisper those last words to me and damn if I didn't find that sexy. I cleared my throat. "We should split up and mingle. I'll meet you back here in say . . . twenty minutes? We can compare notes then."

"Sounds like a plan."

Gib and I parted, and I headed straight toward a woman sitting in a chair in the back row, wearing a black mohair sweater, knitted skirt, and a pillbox hat with a mesh veil.

The veil did nothing to hide her regally beautiful face, which I recognized from the online research I'd done two days before. Walking to a seat just down from where she was sitting, I reached into my handbag and pulled out a tissue. "Here," I offered. The poor dear was trying to hold back tears and failing.

She startled slightly before taking note of the tissue in my outstretched hand. "Thank you. I didn't expect to cry, even though I loved him dearly."

"Grief is a tricky master. He'll show up when you least expect him. I know that from experience."

She dabbed at her eyes with the tissue for a moment before indicating the casket at the front of the room. "Did you know him?"

"Yes. He was a classmate of mine at Carnegie Mellon." Reaching out my hand again, I said, "Dovey Van Dalen."

She took hold of my hand. "Gina Ariti. It's nice to meet you, Dovey."

"Likewise. Are you Augustus's sister? He mentioned his sister quite often when we were in school." I knew she wasn't, but I felt it important to appear innocent on the topic.

"No," she said, her lower lip trembling. "I'm his ex-sister-in-law. Ambrose and I were married for over twenty years before he asked me for a divorce."

"If you're here I suspect the split was amicable?"

She barked out a mirthless laugh. "Hardly. We've grown to despise each other, and I wouldn't be here if it was anyone other than Augie who'd died. Ambrose is furious that I came, of course, but I don't care. He can't kick me out without causing a scene, so here I sit, mourning the loss of someone dear to my heart."

"You poor thing," I said, scooting over to sit next to her. "I'm so sorry for your loss. For what it's worth, I think you're quite courageous to be here."

Gina took a shuddering breath. "I'm also here to support my daughter. She loved Augie too."

I made a point of looking over my shoulder toward the Aritis. "Which one is your ex?"

Gina rolled her eyes. "The one with the blonde on his arm."

"Ah," I said. "And which one is his sister?"

She studied me for a moment before she said, "Eleni committed suicide the day after Augie died."

I sucked in a sharp breath and put a hand over my heart. "Oh, no! You're mourning *another* death in the family? I can't fathom how you all must be feeling right now. I'm so very sorry, Gina."

Her lips turned up into something of a forced smile. "We're all mourning Eleni's death far less than Augie's."

My brow furrowed. "Why? Augie always spoke so fondly of her."

Gina sighed heavily and tugged at the tissue in her hands. "It's family stuff."

"I understand," I said, reaching into my handbag again and pulling out some loose change and my trinket silver dollar. "Would you mind holding this?"

Gina held out her hand and I placed the money into her open palm. I went back to rooting around in my handbag, waiting for Gina's gaze to become unfocused, and I only had to wait a moment or two.

"Gina, you're going to tell me all you know about the rift between Eleni and the rest of the family."

"I'm going to tell you all I know about the rift between Eleni and the rest of the family."

"And you're going to forget that we ever had this conversation."

"I'm going to forget we ever had this conversation."

I gently took back the change and let it fall into the bottom of my handbag. Gina's gaze came into focus again and she shook her head as if to clear it. "Whew! I must've blanked out there. What were we talking about?"

"You were going to tell me about the rift between Eleni and the rest of the family."

"Ah yes, that. You know I'd never tell a soul what's at the heart of that lest I suffer the same fate as Eleni."

My eyes widened. "You don't think it was a suicide?"

Gina gave me a knowing look. "Eleni was terrified of heights. Years ago, she saw a therapist about it, and he guided her through some *immersion* therapy nonsense. The guy was a quack. He basically forced her to live in the penthouse suite on the fifteenth floor. She won the apartment in her divorce from Konstantinos—the snake."

"Not a fan of his, either."

"Not in the least. He and Ambrose are close, though, so it's easy for me to despise him. Anyway, Eleni was determined to live there, but she never went near the terrace. Not even to let in a cooling breeze in the middle of summer."

"That's some phobia."

"It was, which is how I *know* she didn't commit suicide by jumping from the balcony. She wouldn't have been able to even get that sliding glass door open on her own. Her panic around heights was that acute."

If Gina didn't think Eleni had committed suicide, I wondered who she thought was responsible.

"Do you think it was murder?"

"Of course I think it was murder. I'd never say it out loud, but without a doubt Eleni was murdered."

"By whom?"

Gina's lips pressed together in a hard line. She turned to look over her shoulder at the small group made up of her ex-husband, his new spouse, and his cousins. "One of them."

Remembering Kioni from the coffee shop had mentioned seeing Eleni manhandled by a beefy brute with black hair and olive skin, I turned a little in my seat to scrutinize the group more closely.

No one in the huddle resembled Kioni's description.

Ambrose was a tall man with a trim build. Age had turned his dark hair to a soft silver that, frankly, flattered him. Hanging on his arm was a buxom beautiful blonde in a skintight black knit dress that showed a lot of cleavage and leg, and six-inch heels to give those legs an even longer look.

Next to her stood a man probably in his early forties, with jet-black hair, a long nose, and a patch of stubble on his chin. He wore a wrinkled blue suit and white loafers that looked quite out of place. Beside him was another man perhaps similar in age also with black hair, but he was taller than his brother by a few inches, and rounder overall.

On his left was a woman in perhaps her late thirties. She was quite pregnant, and she looked miserable, standing in a black dress with a full skirt, no makeup, and flat ballet shoes. Draped at the crook of her arm was a Hermès Himalayan Diamond Birkin, a handbag so rare that even pre-owned it could fetch up to a half million dollars.

None of the five looked anything like who Kioni had described so I wondered anew who the brute was.

"Why do you suspect that Eleni's own family killed her?"

Gina bounced her eyebrows. "I'm not going to tell you that it's because Eleni was going to confess all the Ariti family's sins to the authorities. From what I hear, she'd been threatening Ambrose for quite some time. The Aritis don't take kindly to threats, even the ones that come from within the family."

"I see. But, Gina, specifically what did Eleni have on the family that she wanted to expose?"

Gina eyed me slyly. "Think about it, Dovey; the family fortune comes from the manufacturing of pharmaceuticals. They mass-produce all kinds of drugs, *including narcotics.*"

I cocked my head, trying to puzzle out what she was hinting at. And then it dawned on me.

"They're selling narcotics on the black market."

Gina tapped her nose, then pointed at me in confirmation.

"Here in the States?" I asked.

"No. At least I don't think so. Ambrose is head of operations, and he likes living in the U.S. He's never applied for citizenship, and I'm certain he has no intention of being deported, so I highly doubt he'd jeopardize his favorite playground."

"Back home in Greece, then?"

Gina sighed as if she carried a heavy burden. "No. Again, he wouldn't jeopardize any territory that he has an affection for. It's my understanding that most of the drugs make their way to Africa and Asia."

"Is the whole family in on it?" I asked quietly.

Gina motioned with her chin toward the group of family members. "You mean the cousins?"

I nodded.

"Of course they are. Evander and Lino in particular. Kyrie makes sure the drug money gets laundered—which isn't very difficult in Greece—and all of them share in the profit."

"Did *you* know about it when you worked for the firm?"

"No. But I suspected."

At that moment, Gina's brow furrowed and I could tell the effects of the silver dollar were beginning to wear off.

I stood up and gave her a slight bow. "Thank you, Gina. You've been a tremendous help."

Before she could respond I moved out of the row of seats, heading to the back of the room where I could decide who to interview next.

While I stood there, I heard a small cry from behind me in the hallway. It was a somewhat muffled sound, but the hair rose on the back of my neck.

Turning, I headed out into the hallway and nearly ran right into Hermia, who looked nothing like the pulled-together woman I'd been speaking with not ten minutes earlier.

Disheveled and in distress, the poor girl was bleeding from a wound in her shoulder that was severe enough to allow blood to leak down her side and dribble onto the floor. In her hand was a scalpel and she was holding it in such a way that I knew she was about to stab herself. Again.

Soaked in blood and sweat, she gripped the scalpel with one hand and her wrist with the other. It was like her left hand was trying to stop her right hand from plunging the scalpel into her heart. And I knew, without a doubt, that someone had just exposed her to Pandora's Promise. Which meant she was perhaps only a second away from killing herself.

CHAPTER 12

Launching myself forward, I grabbed at the wrist holding the scalpel. "Hermia, don't!"

Her wide, wild eyes were fixated on mine, and through gritted teeth she whispered, "Help me!"

I pulled on her wrist, trying to keep it from causing her more harm, and behind me I could hear a commotion as people began to realize what was happening.

Using both hands and all my strength, I managed to pull the scalpel away from Hermia, but the second I had the blade in my hand she tackled me.

Surprisingly strong, Hermia took me to the floor. Clawing and scratching like an enraged cat, she tried to get the scalpel back, but I wasn't yielding. I rolled to the side, using one arm to fend her off while trying to shield the scalpel from her desperate attempts to grab it. All the while, Hermia's eyes remained wide, holding an expression that vacillated between panic and aggression.

Seeing no other way to deal with the chaos of her flailing limbs and scratching nails, I called up a spell I've had to use once or twice before on an unbound. Firmly grabbing her hand with my free one, I pulled her close, pushed my essence into the small space between us, and softly sang,

"Unbound girl who's in too deep,
"It's time for you to go to sleep."

Hermia's gaze immediately lost focus, then her lids closed, and she fell limp against me.

"*Hermia!*" Gina screamed somewhere above me, and that was followed by a tangle of hands and limbs pulling us apart. Somehow, I ended up in Gib's embrace. "Are you hurt?" he asked, looking me over with worried, furrowed brows.

"No, I'm fine." But when I looked at my hand, clutching the scalpel, I saw that I'd cut myself.

"Did you stab my daughter?" Ambrose shouted at me. He was standing hovered over Hermia, his hands clenched into fists, like he was ready to attack me.

"No!" said a familiar voice. I looked up to see Toby at the foot of the stairs. "Hermia was using the scalpel to hurt herself. I wouldn't have believed it if I didn't see it, Ambrose. That woman was trying to get the scalpel *away* from your daughter."

My gaze traveled to Hermia, whose head was being cradled by her mother, while Gina cried out, "Someone call an ambulance!"

Several people pulled out their phones and a woman stepped forward to crouch down next to Hermia. "I'm a nurse. I need to put pressure on that wound! Someone, give me a shirt or a jacket!"

Without hesitation Gib shrugged out of his blazer and handed it to the woman. Then he took me by the elbow and guided me to a chair. "You're cut," he said after sitting me down.

"I'm fine." And I was. The cut was a deep one and bleeding quite a bit, but it takes a lot to permanently harm a mystic, and we heal much faster than our unbound cousins, so it wasn't something I felt needed to be fussed over.

"Let me look," he insisted. I uncurled my hand which had

still been clutching the scalpel and it dropped to the floor. Gib picked it up. "Where'd she get this?"

"We're at a funeral home," I reminded him. "She must've found her way to the embalming room."

He looked over his shoulder to where Hermia lay bleeding from the wound near her shoulder. "Why would she do something like this?"

I shook my head. "I don't know."

The truth, however, was that I *did* know. Someone had come to the wake with the intent to murder Hermia using the Promise. It was the only logical way to explain the woman's behavior, and her wild, pleading eyes before I pulled the scalpel out of her grip. Looking around at the faces gathered, I doubted I'd find a guilty culprit. But maybe the absence of someone would be telling.

Gib gave me a pat on the knee before getting up. "Stay put. I've got a first aid kit in my car."

The second Gib was away down the stairs I stood up and began to work my way through the crowd, keeping all my senses open and surveying everyone to see who might look either guilty or smug.

Scanning every face, I found neither expression. In fact, the mood of the crowd seemed to be one of shock and concern. Moving back to the chair Gib had put me in, I waited for him to return, which was nearly immediately after I sat down again.

In the distance I heard an ambulance siren closing in on our location. While Gib wiped away the blood on my hand and pressed some antiseptic into it, I kept my focus on Hermia. I was deeply concerned for her. She'd be taken to the hospital—a place with an abundance of sharp instruments—and when she woke up from the spell, she could easily try to kill herself again.

I had no idea if the effects of the Promise wore off after a time, and that troubled me greatly, because if it didn't wear off, Hermia would eventually find a way to do the deed.

Paramedics arrived and loaded the young woman onto a stretcher while the nurse continued to press on the wound with Gib's blazer.

He and I stood a little away from the crowd hovering in the doorway as the stretcher was loaded into the second-floor elevator and taken away.

"Why would she do this?" Gina asked her ex-husband.

"How the hell should I know?" he snapped. I realized that Ambrose was the type of man who dealt with his fear by wrapping it in anger.

A uniformed officer appeared at the top of the stairs and gave a speech that he needed to get statements from any witnesses, and every head in the doorway and on the landing swiveled to me.

Luckily, Toby pushed his way toward the cop and said, "I saw the whole thing, Officer. I was right where you're standing when I witnessed the young woman try to stab herself a second time and was saved by that woman."

He pointed to me for emphasis, and I did my best to offer him a grateful smile, but my mind was elsewhere.

It took an interminably long time to wait my turn to be interviewed by the officer and released with the warning that a detective might want to follow up with me later.

I wasn't worried. Well, at least I wasn't worried about being further questioned. I *was* worried about Hermia.

Before leaving, I managed to sneak over to the guestbook and snap a photo of all the names there. I doubted that the mystic wielding the Promise would sign their name for the record, but I was somewhat desperate for a clue as to the killer's identity, and grasping at straws was better than giving up.

One thing was very clear to me, however, and that was that a mystic was targeting this family of unbounds. For what reason? I couldn't fathom, but it was clear that someone meant to wipe out the entire family.

"Coffee?" Gib said after he'd escorted me to my car. I knew he wanted to talk about any discussions I'd had with the family. But I had a different task in mind.

"Rain check?"

There was a flash of disappointment in his expression which he quickly masked with a smile. "Absolutely. I'll be in touch."

With that he turned and walked toward his car. I hopped into Luna, pulled a U-turn, checked to make sure that Gib wasn't following me, then headed straight to SPL headquarters.

Once inside, I rode the elevator up to the seventeenth floor, stepped out, and stood in front of a large, marble desk where an ancient mystic sat fast asleep in a large leather chair, snoring like a buzzsaw.

I tapped on the desk a few times. "Qin Shi. Qin Shi, wake up, please."

The mystic continued to snore.

I sighed. "*Qin Shi*! Wake up!"

In a flash the ancient mystic jumped out of his chair, landing beside the desk with his arms raised in a defensive posture. In each hand he held a trinket—a gold lighter and a silver orb, both of which, I assumed, were lethally charged.

"Oh! Dovey!" he said when he realized it was me.

"Hi, friend. Sorry to startle you, but I need your help."

Qin pocketed his weapons. "A trinket?"

"Yes."

"Purpose?"

I took a deep breath. I was fairly certain Elric wasn't going to like what I was about to ask for. "An unbound was exposed to one of the Pandoras."

"Ahh," he said. "She's dead and you need to bring the unbound back? Dovey, you know those trinkets are strictly for mystics."

"Actually, she's not dead, Qin. At least not yet. But I worry she could be soon unless I give her a trinket to thwart the effect."

He squinted at me. "Did you run this by the boss?"

"I'm going to tell you that I did so that you don't have to lie to him when he questions you."

Qin offered me a toothy smile. "Living dangerously. I like it."

While motioning me forward, he stepped up to a set of enormous doors made of bronze. Qin set his hand on the one to the right and closed his eyes. There were a series of clicks, then the sound of a latch giving way, and Qin used his index finger to push the mammoth door open.

This was Elric's trinket room. Or perhaps I should say that this was *one* of Elric's trinket rooms. Everyone at SPL knew he had maybe a dozen more hidden all over the continent, each one absolutely packed with trinkets. But *this* space was where he housed his most powerful and prized trinkets.

Qin Shi was the collection's guardian, and although he might look as old as time and move like a feeble old man, I doubted there were more than a dozen mystics in the whole northern hemisphere who could match his power.

His fealty to Elric was absolute, but he was also a little soft on me, which was what I was counting on when I came to him for help.

The guardian mystic led me down a long row of shelves packed with thousands upon thousands of trinkets, each one catalogued and carefully stored. Three-quarters of the way down he lifted a bronze bust of Julius Caesar from the shelf and offered it to me. I winced. "Uh, Qin, I know beggars can't be choosers, but that's not something this unbound is likely to take home with her and keep nearby at all times."

Qin turned the bust around to look at the face. "Pity. I knew him well. Great guy. A little full of himself, and a total party animal." He chuckled placing the bust back on the shelf, giving it a little pat on the head. Turning to me, he said, "You want something small but powerful."

"Yes. A piece of jewelry would be ideal."

Qin tugged on the silver goatee he sported while he thought it through, but then his black eyes sparkled, and he snapped his fingers. "I have just the thing."

Moving back along the row of trinkets we'd come from, he led me almost to the entrance, then around the corner all the way to the very back.

This row was nearly overflowing with jewels in platinum, gold, silver, copper, and every precious and semiprecious gem imaginable. We passed a series of three crowns that simply pulsed with power, and a scepter that I knew had been used in the Mystic Great War.

About a quarter of the way down, Qin paused in front of a three-tiered, velvet-covered bracelet stand. There were about a half dozen bracelets hanging from it, and Qin plucked one from the middle. "Here. This is a level seven. Your unbound can wear this and it will counteract the power of the Pandora trinket."

I took the bracelet from him and marveled at its beauty. Made of yellow gold it was constructed in a weave pattern, as if strands of gold had been braided to form the bracelet, and at each divot in the design was a small inlaid diamond.

I looked over at Qin. "It's beautiful."

"It will offer your unbound protection from the Pandora. Just put a little essence into it and it'll counteract the spell."

I twirled the bracelet to catch the light and make it sparkle. "Will she have to wear this forever?"

"Depends on which Pandora she got exposed to."

"The Promise."

"Huh," Qin said, and I couldn't tell if that was good or bad.

" 'Huh' as in . . . ?"

"I'm surprised your unbound got exposed to something so powerful as the Promise and lived. Most *mystics* could be taken down with that Pandora. She'll definitely need to wear it forever."

"I was afraid of that. I don't know that I can craft a spell strong enough to make her want to wear it for the rest of her life and never, ever take it off."

"Then you're left with only two options."

"And they are?"

"Bind her and make her a mystic or destroy the Promise."

"Those aren't great options, Qin."

"Mixing magic with the unbound seldom is, Dovey."

I left SPL with the bracelet in hand and sped over to the hospital I suspected Hermia had been taken to. It was a little past ten when I arrived, and I noted the sign at the entrance that said that visiting hours were over at ten thirty p.m.

If I was quick, I could get in and out without too much trouble.

Before heading to the information desk, I lifted out my trusty silver dollar and when the clerk behind the desk looked up, I held out my fist to him. "I found this when I came through the entrance. I think someone might have lost it."

He opened his palm, and I dropped the dollar into it. "Oooo, a silver dollar. I haven't seen one of these in . . ."

The clerk's excited gaze went vacant.

Lifting the silver dollar out of his palm, I said, "I need to know if Hermia Ariti is out of surgery."

"You need to know if Hermia Ariti is out of surgery," he repeated. Then he swiveled to his computer and began typing. "Yes."

"Where is she now?"

"She's out of recovery and was put in room three fourteen. The psych ward."

I nodded. I'd suspected as much. "Thank you. In a few moments you're going to become fully conscious again, and you won't remember me or anything about our interaction."

"I won't remember you or anything about our interaction."

I patted the countertop with an open palm. "Good man. Thank you."

Making my way to the elevator, I rode it up to the third floor and stepped out cautiously. The floor was quiet with only one nurse in sight. She had her back to me, and I took the advantage to hurry down the hall to the left to room three fourteen. Pausing at the doorway, I retrieved the other trinket Qin had given me for this mission. A single jack from the child's game felt warm in my hand as I lifted it out. After placing it in the corner of the doorway, I stepped back to look inside the hospital room and everything appeared the same. Reaching forward, I dropped my handbag on the inside of the hospital room floor, backed out into the hallway a second time, and looked in. My handbag was nowhere in sight. *Nice*.

Anyone who walked by Hermia's room would see it undisturbed and would have no clue that I was inside.

Back across the threshold again, I picked up my handbag and moved over to Hermia's bed.

The young woman was alone in the room. She looked pale and fragile lying in the bed, and there was a thick bandage covering her left shoulder. She appeared to be asleep, but there was a furrow to her brow, as if she was in the middle of a nightmare and struggling to climb out of.

I walked over to her bedside and noticed that her wrists had been tied down. It was my guess that she'd awakened from my spell at some point and had probably tried to stab herself again.

I retrieved the bracelet from my handbag, noticing that I had Gib's watch in the side pocket. "Drat. I forgot to give him that." With a sigh and a silent promise to get it to him as soon as I could, I retrieved the gold bracelet and undid the clasp. Once I pushed a solid bit of essence into it, I wrapped the bangle around Hermia's forearm.

Her expression immediately relaxed, and she opened her eyes. "Hi," she whispered.

I smiled down at her. "Hey there. How're you feeling?"

"Fuzzy. And my shoulder hurts."

"I bet. Hermia, do you remember anything about what happened this evening?"

She nodded. "Somebody stabbed me."

My eyebrows arched. "Who?"

She squinted as she focused her thoughts. "I . . . I don't know. I remember being in the ladies' room, and when I came out of the stall, there was a glass of champagne and a ring box on the counter."

"Was anyone else there with you in the ladies' room?"

She blinked and shook her head. "There must've been, but I don't remember. I know I was surprised to see the champagne and ring box, and there was also a note—"

"A note?"

She frowned, trying to recall the details. "My name was written on it and underneath that it read 'Cheers!' "

"What did you do next?"

A corner of her lip lifted upward. "I took a swig. It was good champagne."

"And then what?"

"I opened the box, and then . . ." The furrow of her brow deepened. "Somebody attacked me."

"You remember them attacking you in the ladies' room?"

"Yes . . . I mean . . . no. I think it was a few minutes later. I remember going to this room that smelled awful . . ."

The embalming room, I thought.

"And that's where I was attacked. It hurt so much! I've always had this fear of knives, you know. Being stabbed to death is my worst nightmare."

"I understand. What happened next?"

"I think . . . I think I ran. He must've chased after me, but I made it to the stairs and up a flight, and that's when you tackled him, right?"

"*He*," I repeated, ignoring her question.

"Yeah. I mean, at least I think it was a man."

"Do you remember anything . . . anything at all about what he looked like?"

Hermia sighed, and it sounded so tired. Shaking her head she said, "I don't remember. It's so fuzzy. But I know you got the knife away from him. Thank you for saving my life, Dovey."

I stroked her forehead. She had no idea that she'd attacked herself. No doubt the power of the Promise had scrambled the details. "You're welcome."

She tried to move an arm and realized that she was strapped down. "What the . . . ? Why are my wrists tied down?"

"The wound in your shoulder was repaired in surgery. They don't want you to move around and tear it open."

"I won't," she said. "Tell them to unstrap me and I promise I won't."

"I will. I think it'll help if you tell the doctor that you drank a glass of champagne that was left for you, and you think you might've been roofied."

"I was?" Her face was a mask of alarm.

"I think it's the only way to explain the fuzzy memory."

"Oh, my God! You're right!"

Offering Hermia a line that would get her off the psych ward and explain her self-harm was the least I could do for her. Other than also giving her the trinket.

I tapped on the bracelet around her wrist and said, "I brought you something."

She looked down and pulled on her right arm, but the straps held her in place. "What is it?"

"It's a bracelet." I reached for the strap and undid it, then lifted her wrist so that she could see it more clearly.

"Oh, wow. That's beautiful! Dovey, I can't accept that."

Still holding on to Hermia's wrist, I filled the room with my essence and spun a spell assuring that she wouldn't take it off.

"To dangers locked within a box,
"Hold this bangle tight with knots
"Of magic bound to keep you safe,
"Keep it close and have the faith,
"Don't remove it, have no fear,
"This trinket is the one most dear."

I had no idea how long my spell would last. Even the best spells—excluding a binding spell—faded with time.

I chose not to bind Hermia for the exact reasons I chose not to bind Gib to protect him from Elric's jealousy. I didn't think it was fair to bind a mortal without them fully realizing what that meant. I had befriended a few unbounds in my time and watching them age and eventually die was a difficult burden, not to mention the fact that freshly bound mystics faced a harsh world filled with manipulation, deceit, and sometimes . . . *often* . . . violence.

The only reason I'd prospered had been because of Elric. He'd thwarted every attack against me, and there had been plenty of those—mostly from Petra's side of the chessboard.

My morals wouldn't allow me to bind a mortal without their full agreement, which required exposing our world to an unbound and allowing them to decide. With that, there was a definite risk involved, because if a mortal were to be made aware of our world and choose not to be bound, they could expose us to all sorts of attention that we didn't need.

Elric, in particular, frowned upon the practice of exposing our world to the unbound, stopping just short of forbidding it. Other courts had gone to that length, however, including the court of Vostov. There was a high cost to pay for breaching that trust.

Once I was done reciting the spell, I felt Hermia's skin warm, and her expression became placid. "Will you stay with me until I fall asleep, Dovey?"

"Of course."

Only a few minutes later, Hermia's breathing was deep and rhythmic. As gently as I could, I strapped her arm down again as I didn't want anyone to grow suspicious when they checked on her and noticed that one of her wrists was free.

Then I walked quietly toward the door, removed the jack from the corner, and left.

Once I was back inside my car, I pointed Luna's nose toward the funeral home. It would be closed at this hour, but I felt I had to look.

I parked down the street from the funeral home because I didn't want to draw attention to a lone car in their parking lot this late at night. Making my way around the building to the back entrance, I inserted my trinket key into the lock, pushed a bit of essence into it, and unlocked the door.

I waited within the doorway for several beats, unsure if the funeral home had any kind of security. When I didn't hear an alarm, I moved inside.

In front of me was a staircase leading both down and up. I headed down the stairs first, finding the embalming room at the bottom.

Placing my jack trinket on the floor next to a mop and bucket, I felt around for a light switch and turned it on.

The room was cold and immaculately kept, and there were a series of square doors in the wall opposite me, exactly like you'd find in a morgue.

I avoided those while I gave the room a thorough walk-through and to my surprise, in the sink was a lone and empty champagne glass with a ruby-lipped kiss on the rim.

Hermia had been telling the truth, and I wondered if the wielder of the Promise had used a similar technique with Eleni and Augustus. If he or she had, then they'd cleaned up after themselves. Gib had said that when he was at Eleni's, there'd been no evidence of food or drink in the entire apartment. It was also impossible to tell whether Augustus had been slipped a drug-laced drink because the fire would've masked its existence.

I lifted the champagne glass and carefully washed it clean of any liquid, while keeping the lipstick smear on it. Then I dried out the inside just to make sure before setting it back in the sink where I'd found it. If I wanted everyone to believe the story I'd planted about Hermia being roofied, then there couldn't be even a drop of champagne left in the glass to test for traces of Rohypnol.

Pausing only to pick up the jack in the doorway, I made my way back upstairs to the first floor and walked through a kitchen area to the central hallway, winding my way around the entire first floor, pausing in the viewing room for Mrs. Betty Bettendorf.

Her coffin was closed and the small sign near the door told me that tomorrow evening would be the final day for her viewing before her funeral the day after that.

Heading to the stairs, I made my way to the second floor and walked right to the ladies' room. I didn't expect to find the Promise in there, but I still felt the need to be thorough.

After giving the ladies' room a good look, I walked back into the hallway and over to Augustus's viewing room, searching the space from end to end, finding nothing more valuable than a dime on the floor.

With a tired sigh I finally quit the funeral home, leaving the same way I'd come in, and walked back toward my car, my thoughts a tired tangle of more questions than answers.

Ten feet or so from Luna I raised my key fob and unlocked the doors. The next thing I knew, I was flying through the air, headed straight for a tree.

Chapter 13

Barely managing to get my arms up before crashing into the tree trunk, I heard a sickening crunch as several bones in my hand broke on impact.

White-hot pain erupted, traveling from my hand down my arm all the way to my shoulder and I cried out as I fell flat on my back to the ground.

Footsteps behind me alerted me that I was in mortal danger, and it took everything I had to block out the pain and get to my feet. Holding my broken hand against my chest, I barely managed to get my bearings before a red ball of energy came sailing toward me.

Reflexively I threw up my own ball of golden energy and as the two orbs met, they exploded, knocking me and my assailant back to the ground.

"*You damn witch!*" Lavender screamed while she rolled over onto her knees and struggled to regain her feet.

I got to my knees as well, my chest heaving from exertion and pain. Working to get even one foot underneath me felt like more than I was capable of at the moment, but if I didn't, I'd be at the angry mystic's mercy, and I doubted Lavender had any of *that* in mind for me.

Ignoring her insult, I gritted my teeth, hissing air as I pushed up off the ground, and got my footing under control.

The crazed woman was already racing toward me again, with murder in her eyes. I called up another orb of energy, infusing it with a spell that Elric had taught me, and aimed for Lavender's feet.

She saw it coming and her eyes widened but her reaction time was off, and the orb exploded right where I'd aimed it.

Lavender flew straight up in the air, landing on the roof of the funeral home, and I grabbed my handbag from the ground and bolted for Luna. Somehow, I managed to get inside the car and get her started. Within seconds I had peeled off down the street.

I had no idea how Lavender found me, but I had to make it to SPL before she got off that roof and came after me again.

Zigzagging my way through the light traffic at this time of night, I was able to gain the freeway and pushed Luna's speed all the way to HQ.

My panic didn't subside until I'd reached the underground garage and parked Luna near the building's underground entrance.

Only then did I feel safe enough to leave my car. If Lavender attempted to confront or murder me on SPL property, she'd be fed to the dragons. Literally.

Hugging my injured hand, I got out of the car and limped painfully to the elevator. Every part of me felt pummeled and bruised. When the doors opened, I shuffled forward and pressed the button for the seventeenth floor, then leaned against the brass-lined boxcar while doing my best to push the pain aside.

After what felt like eternity, the elevator sounded a soothing *bing* and the doors parted. I shuffled forward again, finding Qin back at his desk, eating his dinner.

"Twice in one night, Dovey?"

I looked at him and whimpered, in too much pain to explain.

Immediately he was out of his chair, hurrying to me. "Who did this to you?" he asked, lifting my injured hand to take a look.

I cried out in pain as he moved my fingers, but managed to grit my teeth and say, "A thief."

"One of ours?" he asked with raised brows.

I shook my head.

"Petra's?"

I shook my head again.

"Freelance?" I nodded. Qin snarled. "Figures. Filthy animals." As the trinket room guardian of Elric's most prized possessions, the ancient mystic hated thieves, especially the kind that worked only for themselves.

"Come," he said gently, escorting me over to his big leather chair. I eased myself into the seat as gingerly as I could without causing myself more pain. It worked. Mostly.

"Stay put," Qin ordered.

I wanted to tell him that he needn't worry, I wouldn't be going anywhere soon, but I simply nodded and laid my head back against the headrest.

The trinket guardian was gone longer than I would've guessed, but he finally emerged holding a gold prism about an inch and a half tall by about an inch wide.

"Here," he said, offering it to me. I extended my left hand, and he shook his head. "No, Dovey. The other one."

Hissing through my teeth again, I moved my right hand out away from my chest, then turned it over so my palm was up. Qin set the prism into my palm and there was an immediate warmth from it that seeped through my skin, and into the bone, radiating through every finger, my wrist, my arm, and my shoulder, and continued to snake its way through my entire body.

I closed my eyes to savor the feeling, noting how the warmth pushed all the pain aside as it worked to repair every break, bump, and bruise.

The warmth faded slowly, like a dying fire giving off less and less heat until it left me tingling and even energized. At last, I opened my eyes to find Qin looking at me with a happy smile. "Better?"

I sighed and handed the prism back to him. "Infinitely."

"Good." Qin pocketed the prism, then reached into another pocket, extracting a gold ring with a giant amethyst in the setting. "Here."

I held out my hand again and he placed the ring into it. It also buzzed with warmth. "What's this for?"

"To arm yourself. I know you're against carrying lethally potent trinkets, Dovey, but you could've been killed tonight. What would Elric do to me if he found out that I'd given you trinkets to use on the unbound, but nothing to protect you?"

"I'm not a killer, Qin. Elric knows that."

"No, the boss man *puts up* with that. He definitely doesn't like it."

I sighed and studied the ring for a moment. "How does it work?"

"It can only be activated when you're under attack. It's more for defense than for targeting someone you want to annihilate."

"What does it do when I'm attacked?" I pressed.

Qin folded my healed fingers over the ring. "As long as you can aim it, it will defend you."

I blinked. "Can it cause collateral damage?"

"You mean to innocent bystanders?"

I nodded.

Qin shrugged, which wasn't the answer I was looking for.

"I don't think I can accept this, Qin. Sorry."

He sighed and held out his palm for the ring. I gave it back to him and, trying to sound reassuring, I said, "I'll watch my back. Now that I know I'm the thief's target, I'll be better prepared."

"Who's the thief?" he asked.

"Lavender."

Qin pursed his lips as he frowned. "She's despicable. And ruthless. She's also got two hundred years and twice as much power on you, Dovey. I think you should take the ring."

But I shook my head. I was investigating a case that demanded that I work around the unbound. A ring that powerful could kill anyone nearby.

It could kill Gib, I thought with a shudder. Qin eyed me curiously and I was thankful he couldn't read my mind.

At least I didn't *think* he could read it. Clearing my throat, I got to my feet and bent low to hug the ancient one. "Thank you," I said to him.

He gave my back a few pats, then pulled away and said, "I hear you had a birthday recently."

I laughed, my good humor returning. "I did."

"How many does that make?"

"Two hundred."

Qin whistled. "Look at you. Surviving long enough to reach two hundred. Good for you, Dovey."

I laughed again and gave him another squeeze, then stepped back, ready to leave. "How many birthdays have you had, Qin?"

He reached up to tug on his goatee. "Well, let's see, I don't remember the exact year I was born, but I'd guess it was about fifty years or so before Julius—"

"Caesar?"

Qin nodded. "So, I'm probably in my early two thousands."

I shook my head in marvel. "Amazing."

He shrugged nonchalantly. "I've had a good run."

I bent to give him a kiss on the cheek, then walked to the elevator and stepped inside the boxcar. I started to wave good night right as the doors were closing, but my hand suddenly felt heavy. I looked down and gasped in astonishment. The amethyst ring was on my ring finger. "Oh, you ancient brat!" I exclaimed. I tried to tug the ring off my finger, but it wouldn't budge. It wasn't too tight, I could easily twirl it, but it wouldn't move when I pulled at it.

Irritated, I slapped at the open-door button, but nothing happened. "Qin!" I yelled, and pounded on the door. "Take this thing off my finger!"

The elevator began its descent, even though I hadn't pressed a floor button. Thinking someone must have called the elevator, I waited it out, determined to head straight back up to the trinket room.

None of the floor lights above the door lit up, however, which I found suspicious. At last, the elevator came to a stop, and I knew I was somewhere near the bottom because of how long it'd taken. The doors opened, revealing the parking garage. And no one was standing there, ready to take the elevator up.

I growled and slapped at the button for the seventeenth floor, determined to make Qin take this ring off my finger, but the button refused to light up, and the elevator doors refused to close no matter how many times I pushed the button to shut them.

I growled again and pressed the button for the sixteenth floor, but that button wouldn't light up either and the elevator doors refused to close. "I cannot believe this!"

I waited in the boxcar for almost fifteen minutes, hoping it would cooperate, but it wouldn't. Exasperated, I stepped out of the boxcar, and the second I was free of it the doors banged shut and I heard the elevator lifting, heading to another floor.

"I will give him such a lecture!" I groused, suddenly too tired to fight. I hoped that there was a trinket I could use at home to pry the ring off my finger, but something told me it wouldn't be that easy.

When I did finally make it home, I was too exhausted to worry about it.

I slept in late the next morning, awaking to a loud clap of thunder. Reaching for my phone to check the time, I realized that Gib had texted me only a minute before.

I'm calling in my rain check. Coffee?

I smirked.

I could use a cup, I replied adding a sleepy emoji.

Bette's?

My smirk widened. "Somebody's craving Stella's blueberry cheese Danish."

Thinking on it for a moment, however, I realized that it might be too risky to bring Gib back into my neighborhood, lest Elric learn what I was up to with Qin and come looking for an explanation.

Why don't we try your side of town?

Gib sent me a pin to the coffee shop, cutely called Perk Up, which was only two miles away, and I replied that I'd see him in an hour.

After a quick shower, I took care with my hair and makeup, then trotted over to my closet to select an outfit that was stylish but didn't look like I was trying too hard.

"Bits?" I called over my shoulder to where his bed was on the nightstand. There was a squeak at my feet, and I looked down to see him sniffing up at me. "How *do* you do that?"

He didn't answer, he simply kept sniffing up at me, but I swear there was a distinct quirk to his mouth, giving him a smile.

"Fine, don't share the details. I do need help, though. It's cold and rainy out. What goes with cold and rainy?"

Bits wound himself into a ball and rolled into my closet,

moving straight over to an oversized, white cowl-neck sweater, then to a pair of black leggings, black booties with silver accents, and a leather and suede black motorcycle jacket.

"Love it," I told him. "That's exactly the look I was thinking of."

He squeaked and rolled past me out of the closet and the next thing I knew he was back in his snuggle, burrowing into it like he planned to hibernate for the day.

After getting dressed, I was about to top the outfit off with some silver jewelry when I realized I was still wearing the gold amethyst ring that Qin had stuck me with.

I pulled on the ring, but it held tight, and I couldn't really spend the morning trying to pry it off when Gib was waiting for me at the coffee shop.

Switching gears, I put on some gold and amethyst earrings and a jumble of gold bangle bracelets and was on my way.

Arriving at the coffee shop right on time, I spotted Gib at a table in the back. Seeing me, he got off the barstool, waved me over, and waited until I slid into the chair across from him to retake his seat.

"Wow," he said when we were settled.

"What?"

"Do you always look this good in the morning?"

I laughed, then pointed at him, wiggling my finger. "You're one to talk."

Gib was dressed in a black turtleneck sweater with a midlength ivory wool overcoat, light blue jeans, and ivory suede boots.

He looked delicious.

Grinning broadly he said, "How do you take your coffee, madame?"

I winked. "Tall, dark, and handsome."

Gib laughed. Getting up from the table, he leaned toward me and whispered, "I like mine blond and beautiful."

A thrill coursed through me, leaving goose pimples in its tracks while my cheeks flushed with heat.

If Gib noticed his effect on me, he didn't let on. He simply squeezed my shoulder and headed toward the counter.

Somehow I resisted the urge to fan myself and settled in to wait. Glancing over my shoulder, I saw that the line to the counter was fairly long and moving slowly, which was odd given that it was nearly ten a.m., and the morning rush should've been over. Then again, the rain had probably slowed everyone down this morning, so the rush was happening a little late.

To pass the time I picked up my phone and looked up the weather to see how long the rain and cold temps were sticking around. Hopping on to a local news station's live broadcast, I was surprised to see the lead story for the morning was about a pedestrian who had run out into traffic and was hit by a truck and killed.

The anchor said, "Alejandro Juarez was a maintenance worker at De Vol Funeral Home. He leaves behind his wife and two adult children. Authorities don't know why Mr. Juarez ran into oncoming traffic. A family spokesperson claims there was no history of depression or drug use and his reasoning for the apparent suicide remains a mystery."

I gasped and sat straight up, my gaze locked on the screen and the memory of the mop and bucket at the base of the stairs of the embalming room at the funeral home came back to me.

"He found the box," I whispered. "Or the mystic had stashed the box in the mop bucket at the funeral home last night and came back to retrieve it this morning, making sure there were no witnesses."

"Here's your coffee, madame. And a croissant in case you haven't had breakfast yet."

I startled at the sound of Gib's voice, pulling my gaze away from the screen to look at him.

"What's happened?" he asked, reading my expression.

"The maintenance worker of the funeral home we were at last night ran out into traffic this morning and was hit by a truck and killed."

Gib set down a mug of coffee and a croissant for me, then slid into the seat opposite. "Come again?"

"This man," I said, swiveling my phone around so he could see the lead story.

Gib's eyes darted back and forth across the screen for a minute and then he lifted his eyes to me. "Jesus. That's a hell of a coincidence. If I didn't know better, I'd say that the Aritis are cursed and some of that bad juju is rubbing off on the people around them."

He had no idea how right he was.

"On that topic," he said, "I think we should compare notes from any conversations we had last night."

"Good idea." By now I felt I could trust Gib. I badly needed to solve this case, and it was a blow to my ego that I hadn't already. Enlisting his help by appearing cooperative might yield me the clues I needed.

He took a sip of his coffee, then tore off a chunk of his croissant. "You should go first."

"I'd prefer it if you did." I didn't want to share my information until I knew his.

He nodded, waiting until he'd finished chewing to talk. "I had an interesting conversation with Ambrose's girlfriend."

I cocked my head. "You mean his new wife?"

"No." Gib's lips tugged upward to a smirk. "His *current* girlfriend."

My jaw dropped. "Ambrose brought his wife and a girlfriend to his brother's wake? *While* his *ex-wife* was also present?"

Gib shrugged one shoulder. "He did."

"Bold." The unbound typically had much stricter morals

than mystics, but even by mystic standards that was a shock. "What did she have to say?"

"Plenty. Ambrose has been keeping her on the side for years. She thought she'd be the next Mrs. Ariti, especially when Ambrose filed for divorce. When she learned that he was dating someone else who he then proposed to, she started issuing threats."

"What kind of threats?"

Gib shrugged again. "The usual. She'd tell his fiancée all about their affair, and then she'd tell his ex-wife so that Gina could go back into court and demand more money, et cetera, et cetera."

"A woman scorned. Did she follow through with any of her threats."

"No. Ambrose locked her down with a big pile of money. He told her he'd continue to support her if she kept her mouth shut. Also, he didn't invite her to Augustus's wake, she came just to show him she could."

"The woman has nerve."

"In spades. Although, it could've been the alcohol. She was half in the tank, taking a nip from a flask she kept in her purse every now and then."

I squinted at Gib, a thought needling me.

"What?" he asked.

"I checked on Hermia before heading home last night. She said that there had been a glass of champagne in the ladies' room with a card addressed to her that read, 'Cheers!' "

Gib nodded. "I heard about that. She thinks she was roofied."

"It would explain her crazed violent behavior."

He sighed. "I'm not sure I buy it, though. Do you?"

I had to be careful here. Encouraging the idea that Hermia had been drugged with a hallucinogenic was something I needed to support, because the circumstances behind using the Promise wouldn't be believed or easily explained without exposing myself and my community. "I do believe it. I had a lovely conversation with Hermia yesterday morning and I doubt the woman has a violent bone in her body."

"The hospital ran a tox screen. Nothing showed up."

"How long ago did they screen her?"

"This morning."

"Any trace of the drug could've cleared out of her system by then. Especially if she's had multiple rounds of IVs to get her through the surgery."

Gib raised his coffee cup. Before taking a sip, he said, "Fair point. But back to Samantha—"

"The girlfriend?"

"Yeah, sorry, her name is Samantha Rollins. Anyway, she didn't especially strike me as a murderer, but if she was slipping a hallucinogenic to Hermia, Augustus, and Eleni, then she might have me fooled."

I sighed. "I wish we had one solid clue to help us identify a person of interest."

"Who did you talk to?"

"Ambrose's ex. Gina."

"And . . . ?"

"And there could be another angle."

He turned his palm up and moved his fingers in a "let's have it" motion.

"Gina seems to think that the Aritis are selling drugs on the black market."

It was Gib's turn to look surprised. "Here?" he said, and I knew his FBI hackles had just been raised.

"According to Gina, no. She said they deal mostly in Africa and Asia."

"From here?" he pressed.

"Again, no. The Ariti factory is based in Greece. She said that the drugs are shipped from there."

"Well, we've got no jurisdiction in Greece, but I can make a few overseas phone calls and see what turns up."

"Gina also suggested that the reason Eleni had been ostracized from the family was because she was threatening to expose the drug ring."

"Huh," Gib said, letting that sink in.

I tapped the table with my nail, mentally debating whether to divulge a little more of what I'd learned. "There is another detail that I've left out," I said, after making up my mind.

Gib arched a brow, looking at me expectantly.

"I spoke to the barista at Eleni's favorite coffee shop. It's across the street from her office. She got to know Eleni rather well, which was why she was so alarmed one day when she saw Eleni being manhandled right outside her office."

"Define 'manhandled.'"

"Forcefully shoved into a town car and driven away."

"Did she get a plate number?"

"I don't think so."

"Description?"

"Kioni—the barista—said that the man shoving Eleni into the car was a big muscular guy, somewhere between six-one and six-two, with jet-black hair and likely of either Italian or Greek descent."

"How long ago did this happen?"

"She said it happened three days before Eleni's death."

"Did Kioni ever learn who the man was or what he wanted from Eleni?"

"She didn't."

Gib frowned. "This case is starting to be a real pain in the neck."

"Agreed."

"Well, I can probably shake the tree a little by interviewing Ambrose."

"Do you think he'll talk to you?" It was my experience that wealthy people typically didn't grant interviews to law enforcement, preferring to speak through their high-priced lawyers.

"If I lead with the illicit drug ring thing he might."

"I'd like to come with you."

Gib polished off the rest of his coffee, offered me a wink, and said, "Thought you'd never ask."

CHAPTER 14

Gib and I took his car to the Ariti offices—a modest three-story building off the north end of the beltway. As we walked toward the front door, Gib said, "Let me take the lead on this one, okay?"

"Sure. No problem." If Gib couldn't get the answers we were looking for out of Ambrose, then I'd make it a point to use a trinket to get some answers out of him later.

When we arrived at the reception desk, a woman behind the counter took us both in, her mouth agape. "Wow. You here for a photo shoot or something?"

Gib and I traded confused looks. "Excuse me?" I said.

She wagged her finger back and forth at us. "You guys are models, right?"

"Not quite," Gib told her. "We just play them on TV."

I put a finger to my lips to suppress a laugh. I doubted the young woman would understand the reference.

"I don't get it," she said, her gaze shifting to me.

"It's nothing." I waved my hand in dismissal. "We're here to see Mr. Ambrose Ariti."

"Do you have an appointment?"

"We do not," Gib said, unhooking his badge from his waistband. "But I've got one of these. Will that let me cut to the front of the line?"

Her jaw dropped again. "FBI? You here doing a raid or something?"

"Or something," Gib said. The phrase seemed to be a favorite of hers.

"Well, Mr. Ambrose ain't here."

Gib took a deep calming breath. "Do you know either where he is or when he might be coming back?"

"Word is that he left early to go pick up his kid. She had a psychotic break or something." She tapped her temple for emphasis.

"You believe he's at the hospital?" Gib pressed.

She shook her head. "Naw. That was hours ago. They're probably home by now. You should try there, cuz I heard he's taking the rest of the week off to deal with all the family drama, what with everybody droppin' dead in his whole family or somethin'."

The woman rolled her eyes, and I couldn't help but glare at her. No matter what Ariti's temperament was, two of his family members died horrific deaths and his daughter had barely survived her own nightmarish demise.

"His address?" I asked crisply.

The receptionist frowned. "I don't have it. But you guys should, right?" She pointed to us again.

Gib tapped the counter, offering her a grimacing smile. "We do. Thank you for your help."

With that he turned on his heel and began walking away. I followed and from behind we heard the receptionist call out, "You guys should do some modeling! I bet you'd make a lot more money than what they pay you at the FBI!"

"Or somethin'," he muttered, holding open the door for me.

After we exited the building, Gib popped his umbrella and turned to face me, while shielding us both from the rain. "Let's assess."

I tilted my head in curiosity.

"Our next move is either to visit Ambrose at his home or run away to become fashion models."

I giggled. "Didn't you already do that?"

"I did, and she's not wrong. I made a lot more doing that than the Bureau pays me."

"My vote is to head to Ambrose's, but I am curious; what made you quit?"

Gib moved to my side and we began walking toward his Range Rover. "Modeling sounds like fun! Glamour! The high life! But the truth is it's just another meat market. After a while, I got fed up with all the superficial connections, backstabbing, gossip, and the ocean of insecurity *everybody* in the fashion industry wades around in."

"Whoa. Stop trying to talk me into getting some headshots."

He rolled his eyes but there was a playful grin on his face. Pausing at the passenger-side door, he opened it for me. "Meh lady," he said, rolling his hand in an "after you" gesture.

I hopped into the front seat, pleased by the chivalry.

When Gib got into the driver's seat, he turned the engine on and let the car warm up while he tapped at his phone. "Got it."

"Ambrose's address?"

"Yep. Hopefully that receptionist hasn't already texted him about us."

"Why is it bad if she does?"

Gib pulled out into traffic, the wiper blades knocking back and forth in a soothing rhythm. "People will tell you a lot more when you surprise them than when they know you're coming. When they're expecting you, they have time to think about getting their story straight. Surprising them at their front door kicks in their natural tendency to talk to you, simply to claim their innocence. And they *always* give up more info without realizing it."

"Did you tell anyone at the wake last night that you work for the Bureau?"

"Nope. Well, except Toby, but that was indirectly."

"Indirectly?"

"I gave him my card," he reminded me.

"Do you think he told anyone else?"

"Doubtful. From what I gathered, Toby wasn't a welcome member of the family, even though he and Augustus had been together for almost two decades."

"Such a shame. This family is overflowing with dysfunction."

"True."

We made small talk on the way to Ambrose's home, and I realized how comfortable I was in Gib's presence. He was easy to be around. And I *liked* him. Which was trouble. But I couldn't seem to keep my distance. More than that, I didn't *want* to keep my distance. I told myself that once this case was solved and I got the Promise back to its rightful owner, I'd make a clean break.

But I didn't want to. I didn't want to at all.

We arrived at the gated community where Ambrose and his new wife lived, and Gib presented his badge to the guard at the gate.

"He expectin' you?" the guard asked. He was a tall, imposing man who seemed to take his job very seriously.

"Yes, Stan," Gib said, taking note of the man's name tag pinned to his blue shirt as he fed him a lie.

"You got a warrant?"

"No, Stan. It's not that kind of visit. Now, how about you open that gate so that we aren't late, and then we can have a little chat with Mr. Ariti and get out of his hair for the rest of the day."

The guard offered Gib a stern frown but pressed the button to open the gate, and we zipped forward.

Gib wound his way through the neighborhood and even I marveled at the extravagance of the community. The homes were massive estates in all sorts of architectural styles, some gauche, some classic, some modern, and some just funky.

The Ariti estate was toward the back of the subdivision. His home was quite contemporary; lots of white brick and teak wood aligned in sharp angles and boxy wings.

"I've been in this neighborhood before," Gib mused.

"You have?"

He nodded. "I had a teammate on the baseball team who would throw big pool parties at the season's end."

"Are you still friends with anyone from your high school?"

Gib didn't answer me right away, and I noted the pause. "No."

He didn't elaborate, just like he didn't elaborate about his deceased wife. I realized that as charming and disarming as he was, there were still some demons that he was obviously dealing with.

We rounded a corner and Gib parked at the foot of the driveway. A few moments later we were on Ariti's front steps.

Gib rang the doorbell, and it was answered promptly by a small Hispanic woman in a maid's uniform.

"*Sí*?" she asked.

"Good morning, Ms. . . . ?" he said, trying to draw out the woman's name.

She tapped her chest. "Henrietta."

"Good morning, Henrietta. I'm Special Agent Barlow, here to speak to Mr. Ariti. Is he home?"

Gib held up his badge for Henrietta to inspect, and I noticed how pale she became and how frightened her expression was. I suspected she must've come from a country where the police were much feared.

"Uh . . ." she said. "I see for you. You stay here, okay?"

I offered her a warm smile and a gentle tone. "We will, ma'am. Thank you."

Her gaze darted to me, but it was clear I'd done nothing to quell her fear. She nodded though and closed the door.

We waited under the shelter of Gib's umbrella, listening to the patter of rain as it tapped out a rhythmic tune on the umbrella's skin.

At last, the door was opened, by Ambrose himself. "You FBI?"

It came out more like an accusation than a question.

Gib offered up his shield again. "Special Agent Barlow, sir. Do you have a moment to speak to us about the death of your brother and sister?"

"Do you have news?"

"Well, sir, not per se. But I *have* been finding some irregularities that I'd like your insight on."

Ambrose narrowed his eyes assessing Gib, and I wondered why he seemed so irritated by our presence.

"Mr. Ariti," I said, winning his attention. "My associate and I don't believe that your brother's death was the result of an accident. Nor do we believe that your sister committed suicide."

"What evidence have you discovered?" he barked at me. His tone was clearly defensive, and it made me wonder what he was hiding.

Gib clipped his badge back onto his waistband. "For starters, the coincidence of both your siblings dying tragically within a two-day period and then your daughter possibly being drugged up enough to cause herself some harm has us thinking that there might be more to all this. Wouldn't you agree?"

"I had *nothing* to do with my brother and sister's deaths."

Wow. Dost thou protest too much, Mr. Ariti? I thought.

"No one said you did," Gib replied. "What I'm most concerned about, sir, is that if the fire at Augustus's gallery wasn't an accident, and your sister was forced off her terrace, and your daughter was intentionally drugged, who's to say that you won't be the next target?"

Ariti's jaw clenched, and his hands balled into fists. I had the feeling he'd been thinking that too.

Stepping aside without saying a word, he motioned us into

the house. Gib shook out the umbrella before leaving it on the front step allowing me to step through the entrance ahead of him.

The first thing I saw was the retreating form of the new Mrs. Ariti, walking toward a door at the end of the hallway. When she opened it, I got a whiff of chlorine.

It must be nice to live in a house with an indoor pool. Or a hot tub. Or perhaps both.

Ambrose led us down a hallway on the left, past a grand staircase and into a very large home office. An ornate desk sat in front of shelving lined with books, framed photos, and a whole host of medals and trophies. Many of the trophies were topped with swimmer figurines, and an abundance of the photographs showed a much younger Ambrose, standing atop a winners' podium with a medal around his neck. My eyes widened to see one photo with the Olympic circles in the background and Ambrose standing proudly on the second-place block.

That explains the indoor pool.

He motioned us to a dark red leather sofa, while he took a seat behind his desk.

"How is Hermia?" I asked as we sat down.

Ambrose sighed heavily, and it was easy to see the toll the last few days had taken on him. "Resting. But she appears to be of sound mind, so I doubt we'll have another episode like yesterday."

He took a slight pause before he added, "Thank you for getting the blade away from her. I don't think I could take another death in the family."

Gib leaned forward, resting his elbows on his knees. "That's what we wanted to talk with you about, Mr. Ariti. As you know the FBI has assigned me to investigate the death of your brother and sister—"

"At my request, Agent Barlow."

Subtle, I thought. He was reminding Gib who the real power player was here.

Gib nodded agreeably. "Yes, sir. During our initial investigation we've come across some information that may or may not be related to your siblings' deaths."

"Such as?"

Gib cocked his head slightly. "Such as a source disclosing information about a black-market drug deal your pharmaceutical company is funneling from Greece to Asia and Africa."

Ambrose steepled his fingers and rested his elbows on the desk, while his narrowed eyes glittered with malice. "I would be very careful about what you're accusing my family of, Agent Barlow."

"No one's accusing you or your family, sir. We're simply trying to find a path that explains the last seventy-two hours, within which your siblings both died under suspicious circumstances, and your daughter was roofied into causing herself harm."

"Not to mention the fact that we have it on good authority that your sister was ostracized from the family because of her ongoing threat to expose these alleged illegal drug sales," I interjected.

The way Ambrose was glaring at us made me grateful that Gib was carrying a gun.

"Eleni was a troubled woman," he said. "She was paranoid. Probably bipolar, which is why her marriage crumbled. She was given to wild stories about how the family was cheating her out of her fair share. She was never *once* paid less than any of us, but she always wanted more. She was ostracized from the family for making up these ridiculous allegations. I hadn't spoken to her in more than two years and the only correspondence I ever planned to have with her for the rest of her life was to send a wire transfer to her bank account once a month.

"So, Agent Barlow, and Agent . . . ?" Ambrose stared at me blankly.

"Van Dalen," I supplied without letting him know I wasn't an FBI agent.

"Van Dalen, while you might find it a shock that Eleni jumped to her death, I do not. As I said, she was a troubled woman, and it was likely Augustus's demise that left her suicidal."

"They were close?" Gibs asked.

"Augustus was the peacemaker in the family. He saw good in everyone. It's why I called your boss and demanded an investigation. I will *never* believe that Ambrose set that fire by himself. It's my theory that someone was there to rob him. I'd spoken to him an hour before the fire. He'd been going over his books, which leads me to believe he was surprised by a burglar, overpowered, perhaps murdered, then the fire was set while he lay dead or dying in his office. I only hope that he didn't suffer. I cannot think of a more hideous way to die, especially since my brother was deathly afraid of fire."

"Are you aware of anyone threatening your sister, Mr. Ariti?" I asked. He wanted to focus on Augustus, but I wanted to focus on Eleni, because I felt in my gut, she was the one who this whole case revolved around.

Ambrose directed that lethal glare on me. "I didn't keep tabs on my sister."

"It's just that we have an eyewitness who saw Eleni being manhandled in front of her office," I pressed.

Ambrose sighed heavily again. "Was this on the day of her suicide?"

"No. Three days before."

He turned his palms up. "As I said, my sister suffered mentally. Her ex-husband is my V.P. of international sales. He endured *years* of her verbal and physical abuse before he couldn't take it anymore and filed for divorce. He was willing to walk away with nothing because of her prenup rather than continue to live with her. It's one of the reasons I've kept him on at the company. He's a good man, and he was good to my sister even when she didn't deserve it."

"I see," I said. I didn't like Ambrose. I didn't like him one bit. "But your wife did, right? She deserved to be fired from her job working at your company, correct, Mr. Ariti?"

Gib eyed me sideways, and I knew I was way out of bounds here, but the man was a first-class jerk. I refused to believe that Eleni was the bad guy. Nothing in her journal indicated she was anything but lovely, thoughtful, generous, and kind.

"My *ex*-wife. Gina landed on her feet. She'll be fine." Ambrose's anger was palpable. Bringing Gina up had struck a nerve.

I wanted to press Ambrose on the topic by divulging that I was aware she was quite philanthropic, but as I opened my mouth to speak a bloodcurdling scream erupted from somewhere in the house.

All three of us were on our feet and bolting toward the sound as whoever had screamed was giving a repeat performance, over, and over, and over again.

Gib was the first to get to the central hallway. He rounded left, and the screaming subsided to agonizing sobs.

Ambrose was ahead of me as well, but I was hot on his heels, readying the amethyst ring should I need to defend us with lethal force.

At last, I turned the corner and there stood Henrietta, sobbing hysterically, her entire form shaking in fear and anguish. When she saw Ambrose, her hands balled into fists, out in front of her as she was wracked with sobs. "I didn't know she was down there! I didn't know! Mr. Ariti, *I didn't know!*"

My gaze darted from her to farther down the hallway, landing on the open door and the smell of chlorine. A loud splash sounded from the doorway and while Ambrose was momentarily halted by his maid, I darted around the pair and raced for the door.

Stopping within the doorway, I saw the large indoor pool, and at the bottom of the deep end was the new Mrs. Ariti, lying face down as Gib swam to her side and struggled to lift her off the pool floor. Her body was completely bloated with water, and she didn't appear to be buoyant, which meant she must be quite heavy.

Looking desperately around for anything that might help, I saw a leaf skimmer on the wall and ran to it, pulling it off the hooks to rush it back over to the side of the pool. I thrust it down toward Gib.

He saw the net and hooked one arm around it while also wrapping the other arm around Mrs. Ariti.

Ambrose reached my side just as I began to pull. He cried out at the sight of his wife's limp and water-bloated body. "*Cheyanne!*"

"Help me!" I demanded, struggling with the combined weight of Gib and Mrs. Ariti.

Ambrose grabbed the skimmer out of my hands and pulled the pair up. Gib's head emerged first, and he sucked in a huge lungful of air.

I bent down at the edge of the pool, reaching out my hand toward him, and shouted over my shoulder toward the door, "Henrietta! Call nine-one-one!" I hoped the maid was able to calm her hysterics enough to do that.

A moment later Gib let go of the skimmer and grabbed my hand. Ambrose threw the net aside and got down on his knees too. "Give her to me!" he begged, his voice cracking with emotion.

Gib kicked hard and rotated Mrs. Ariti toward her husband. Every inch of her was bloated and blue, and her eyes were open but unfocused.

Ambrose let out a sob, grabbing his wife by the shoulders to pull her flush with the wall before he tried lifting her out of the water.

The woman was so bloated, however, that she was too heavy for him to pull her out. Gib planted hands on the lip of the pool deck, and I got out of the way as he sprung himself up, then moved over to help Ambrose. With a bobbing motion, they managed to get Mrs. Ariti out of the pool and onto the deck.

"*No!*" Ambrose wailed, cupping his wife's face between his hands. "Cheyanne! Baby, don't die! Don't die!"

It was obvious to me that she already had, and no amount of pleading was going to bring her back. Seeing his devastation, which was hard to watch, I was moved enough to entertain the thought of heading to SPL for a trinket that might be able to bring Cheyanne back to life—but trinkets that can bring back the dead are quite rare and very, very expensive. There was no way I could justify to Elric that I'd used one on an unbound, not to mention the fact that bringing Cheyanne back to life from her current state of such obvious demise was bound to draw attention we mystics didn't need.

Still, Gib began CPR. I knew he needed to try to resuscitate her until the paramedics arrived. With every pump of his stacked hands on her sternum, water gushed out of Cheyanne's mouth, and the sight was more than I could bear.

Getting up, I headed to the door to see if Henrietta had called 911. I found her slumped against the wall, cradling the phone and sobbing.

I moved over to her and squatted beside her, resting a hand on her shoulder.

"I didn't know!" she wailed. "I didn't know!"

"Of course you didn't," I said gently, easing the phone out of her hand. The screen was still active, and I could see that she had called 911.

I set the phone aside and wrapped my arms around her shoulders while they shuddered with grief. "I'm so sorry, Henrietta." And I truly was. But as my own shock began to ebb, I felt goose bumps line my arms. Squeezing her shoulder, I said, "Did anyone come to visit today besides us?"

She shook her head while making a keening sound.

"Were any packages delivered today addressed to Mrs. Ariti?"

The keening paused for a moment. "*Si.* I put them in their room."

I let go of her shoulder and stood up. "I need to see those packages. It's important."

Henrietta wiped her eyes, then pointed toward the staircase. "Upstairs."

"Show me?"

With my help Henrietta got to her feet and I supported her by the arm as we made our way to the second floor. When we reached the landing, Henrietta turned us right and we walked to the end of the corridor.

The master bedroom was a massive affair, with a grand bronze bed frame, cozy seating area, coffee bar, and his and her closets. Lying on the taupe-colored bedspread were two opened boxes, each containing brand-new handbags.

"Just these two?" I asked the stricken maid.

She nodded dully.

Stepping away from the bed, I toured the room, keeping my hands to myself so that Henrietta could see that my intention was only as an observer. There were no ring boxes lying out in the open, but I stopped short of pulling open drawers and sorting through the couple's personal items. Instinctively, I had the feeling the Promise wasn't here.

Still, I wanted to do a thorough inspection, so I checked behind the curtains of both windows, one looking out over the front lawn, the other looking out over the garden, tennis court, and guesthouse, but there was nothing there that felt like it was off.

"Henrietta?" I asked, standing at the window overlooking the front lawn as an ambulance and a police car pulled up.

"*Si*?"

"Was Mrs. Ariti afraid of the water?"

"*Si*," she said softly. "She didn't know how to swim. Mr. Ariti bought this house because of the pool. He was once a great swimmer, and he was going to teach Mrs. Ariti how to swim." Her voice broke on the last few words, and she began to sob again.

I moved over to her and wrapped my arm around her shoulders. "The police and paramedics are here. I'll show them to the pool. You take your time pulling yourself together, okay?"

Henrietta nodded, then buried her face in her hands.

By the time I walked out of the bedroom, my own eyes were misty.

The doorbell rang and I hurried to answer it, letting in the first responders and leading them to the pool door. I stepped aside so that they could enter, but caught a glimpse of Gib, his water-soaked sweater clinging to his muscled form and his head red with exertion, while he continued to try to pump some life back into Cheyanne Ariti.

Beside her kneeled Ambrose, his posture bent, his wife's hand held to his forehead as he wept, and wept.

Chapter 15

Gib and I each gave a statement to the detective who'd been called to the scene. My statement was perhaps the most critical in absolving Ambrose of any suspicion in the death of his wife. I'd seen Cheyanne exit the hallway through the door of the pool, and we'd been with Ambrose from that point forward.

As for Ambrose, he was far too inside his own grief to even be aware of what was happening. He sat forlorn on the third step of his staircase, staring blankly out into space while tears leaked down his cheeks.

Even though Gib had spoken to the woman claiming to be Ambrose's current girlfriend, it was obvious to me that Ambrose had dearly loved his new wife.

I waited in the parlor off the hallway for Gib to finish his interview with the detective and once he was done, I got up from my chair and handed him a towel and his coat from the pool deck. "Here."

He took it and rubbed it against his hair. "I'm not dripping anymore. Mostly just damp now."

I nodded. "Are we okay to leave?"

"We are." Gib looked down at his wet clothes. At least he'd shimmied out of his coat before he dove into the water. His shoes were likely ruined, but everything else could probably be washed and good as new again. "I could really use a warm shower and a fresh pair of clothes."

I motioned toward the door with my chin, and we left the house.

Gib had to do some maneuvering to get around the police cars in the driveway, but he managed.

The steady rain had given way to a drizzle, which kept the wipers moving in their slow, rhythmic motion.

Neither one of us spoke; we seemed to both be lost in our own thoughts. I couldn't help but feel terribly guilty that Cheyanne had been murdered because I hadn't discovered who the mystic was wielding the Promise to eliminate members of the Ariti family one by one.

"Hey," Gib said softly, pulling me out of my thoughts.

"Yes?"

"This is my place. The coffee shop where your car is parked is three minutes away, but I'd like to invite you in and talk about the case, if you're willing."

Belatedly, I realized Gib was idling next to a white brick town house with a wood and glass front door and small cherry blossom tree screening the front window behind it.

"Oh! I didn't realize . . . I mean, I suppose that would be fine."

But if my accelerated pulse were any indication, it wasn't fine. It was trouble.

Gib smiled at me and pulled over to the curb. We got out and I followed him up the stone stairs to his front door, which had a combination lock. He punched in the code and opened the door, allowing me to go in first.

My first impression of Gib's house was exactly as I'd expected. Polished black walnut floors that creaked when tread upon, crepe-colored walls crowned by three-inch molding, a tasteful chandelier hovering over the foyer, and down the hall a glimpse of a modern, minimalist kitchen.

As I moved farther down the central hallway, allowing me a view into the living room, I could see that the minimal style was consistent. His living room housed a low, charcoal-gray leather sofa with umber throw pillows and a sheepskin rug dyed black.

On the far wall was a fireplace that appeared to have been recently used, and at the back of the room were three sets of built-in bookcases, crammed with books in an array of topics and genres.

"Will you be okay in here if I scoot upstairs for a quick shower?" he asked.

"Of course."

Gib moved toward the stairs and pointed to the kitchen down the hall. "I've got an espresso machine if you want to warm up, and there's water and juice in the fridge."

"Thank you." A cup of something warm was exactly what I needed.

He saluted me from the stairs before hurrying up for his shower.

When I made my way to the kitchen, I found that it was bigger than I expected. There was a high-top table with chocolate-leather-upholstered bar chairs and hung on the back wall was a photo of a beautiful woman with long black hair, brown eyes, and a thin build. In the background was the Eiffel Tower, and she was blowing a kiss to the camera.

Something ugly coiled in my stomach as I looked at the framed photo. Something I'd thought myself numb to by now. But there it was and it was as green and ugly as I remembered it.

Intuitively I knew that she must be Gib's late wife, and to feel jealous of a dead woman, especially when I wasn't romantically involved with Gib, was ridiculous.

And yet, here I stood, being ridiculous.

The sound of a shower being turned on pulled me from my dark thoughts, which allowed me to head over to the espresso machine and begin to make myself a cappuccino.

I found milk in Gib's fridge and got my beverage nice and frothy, just the way I like it.

When the shower turned off, I began to make another cup for Gib. I didn't know if he liked cappuccino, but I remembered that he'd been generous with milk and sugar in his coffee this morning at Perk Up.

I was just sprinkling a little nutmeg and cinnamon from the spice rack on his cappuccino when I heard him approach from behind.

"I made you a cappuccino," I sang, while I poured the frothy milk from the small silver pitcher.

"Thanks," he said, coming to stand next to me bare-chested, dressed only in jeans.

My jaw dropped. So did the pitcher.

"Ah!" I cried, jumping to avoid getting splattered. "I'm so sorry!"

We both bent down to retrieve the pitcher and nearly knocked heads. I was the first to stand up straight and all I could do was marvel at this *magnificent* man.

His sweater had clung to him when he climbed out of the pool, but it hid quite a lot that was now completely exposed.

Gib's body looked like something etched from marble. His physique could put Michelangelo's David to shame.

"It's okay," he said, the hint of a grin tugging at the corners of his mouth.

I had a feeling he knew what'd caused me to drop the pitcher.

He took the pitcher to the sink and grabbed a roll of paper towels, bending down again to mop up the splattered milk.

And I simply stood there, ogling the poor man, watching the way his back and shoulder muscles bunched as he moved. The tapered lines of his abdominals, the smooth square cut of his pecs, the biceps that bulged when he bent his arm.

Watching him was like staring at the aurora borealis, inviting a certain marvel and wonder all its own.

Once he'd mopped up the floor, Gib set the paper towels back on the counter and headed over to the kitchen table. Belatedly I saw that he had a basket of folded laundry there. He took out a charcoal-knit, V-neck sweater, putting it on to cover himself, but it hugged his chest tightly.

Oh, how I envied that sweater.

"Did you want some food, Dovey?" he asked.

I shook my head, trying desperately to clear it of illicit thoughts. "Hmm?"

"Food. Would you like something to eat."

"Yes. Yes, that would be nice."

Gib pointed to a stack of paper to the left of the fridge. "Pick out anything from those menus and I'll call in a delivery."

Thank God, I thought, turning to the stack. Anything to distract from my embarrassing reaction to his half-nakedness.

I could sense him coming close to me from behind and I stiffened. I didn't want to give him the wrong idea. Yes, I found him beautiful. Charming. Sincere, and kind, but that didn't mean that I wanted to get involved with him.

But here's the hard part. I did. I did want to get involved. Not marriage involved, but he'd been the first man in almost two hundred years whom I'd found myself attracted to in the same way I'd first been attracted to Elric.

Elric.

Damn. I'd almost forgotten about him and how much the most powerful mystic in the world hated competition.

That reminded me about Gib's watch . . . which I'd left at home in my other handbag.

Turning to face him, I offered the first menu on top of the stack. I hadn't even looked at it, but his nearness was going to be my undoing if I didn't get myself under control.

He looked down at the menu. "Pizza?"

"Sure," I said. It wasn't my first choice, but I'd eat every slice before I admitted that my ability to focus was currently completely compromised.

He turned the menu over, then flipped it back. "Which one?"

"You decide."

"I'm a fan of the butternut squash and goat cheese."

I perked up. That sounded delicious. "Sold."

He reached for the cappuccino I'd made him and took a small sip. "Mmm," he said, cheering me with his cup. "You make a great cappuccino."

I smiled, cleared my throat, and said, "I have your watch."

"Oh, yeah? Good, I've been missing it. Did you have it repaired?"

"Yes."

"Can I pay you for the repair?"

"No. It's on me."

"You're really kind, Dovey. Thank you."

An awkward silence rose between us as he looked at me expectantly, and I finally realized he was waiting for me to hand him his watch. "Uh . . . I don't have it with me. I meant to give it to you last night, but . . ."

He nodded like he completely understood. "Chaos."

"Yeah. Anyway, it's in my other handbag. I'll remember to bring it the next time we meet."

Gib grinned. "Next time?"

"Well, yeah. We're working the case together, right?"

"We are," he said, but that knowing smile didn't fade, and I felt my cheeks flush.

I pointed to the menu in his hand. "Maybe you should order that pizza now."

Gib called in an order, then he led me into the living room. I took a seat on his couch, and he took a seat across from me in a low-back club chair.

"I feel like we're running in circles on this case," he began.

"Agreed."

"I don't know how to explain almost every member of the Ariti family dying by suicide. Someone must be drugging these people and somehow manipulating them into killing themselves."

"It's the only possible theory that could explain it," I lied.

"Henrietta told me there was no one else in the house besides the five of us, so how was Cheyanne drugged?"

"I have no idea." But I did.

Mystics can make themselves invisible to mortal eyes. It takes a powerful trinket—something above a level six, but it's more than plausible that the mystic wielding the Promise had utilized a trinket like that to get into the house, expose Cheyanne, and get back out without anyone being the wiser. And then I suddenly thought of Sequoya with the ballpoint pen that allowed her to disappear. For a moment I entertained the thought that she might have something to do with this, but then I immediately dismissed it because Elric would *kill* her if she ever betrayed him, and Sequoya was a self-preservation specialist.

Still, it proved that those trinkets were available if anyone had something of equal value to trade.

Gib raked a hand through his hair. "We don't even know what drug was used. Augustus's body was too badly burned to pull a tox screen, Eleni's tox screen came back negative for all known hallucinogenics—"

"She could've been helped over that balcony, Gib."

"True, but Hermia wasn't helped into stabbing herself and Henrietta swears it was just the five of us in that house when Cheyanne jumped into the pool."

"Will they do a tox screen on her?"

Gib shrugged. "You saw her," he said. "Her body was so bloated with water that I doubt it'd come back with anything."

"How did she become *that* bloated though?"

"It's common among drowned victims. They try to suck in air and keep sucking in water and their whole bodies fill up with it, that's why it's hard to find them when someone goes missing in a lake. They lose buoyancy and sink, and it's not until later when their bodies fill with gas from decomp that they float to the surface again."

I shuddered. "What an awful way to die."

"Agreed."

"What about Ambrose's girlfriend on the side?" I asked next.

"Samantha Rollins."

"Yes, her. She definitely had a motive for killing Cheyanne."

"She did. But I still don't know that I buy it. She didn't strike me as particularly smart, and like I said before, she was half in the bag at the funeral. I don't think she'd be able to pull something like this off."

"Could her disposition have been an act?"

Gib pressed his lips together, thinking on that. After a moment he shook his head. "I don't think so. I've been trained to spot a lie, and I didn't pick up on anything from her that even hinted that she wasn't telling the truth."

The doorbell rang and Gib got up. "That'll be the pizza."

I waited while he paid and tipped the delivery driver, then went into the kitchen to retrieve a set of plates and napkins before returning to plop the pizza box down on the table. "This'll knock your socks off."

After being served a slice, I took a tentative bite and was in fact impressed. "Wow. This is amazing."

"Told you," he said, folding his own slice and taking a big bite. "I get a pizza from this place at least once a week."

"How does someone with your physique eat pizza once a week?"

He grunted and smiled while he chewed. "I spend a lot of time in the gym."

I smirked. "If only it showed."

He lifted his chin to laugh. "You're one to talk, Dovey. You look like you're in great shape."

His gaze focused intently on me, and I felt a blush coming on, so I decided to change the subject before we went too far with this conversation. "Have you pulled Eleni's financial records?"

"I put in the request to her bank. I'm waiting for them to send the file over. Why?"

"I want to know who this thug was that Kioni saw pushing Eleni into the car."

"You think it was about money," he said, more a statement than question.

"I do. If she was trying to blackmail her own family, what's to say she wasn't blackmailing someone else too."

"Good point. I checked out her office, which is pretty sparse. No ledger or other incriminating evidence there. I didn't even find a laptop."

Inwardly, I blanched. I had Eleni's journal lying on my desk at home. I couldn't very well tell Gib that, but maybe I could suggest he take another look.

"Are you sure you looked thoroughly enough?"

"I'm not known for skimming over evidence, Dovey." His tone wasn't defensive, it was much closer to playful. But then he frowned and said, "Although, now that you mention it, for some reason I don't remember much about being in her office. It's the weirdest thing, the memory feels fuzzy, but everything else about that day comes back to me just fine."

My silver dollar had no doubt left a lingering effect on Gib's memory. "After you get her financial records, maybe it'd be a good idea to go back and do another round of snooping—to make sure you were thorough the last time."

Gib nodded slowly and then he sighed. "I can also review footage from any cameras in the area."

"You think the guy who pushed Eleni into the car might've been caught on camera?"

"That's a busy corner. There's got to be a camera that recorded what happened. You said this took place on the twentieth, right?"

I counted backward from what Kioni had told me. "No, it would've been the nineteenth."

And then another thought occurred to me. "Will you get Ambrose some security so that he doesn't wind up being victim number five?"

"No. There're strict rules for assigning a protective detail. They're mostly used to protect informants, and Ambrose isn't offering up any information that would meet the criteria. I did mention to him that he needed to hire some security of his own. I also told him that his cousins should do the same."

A mystic wouldn't be stopped by an unbound's security detail; however, if these murders escalated to a larger group of unbounds beyond the Aritis family, Elric would hear about it. He wouldn't tolerate being exposed by a rogue mystic inviting scrutiny. Eventually, he'd have the mystic hunted down and assassinated.

I folded my napkin and set it on the plate. "I should get going."

Gib looked at his wrist—which was bare—and grinned at me when he realized he wasn't wearing his watch. "Old habit."

I wiggled my phone at him. "It's going on two o'clock."

"Wow. I didn't realize it'd gotten so late. Let me grab my keys and I'll drive you back to your car."

A few minutes later, he pulled up next to Luna and said, "This might sound weird, Dovey, but even though today was a tragic day, I still enjoyed getting to hang out with you."

I looked into Gib's eyes, and it was all I could do to hold back running my fingers through his hair. I didn't feel flush this time, I only felt desire.

"Me too," I said softly.

"I'll be in touch."

I smiled. "Good."

Gib waited until I got inside Luna and waved to him before leaving, and for a long time I sat there, just listening to the rainfall, wondering how I could turn off these feelings for him.

Logically, I knew that I needed to have as little to do with him as possible—mystics and the unbound don't get involved. I *wouldn't* bind him without his permission, and since I *wouldn't* divulge mystic secrets to gain his permission, the point was moot.

But my heart was searching for a way to override common sense. I wanted to be near him, close to him, able to kiss him and see where things led.

I realized that, for the first time in my life, I regretted being bound. And I didn't know what to do with that.

CHAPTER 16

I went straight home. Bits uncurled himself as soon as I checked on him. He moved to the edge of the nightstand and stood on his hind legs to let me know he wanted to be picked up.

"Hello, you rascal," I said, carefully getting my hand under his soft belly to avoid his spikes. He sniffed my hand and looked up at me expectantly, as if to say, "Hey! Where're my snacks?"

I laughed and walked him downstairs to the kitchen, set him on the counter, and prepared a meal for him. He made his typical impatient chuffing noises while I readied his meal. "I know, I know, Bits. You're hungry. I got the memo."

He paused his chuffing to stand up on his hind legs again, his pointy nose wrinkling as he sniffed at me like he could smell that I'd been up to no good.

"Oh, please. Don't look at me like that, Bits. I haven't done anything wrong."

Yet.

But I wanted to.

I definitely wanted to.

After setting Bits's lunch down, I hurried upstairs to retrieve the handbag that held the journal. I planned to sneak it back into Eleni's office before Gib had a chance to do his second inspection.

When I opened the handbag, I was reminded that I'd also taken Eleni's tarot cards from her desk drawer, which *then* reminded me that I needed to confer with Ursula about something I'd heard long ago, but I wasn't sure if I remembered it correctly.

Heading back downstairs, I waved goodbye to Bits, got back inside Luna, and drove to Ursula's. I figured that since her house was on the way to Eleni's office, I'd start with her.

When I arrived, she threw open the door and hugged me. "Hello, gorgeous girl! I was just thinking about you!"

I hugged her back, laughing at her enthusiasm. Pulling back from her but holding on to her shoulders, I said, "From now on, I want to be greeted this way whenever I come over."

She beamed a magnificent smile at me. "As you wish, Princess Buttercup."

We laughed together and she waved me inside. "Coffee? Tea? Wine?"

"No, thank you, Ursula. I can't stay long."

"Oh, poo. I'm bored out of my mind today and was hoping for some company."

"I can swing back by once I'm done with an errand, which is what I want to talk to you about."

Her brow arched. "Lay it on me, baby."

"I believe I heard something a long time ago, but I want to make sure I've got the details right."

"Which is . . . ?"

"I heard, maybe a hundred years ago, that those born with the gift of sight are able to activate some of the more powerful trinkets."

Ursula nodded. "That's true."

"It is?"

"Oh, yeah."

"So, all this time I've been thinking that the Promise could only be wielded by a mystic because it's too powerful a trinket to be activated by someone unbound, but now you're telling me that an unbound with the gift of sight *can* activate it?"

"Yes," she said simply, then elaborated. "It's one of the primary reasons we don't mix with the unbound. If the intuitive ones knew that they could harness a powerful trinket's power without having to be bound, we'd have *a lot* more stolen trinkets, Dovey, and big chaos in the unbound world, which would then cause big chaos in the mystic world. It'd be a whole domino effect."

"How can you tell if an unbound has psychic abilities?"

"Other than the roadside palm readers who put a neon sign in their front window, advertising their skills?"

I grinned. "Yes, other than that."

"Well, it's usually passed down from generation to generation, typically showing up more in the women than in the men."

"I see."

"Why're you asking, Dovey?"

I opened my handbag and took out the tarot cards. "I found these in Eleni Ariti's office."

Ursula looked from me to the cards, then back again. "You think Eleni was psychic?"

Moving over to Ursula's kitchen table, I laid out the top several cards for her to see. Pointing to the first one, I said, "Ambrose died in a fire." Then to the next one where a woman was falling from a tower. "Eleni died falling off her terrace." I turned over the next card, pointed to it, and said, "Hermia tried to stab herself, and"—flipping the next card—"Ambrose's wife drowned today in the family pool." For the finale, I turned over the next card showing the shrouded skeleton wielding a scythe.

"Wow," Ursula said, gazing at the display of cards. "Yeah. She was psychic all right."

"So, she would've been able to make the Promise work, right?"

"Yes. Do you think she used the Promise to kill her brother?"

I inhaled a deep breath, letting it out on a sigh. "I do not know, my friend, but I doubt it because Eleni was dead prior to Hermia—her niece—being exposed and Cheyanne Ariti's death was this morning."

"Anybody else in the family play with tarot cards?"

I shrugged. "One of Ambrose's cousins is a woman. The other two are males."

Ursula bit her lower lip. "What would a member of the family achieve by murdering the other family members?"

"Money and power."

"Those are good motives, Dovey. Maybe you should figure out where the cousins live and do a stakeout or two."

I shook my head. "They live in Greece. I think they were here for some family meeting, or they were here for Augustus's funeral, it's hard to tell."

"Do you think they were here when the murders began?" Ursula asked.

"Again, I don't know. Maybe?"

"It might be worth checking to see if any or all of them had come into town prior to Augustus's murder."

I nodded, then leaned in to give Ursula a kiss on the cheek. "Thank you."

"Anytime. And come back over after you run your errand."

"Will do," I said, moving to the door. Before leaving I waved over my shoulder and said, "Keep the wine cold!"

Back inside Luna, I made the decision to delay going to Eleni's office for a bit while I checked in with Hermia. I wanted to see how she was recovering, but I also hoped to ask her about any psychics in the family beside Eleni.

Fifteen minutes later, I was parked on the street near Augustus's town house and walking toward the front door when all of a sudden, I felt a prickling sensation that someone was watching me.

Pausing, I looked behind me but didn't see anyone either parked in a car or walking down the sidewalk. Turning in a slow circle, I scanned the area to see who might be watching me, but I couldn't spot a single suspicious person.

Closing my left hand into a fist, I felt the ring on my finger pulse with power. If Lavender was stalking me, I'd need to be very, very careful.

I stood still for a minute or two, waiting and watching, that prickly sensation neither ebbing nor getting worse. After another two minutes, I'd had enough of holding still so I took a deep breath and marched down the sidewalk to Augustus's door, knocking loudly.

I waited for a bit, but no one came to the door. I wondered if perhaps Hermia had fallen asleep, so I went back to Luna and got in, locking the doors before doing a search on Hermia to see if I might find her phone number.

"Gotcha," I said when I'd found it. Calling the phone number, I counted out the rings and Hermia answered on the third one.

"Hermia?"

"Yes, who's this?"

"It's Dovey Van Dalen. I wanted to check in on you."

"Oh, Dovey, I'm sorry but this isn't a good time. My dad's wife drowned in their swimming pool this morning. He's almost completely catatonic over it."

"Are you with him now?"

"I am. Mother is even coming over, and all three of Dad's cousins are here too."

"That's good. I'm glad you'll all be there to support each other. I don't want to keep you, but I need to know something that might sound like a strange thing to be asking."

"Okay."

"Do you know of any family members who ever claimed to have psychic abilities?"

"Wow. You weren't kidding on the strange question."

"I know, but it's important. So . . . do you?"

There was a slight pause, then Hermia said, "My grandmother on my dad's side of the family used to do readings for people in her village over in Greece. And Aunt Eleni always claimed to have *the gift*."

She enunciated the last two words, as if she thought her aunt's claims were ridiculous.

"How about your dad's cousins? Do you know if any of them claim to be intuitive?"

Hermia huffed out a humorless laugh. "Oh, yeah. Evander and Lino won't make any major decision until they've checked in with Kyrie's *feefees*. To be fair, though, she's usually right, and she *has* increased the profit share at the company significantly since she became a member of the board."

"When did your father's cousins come into town?"

"A week ago. All members of the board meet here once a quarter. It was just coincidence that they were here when Uncle Augie died."

And Eleni, I thought to myself.

"Thank you, Hermia. I don't want to keep you from your family any longer. You have my sincerest condolences."

"Dovey?" she asked before I could end the call.

"Yes?"

"Dad says you were here when Cheyanne died. I still can't get over it. I mean, I hated her because I thought she was a gold-digger, but I didn't wish her *dead*, you know?"

"I do."

"Was she acting weird? Did she say something that would've given anybody a clue?"

"To be honest, Hermia, when Agent Barlow and I stepped inside all I caught of Cheyanne was her heading to the pool."

"It doesn't make any sense," she said. "Cheyanne didn't know how to swim. She was terrified of deep water."

"I know. I can't explain it either," I lied.

"And I don't understand what's happening to my family right now. How is it even possible that three people in this family are dead in just, what, four days? And how could someone go unnoticed enough at Uncle Augie's wake to try to kill *me*? How could all of this happen without anyone seeing anything suspicious?"

"That is exactly what Agent Barlow and I are trying to answer, Hermia. Neither one of us intends to stop until we've figured all of it out."

"You promise?" she asked, her voice shaking with emotion. I imagined she might have a little PTSD from what she went through last night.

"I promise."

And I meant it.

After getting off the call with Hermia, I drove to the alley behind the building where Eleni's office was, parked, and made my way to the back entrance. Stepping inside, I rummaged around in my handbag for my key trinket that would unlock any unbound's door, then headed up the stairs to the second floor.

After making sure no one was in the hallway, I moved quickly down to Eleni's door and inserted the key into the lock. It opened easily and I stepped forward only to bump right into the massive chest on a massive man.

I gasped in surprise, stepping back, ready to take action against the man who fit Kioni's description of him to a T . . . when I felt a hard blow to the back of my head, and it was lights out for me.

I woke up sometime later, my head throbbing like the entire percussion section of an orchestra was pounding away inside my head.

It took me a minute to figure out that I was tied to a chair and gagged with a disgusting-tasting rag in my mouth.

My head lolled on my neck, and for a moment I was so dizzy I thought I might vomit.

"She's awake."

I didn't recognize the voice, and I didn't raise my chin because I was focusing on not vomiting with a gag in my mouth. That would be an unpleasant experience on top of an already unpleasant experience.

So while I sat there blinking, I was able to get a feeling for where I was.

The floor beneath my feet was concrete, and the air was chilly and damp and the lighting was dim.

When whoever was in here with me had spoken, his voice had echoed a bit, which told me I was likely in a large open space.

"Who are you," the voice commanded.

I lifted my head, blinking and blinking to clear my vision. It worked.

Mostly.

Across from me in a chair sat someone who looked quite familiar, but I couldn't tell from where. He had black hair, olive skin, a brooding expression, and he was eyeing me with an intense malice that, were I not a mystic, might've frightened me.

As it was, I didn't think I was in the kind of danger that would cause me to panic. I mean, sure, this was bad, but I didn't think it was any worse than being in a crypt with a fifteen-foot serpent.

The trouble was, with my hands bound behind me, I didn't have access to any trinkets. Sure, I had the amethyst ring, but I needed to be able to *aim* that, which wasn't something I could do with bound hands. Calling up a ball of energy to lob at my assailants was also out. My hands needed to be free for that to happen.

So I needed to be patient, and wait for an opportunity to strike back.

The man motioned to someone out of my peripheral vision and heavy footsteps approached me. I braced for any form of violence that was about to be rained down on me, but all that happened was that the gag was yanked out of my mouth and shoved down to my neck.

I worked my jaw a little and stared at the guy in the chair, hoping he understood that I was neither intimidated nor scared.

He leaned forward and rested his arms on his knees. "I'm only going to ask you one. More. Time. Who are you?"

"Your. Worst. Nightmare." I added a grin just to let him know that he wasn't about to get squat from me.

From just beyond my peripheral vision came a fist that punched the side of my face hard enough to fracture a molar. I grunted in pain, but didn't cry out, even when my mouth filled with blood from the broken tooth. I spit the remnants of the tooth and some of the blood out toward the seated thug, and his glare only intensified.

"I figure it'll only take about ten minutes to break you," he said. "Gus doesn't care that you're a woman. He might even like beating you up better because of it."

I turned my head to look behind my left shoulder and there was the bruiser that I'd bumped into when I'd entered Eleni's office.

"Did you rough Eleni up like this?" I asked to no one in particular.

"No," the guy in front of me said. "But she deserved it. We're done playing nice. Where is my money?"

"I have no clue."

Another punch struck me from the side, and white-hot, blinding pain erupted behind my eye. I grunted again, my head hanging forward, the dizziness returning, and the world spun me into darkness.

Again.

When I came to for the second time, I heard a man speaking on the phone, not in English, but in Greek. I speak a smattering of over a dozen languages. You live long enough, it's not as hard as it seems.

The gist of his conversation was about me. I think. And I thought that because he was talking about where to dispose of the body. He made a few suggestions, the Potomac, the dump, or simply dropping me into a manhole for the rats to take care of my remains.

My head was killing me, and I couldn't see out of my left eye, but I believed I could whisper, and if I focused through the pain, I could cast a simple enough spell to get myself out of these restraints.

Closing my good eye, I mentally worked through the spell, not wanting to speak it until I knew it was ready.

It only took me a few moments to get the wording down, then, without lifting my head or moving any other muscle, I concentrated on pouring some of my essence into the ropes that bound me, and whispered . . .

"Ties that bind,

"You must unwind,

"To free me from this station,

"Let go, relax,

"From my thorax

"The time is now *so hasten!"*

"Is she awake?" the guy in the chair demanded, snapping his fingers. "Nick. Check her."

Footsteps approached again and I held very, very still, unwilling to allow myself to brace for any violence about to come my way. They couldn't know that I was ready to unleash hell upon them.

A hand grabbed me by my hair at the top of my scalp and yanked my head up. It was all the help I needed. Gathering a ball of energy into my right palm, I shot up from the chair like a rocket, the ropes falling away, and I caught the big brute totally by surprise, shoving that energy right under his chin.

There was an explosive sound and Nick's head snapped back with a loud crack, and he dropped to the ground like a sack of flour.

Before his body even hit the floor I was whirling in a circle, picking up the chair I'd been tied to before flinging it at the man who'd sat across from me. It hit him square in the face, and he careened backward, toppling over.

I was about to make a run for it when massive arms wrapped around me from behind and squeezed my rib cage with unrelenting strength, making it impossible to expand my chest for a breath.

I struggled and kicked, but I couldn't make my heels connect, and I couldn't wield another orb because my arms were held down, and I couldn't cast a spell because I didn't have any air to use to speak the words.

Whoever was holding me kept squeezing the life right out of me, and there was a part of my brain that thought it so ridiculous that, after two hundred years, I'd get killed by an *unbound*!

Darkness began to creep toward the edges of my vision and tiny sparks of light flickered behind my eyes. The man who'd been calling the shots moaned, then rolled and shoved the chair I'd hit him with aside. When he sat up, his face was a ruin. I'd definitely broken several bones and blood openly poured out of his nose down his chin and even more dripped from an open gash just under his eye.

"I'm going to *kill* you!" he screamed.

"Take a number!" a woman's voice called from the door across the expansive room.

I knew that voice.

"She's *mine*!" she shouted.

Lavender. Sweet, wonderful Lavender had no doubt been the one who'd raised my hackles on the sidewalk near Augustus's house, and she had no doubt tailed me first to Eleni's office, then in whatever vehicle these brutes used to transport me here.

And I didn't even care that the mystic wanted to kill me. As long as she got me out of the vise of this man's arms, I'd take my chances with her.

"Who the hell are you?!" Mr. Wrecked Face yelled.

"Your. Worst. Nightmare!"

Okay, so mystics use that phrase a lot.

Mostly because it's effective.

And true.

Wrecked Face snarled at her and turned to a small table that'd been by his chair, where he'd set his gun.

I saw a bright yellow orb flash by me, hitting Wrecked Face in the chest, lifting him in the air and sending him flying ten feet away.

Vise Grip immediately dropped me to face the new threat, and I crumpled to my knees at his feet.

"Oh, so you wanna play too, big guy?" Lavender snickered.

I gasped for air as I sat on the ground and saw Lavender beginning to gather another orb in her hand.

Behind her was a door that I prayed led to the outside. Once she took care of Vise Grip, I'd never get past her alive.

I gulped more air and hid my right hand behind my back, straining to create an orb of my own. I figured I'd only have one shot, so I had to make it count. Meanwhile, Vise Grip flexed his shoulders and massive arms in challenge, and he began to charge toward Lavender like a raging bull. Her lips curled into a welcoming snarl and as he closed in on her she lifted an orb of energy, sending it straight for him.

In that moment I launched my own smaller orb right at hers, and luckily my aim was true. The two orbs collided, and a burst of energy reverberated through the air, sending both Lavender and Vise Grip hurtling back.

Vise Grip recovered first, and he picked up right where he left off, charging toward the mystic, his arms outstretched in front of him, ready to close around her neck. I wasted no more time sitting there gulping air. Scrambling to my feet, I ran toward the exit, keeping Vise Grip between me and Lavender.

She was torn between watching me flee, and the brute closing in on her *fast*.

Somehow I managed to get to the door first, hearing the clash of bodies behind me as I threw my weight against the door.

It opened, thank God, and I tumbled out into the open, stumbling into a dark, damp alley, and nearly knocking into an oil barrel. Grabbing on to it, I hurled it toward the door where it toppled over, acting as an obstacle that I hoped might slow Lavender down.

Then I took off at a dead run. Moving as fast as I could possibly go, I ran around the warehouse to the main street and kept on running, searching anywhere for a street sign that might let me know where I was.

I couldn't find one, and behind me, in the distance, I heard Lavender scream my name. She'd made it outside too.

Suddenly in front of me a pair of headlights appeared, racing toward me at alarming speed. I waved my hands in the air, both trying to flag the car down and let the driver know I was in the road.

The car came to a screeching halt, and to my astonishment, I recognized the yellow Mustang and the driver in it.

"Dex!"

He jumped out of the car and rushed around the hood to

catch me as I collapsed into his arms. "Dovey! What's happened to you, love?"

"Lav . . . en . . . der," I gasped, still fighting for air.

The screaming of my name reverberated off the walls of the warehouses that lined the street.

Dex's head jerked toward the sound. "Come on," he said, all but carrying me to the car. Opening the door, he eased me inside, then ran around to the driver's side, got in, spun the car around, and we took off like a rocket.

CHAPTER 17

"Dovey, where should I take you?" Dex asked.

I put a hand to the left side of my face. As much satisfaction as I'd gotten from ruining my kidnapper's face, I was starting to feel the effects of all that adrenaline wearing off and it *hurt.*

I moaned pathetically and Dex laid a hand on my shoulder. "Headquarters?"

I shook my head. Every time I entered that building before securing the Promise was another chance for Elric to be disappointed in me and start asking questions I *really* didn't want to answer.

"Ursula's?"

I nodded and shook my head in a sort of undecided bob.

"Don't you worry on it, lass. I know where to go."

I closed my eyes and tried to compartmentalize the pain. My feet hit something on the passenger-side floor, and I tilted my good eye toward it to see what it was.

"Puppy food?"

The serious expression Dex had been wearing fell partially away. "Yeah, Ezzy and I got a new pup. She's a sweet lass."

"Ezzy," I repeated.

Dex looked over at me and I swear there was a hint of guilt when he explained, "Esmé Bellarouse. My partner. She just got hired at SPL."

"Oh, yeah. I remember now. She survived the interviews and she's Elric's new thief, right?"

Dex's chest pumped up with pride. "She did and she is."

"Good for you both." I fell silent for a bit before deciding to ask Dex a question I'd been burning to bring up to him for a while now. "Can I ask you something?"

"Of course."

"You know Ursula really digs you, right?"

Dex blushed and he cleared his throat. "Ursula is a sweetheart."

"So why aren't you two together? And forgive me for asking that, but I've heard that you and Esmé aren't . . . you know . . ."

"More than just friends?"

"Yeah. That."

Dex sighed. "It's complicated, Dovey. And it just got *more* complicated. I can't get into it without breaching some trust, but I fell for Ezzy a long time ago, and she's had my heart ever since."

"But she doesn't feel the same way?"

Dex worked his lower jaw, as if it hurt, and that's when I noticed that there was some bruising on his own face. "It's complicated," he repeated in a whisper.

I let it drop and changed subjects, reaching out to tap his jaw lightly with one finger. "What happened to you?"

He glanced sideways at me. "Got into a little scrap with some mystics who're not big fans of me and Ezzy."

"Wait till I see the other guys, huh?" I said, when he didn't elaborate.

"I'd say yeah to that, except you'll probably never see the other guys again."

"Oh! That bad, eh?"

Dex's grip on the steering wheel tightened. "Wasn't pretty."

"Then I'm glad you came out on top."

"Us too, love. Us too."

A few minutes later, Dex pulled up in front of Ursula's house. If my head didn't hurt so much, I would've made a joke about how uncanny it was that Dex knew she'd be expecting me, but I simply didn't have the energy.

I was exhausted and in pain, and all I wanted to do was go to sleep for a month. Dex walked me to the front steps and the door swung open to reveal Ursula looking alarmed. "Dovey!"

"She's all right, but she'll need a healing trinket. Do you have any on hand, love?"

Ursula beamed at him for using that nickname. I didn't have the heart to tell her that Dex had just used that endearment on me, and probably used it on quite a few other women too.

"I do indeed. Dex. Help her inside and let her lie down on the sofa. I'll dig something out of my stash."

Ursula disappeared into a hallway behind the living room, and Dex eased me very gently down onto the couch. Then he took off my boots, put a pillow under my head, and grabbed an afghan to cover me with.

I could see why Ursula was so into him. He was sweet. "Thank you," I said, squeezing his hand. "You probably saved my life tonight."

He squeezed back but then a surprised look came over him and he lifted my left hand to inspect the ring Qin had put there. "Where'd you get this, Dovey?"

"Elric's trinket room."

"It's loaded with power," he said, laying a hand over it and closing his eyes. According to Ursula, Dex can sense the purpose of most any trinket he comes across. He's also very talented at stripping away comeback spells on a trinket to make sure they don't go immediately back to their owner.

"Supposedly, it's lethal."

Dex swept a hand across my brow, moving aside some stray strands of hair. "And you didn't think to use it tonight?"

I shrugged. "I was kidnapped and tied to a chair with my

arms locked down. I couldn't get the trinket up to point it at anybody, and then, when I had the chance to escape, I forgot about it."

"Next time, try not to let Lavender get a jump on you."

"Thank you, Captain Obvious," I said, wincing when I tried to smile.

Dex chuckled. "Why is Lavender after you?"

I sighed heavily. "She stole something from Arlo, and I stole it back, plus I took a valuable trinket from her, and had her pet serpent killed."

"All that, eh?"

"Afraid so."

Dex gave a pat to my shin as he stood up tall again. "I've got to get back to the pup. She's probably hungry by now. You rest and get well."

"Thank you, friend."

He nodded and left.

Ursula finally came out from the back of the house, pausing in the doorway leading to the living room to look around. "Where's Dex?"

"He got a new puppy and said he had to go home to feed her."

"A new puppy?"

"Yep."

"I would love to find that annoying, but I can't get past how adorable it is."

I smiled, wincing again. "I get why you like him. He's pretty great."

She came over to me holding a little golden acorn that gleamed when it caught the light. "Here," she said, opening my palm and placing the trinket on it. I closed my fingers around it, feeling the warmth of it radiate through me. Much of the pain I was feeling ebbed immediately.

I sighed contentedly. "Thank you, Ursula. I have a few healing trinkets at home, but nothing this powerful."

"It's my best healer. Level eight."

My eyes widened. "Level eight?" She nodded. "Where did you get a level eight?"

Very few mystics have trinkets greater than a level seven. Elric, of course, has trinkets all the way up to thirteen or fourteen on a scale that goes up to fifteen. But only one trinket in the whole world is rumored to be that powerful—the Phoenix, able to bring anyone back to life, fully restored no matter how brutal the injury, lethal the poison, or grave the disease. But the Phoenix is more legend than fact as no mystic has ever stepped forward to proclaim they're the possessor of the most powerful trinket of all which, by extension, would make *them* the most powerful *mystic* of all.

In answer to my question, Ursula's eyes sparkled with mischief. "I once concocted a love potion for a *very* grateful merlin whose adored had caught him flirting and refused to forgive him, and that," she said, pointing to the acorn, "was my tip!"

"Nice tip."

"Indeed. Now, what the devil happened to you, Dovey?"

I raised the acorn to my left temple to quell the throbbing behind my eye. Warmth seeped into my cheek, and I could immediately feel the effects of a lessening of the swelling around my eye.

"I honestly don't know, Ursula."

"How could you not know?"

I sighed, trying to organize my thoughts. "After leaving you I went to Eleni's office and walked into the middle of a robbery."

"Another mystic?"

"No. An unbound. Three to be exact."

Ursula cocked her head slightly. "And you didn't dispatch them?"

"I didn't have a chance. I got clobbered from behind. Knocked unconscious."

Ursula winced. "Ouch."

"I'll say. Anyway, when I came to, I was tied to a chair, my arms pinned at my sides, and concussed enough to make spell-casting . . . difficult."

Ursula moved to my feet, lifting them so that she could sit down and put them on her lap. She rubbed my shin in sympathy. "Then what happened?"

"Well, then I came face-to-face with some menacing-looking guy who wanted to know where his money was."

"What money?"

I shrugged. "No clue. He was poring over Eleni's journal, though, so I believe he might've been the one blackmailing her."

"Was he also the one who *helped* her off the terrace?"

"You mean, do I think he either has the Promise or he outright murdered her, and the Promise is unrelated to that deed?"

"Yes."

I took a moment to think that through. "No to both. I don't believe he's in possession of the Promise because after he had his goon knock me out for a second time—"

"Double ouch."

I smirked and continued. "I woke up to hear him on the phone with someone discussing what to do with my body. If he had the Promise, he would've used it on me, dropped me someplace public, and allowed witnesses to watch me commit suicide. No one would've traced it back to him.

"As for why I don't believe he murdered Eleni, she obviously owed him some money, otherwise why ransack her office, and a guy like that would've kept her alive long enough to get the location of his money out of her."

"How did you get away?"

"I wove a spell to undo the rope that tied me to the chair, was able to get off an orb for the nearest goon who'd been beating on me, threw the chair at the blackmailer, and was nearly squeezed to death by the third goon, which is when our friend showed up."

Ursula nodded like she knew. "Dex."

"No. Lavender."

Her eyes widened and her jaw dropped. "*Lavender?!*"

I moved the acorn to the back of my head where I'd first been knocked out. "The one and, hopefully, only."

"How did she find you?"

"She's been dogging me ever since I raided her crypt. I suspect she wants her trinkets back and revenge for sending Jacquelyn's dragon to eat her pet serpent."

It took a moment for Ursula to speak. Her mouth opened and closed a few times before she asked, "Lavender saved you?"

I chuckled. "Yes, but not intentionally. She got the goon to let me go, preferring to kill me herself, and while she and the goon tussled it out, I fled out the door. I got very lucky that Dex just happened to be driving near the warehouse district when he spotted me and gave me a lift here."

Ursula nodded, a touch of sadness in her eyes. "I believe he and Esmé live over that way."

"You know that Esmé thinks of Dex only as her friend, right?"

Ursula said, "He's her second, Dovey. Her most trusted partner. It doesn't matter how she feels about him. It only matters how *he* feels about *her*. I mean, he just got her a puppy! She's more than just a friend to him."

"I suspect much of those feelings are simply out of loyalty."

Ursula sighed sadly, then rolled her shoulders and sat up a little straighter. "I refuse to dwell on it. Let's get back to your misadventures. What's your game plan after tonight?"

I moved the acorn down to my sternum. My ribs felt tender after nearly being squeezed to death. Closing my eyes, I said, "Honestly? I don't even know. That's a problem for tomorrow."

Ursula rubbed my shin again before lifting my legs to stand up. "Would you like to sleep in the guest room?"

"If it's all the same to you, I'm quite comfortable right here."

"Of course."

I heard Ursula move off into the kitchen and I lay there on her couch exhausted, but unable to sink into sleep. Too much had happened tonight for my thoughts to simmer down, and a growing anxiety was robbing me of peace as I realized I was no closer to discovering the location of the Promise. Elric would not be pleased.

Ursula's footsteps sounded again, coming close. I opened my eyes to see her standing above me, holding a mug of steaming liquid. "Here. This will let you sleep."

I sat up and took the mug, offering her a grateful smile. "How'd you know?"

"I've been in a scrape or two myself, Dovey. No mystic lives as long as I have without nearly dying several times over."

I took a sip of the liquid, which smelled and tasted delicious. "This is heaven."

She grinned at me, stroked the side of my cheek, and said, "You sleep. I'm going to make the house impenetrable to the likes of Lavender, just in case she comes looking for you here."

I took another long sip from the mug, my eyelids feeling heavy already. "Good plan."

A few minutes later, I was fast asleep.

Chapter 18

Early the next morning, after a wonderfully peaceful night's sleep, Ursula drove me to my car, still parked in the alley behind the building where Eleni had her office. From there, armed with the amethyst ring on my finger, I headed back to the warehouse district.

I wanted my handbag and Gib's watch back. I wasn't worried about any member of the crew that'd kidnapped me. Lavender would've dispatched any survivors, but I was nervous about encountering her again.

Glancing in my rearview mirror, I caught my reflection and was relieved to see the acorn had done a good job of putting me back together. There was still a dappled bruising around my eye, but no lingering headache, dizziness, or pain. Even my broken tooth had been restored.

Cruising down the central avenue of the warehouse district, I took a while to get my bearings and find the warehouse I'd been kidnapped to, but at last I finally saw the familiar barrel that I'd toppled over as a barricade to slow Lavender down when she decided to give chase.

I pulled up right next to the barrel, got out of the car, but left Luna's engine running. After wrapping her doors in a spell that would only allow me to open them, I headed inside the warehouse, which was dark, damp, and still creepy.

I came up short as I nearly tripped over the body of the goon who'd tried to squeeze the life out of me. He lay sprawled on the concrete floor, face down, hiding whatever mortal wound Lavender had inflicted.

Circling his body, I headed across the space toward the toppled chairs where I'd been tied up and my kidnapper had tried to question me.

Just behind the chairs I discovered my handbag. Gasping in relief, I bent and picked it up, discovering Luna's key fob (I'd had to magically get the car running this morning), my wallet, the jack trinket I'd used at the hospital, and my smartphone, but nothing else.

Gib's watch was gone. Cursing under my breath, I looked around but didn't see it on the floor. Then I headed over to where the body of my kidnapper should've been lying, hoping he had the watch on his person, but, other than a small pool of blood, there was no sign of him.

"Really?" I grumbled. Immediately I had to wonder if he'd survived being tossed in the air and thrown ten feet away. He'd already been grievously injured, but perhaps not grievously enough.

Not leaving it up to chance, I began to walk the expanse of the warehouse, thinking maybe he'd crawled off somewhere and succumbed to his injuries, but there was no sign of him.

There *were,* however, plenty of other things to take note of.

Stacked on pallets in neat little squares were unopened boxes. I paused to open one and inside I found smaller boxes, all with a label for medical narcotics.

Stepping back from the box I'd opened, I looked at the rows of larger shipping boxes and counted well over a hundred of those.

Stamped on the side of the boxes was the company name, ARITI PHARMACEUTICALS INC.

I guess the trade in black market drugs has now expanded to the U.S.

A chime from an incoming text caused me to jump. Pulling my phone out from my handbag, I looked at the display. It was a message from Gib.

Can you meet with me? There's been another attempted murder.

I quickly typed a reply, agreeing to meet after I had a chance to shower. There was no way I was going to meet Gib wearing the now bloodstained clothing from yesterday. After sending the text, I hurried out of the warehouse and headed home.

Showering quickly, and applying makeup to cover my bruised eye, I selected black leather leggings and knee-high riding boots with a low heel, a white tank top with a plunging neckline, and a wide collar, white-fur-lined black leather jacket that fit me like a second skin.

Today, I wanted to look ready for battle because my gut was telling me there was more violence on the horizon.

Last, before I left the house, I headed to the washer to pull out the clothes that I'd thrown in after my up-close-and-personal time with a certain serpent. Digging through the pocket of my puff vest, I pulled out the trinket I'd lifted off Lavender and tucked it into the pocket of my leather jacket. Grabbing only my wallet, keys, Swiss army knife, and phone, I headed out the door.

Gib and I had agreed to meet at a park, midway between our homes, and when I arrived, he was already idling in the lot. I pulled in next to him, cut the engine, and got out to move to his passenger-side door.

He unlocked it and I scooted in.

"Whoa," he said, looking me up and down like a hungry wolf.

"What?"

"Helloooooo, Catwoman."

I rolled my eyes, not wanting to laugh and encourage him. "Who was the target this time?"

He blinked and shook his head to get his focus back. "Konstantinos Katapotis. Eleni's ex-husband."

"He's still alive?"

"He is but he's in rough shape."

"What happened?"

"It looks like a hit-and-run. A passing car saw him lying face down in the street near the warehouse district and called it in."

A jolt of recognition went through me. "The warehouse district?"

"Yeah. The Aritis own a warehouse in that area."

"What're his injuries?"

"Multiple facial fractures and a blunt force trauma to his ribs."

My mind raced, trying to piece the puzzle together. "Gib?"

"Yeah?"

"We know that Eleni had an ironclad prenup so that when she divorced Konstantinos, she kept everything, right?"

"That's what I gather."

"Did he get anything?"

"You want to hear something ironic?"

"If it answers my question, then yes."

Gib scratched the stubble on his chin. "He got a warehouse."

"Huh," I said.

"What's huh?"

I was starting to see the full picture, but there was one other thing that was niggling at me. Something that stood out against the backdrop of consistency, and it all had to do with Augustus's murder.

"I'm starting to see it."

"What?"

"The pieces forming the larger puzzle."

"Want to clue me in?"

"Yes, Gib, but before I share, I need to see the crime scene at the art gallery one more time."

"Why? What're you thinking?"

"There's something that's been bothering me, and I haven't been able to put it all together until now. But I need to see it to confirm my suspicion."

Gib pointed out the windshield. "Ride with me or drive separate."

"Together."

He smiled. He was so gorgeous when he smiled. "Together it is, then."

He'd whispered the words, to make them more intimate, and a small thrill went through me.

I didn't know how I was going to be able to disconnect myself from this man, even once the case was over. Reason told me we'd probably never run into each other again—none of my previous cases had involved the FBI. But I wanted to run into him again. And I wanted to kiss him. And I wanted to feel his arms wrapped around me. And I wanted much more than that.

All of what I wanted was doomed to end poorly, however. There was no way to reconcile the fact that I would remain a mystic and he would remain an unbound, a pairing that was destined to fail before it even began.

Knowing all that, however, did nothing to dampen my wish to remain close to Gib. It was a problem without a solution, and it was a problem for both of us that was likely to cause a host of *other* problems for both of us.

With effort, I pulled my gaze away from his, swiveled straight in my seat, and buckled the seat belt. Making a forward motion with my finger I said, "Tallyho."

We arrived at Augustus's gallery a short time later. The board I'd pried loose from the door was back in place, and all the windows had now been covered over as well.

I got out and walked to the large board that'd been placed over the front window. "Can you get this off?" I asked Gib over my shoulder. "I need to see something from this vantage point."

I could've used my trusty Swiss Army knife, but then I'd have some explaining to do.

Gib nodded, then went to the back of his Range Rover, opened the rear door, and took out a toolbox. Rummaging through it, he pulled up a hammer, tucking the toolbox back into his SUV before coming to my side and beginning to work on the nails.

It took a bit of time, but at last he got the board free, and lifted it away from the building so that I could look through the opening.

The window was likely intentionally oversized to give a good view of the artwork inside. I moved along the length of it, finally finding the angle I was looking for when I could plainly see the spot where Augustus had died, the outline of the gas can next to the severely charred area where he'd perished.

"Just what I thought," I said.

"What did you think?"

Instead of answering Gib's question I said, "I need to speak to Ambrose. Do you have his number?"

Gib nodded. "Want to clue me in?"

"I will but let me confirm a thing or two first."

Gib lifted his phone from his pocket, pulled up Ambrose's number, and handed it to me. I hit the green button and waited through the rings until Ambrose picked up.

"Yes?" he said.

"Good morning, Mr. Ariti. This is Dovey Van Dalen. I'm the associate of Special Agent Barlow who spoke to you yesterday at your home."

"I remember," he said. He sounded so weary and sad, and

I didn't blame him. His world was quickly disintegrating around him.

"I'm calling because I want to make sure I'm remembering correctly. When we spoke, you had mentioned that you suspected that your brother's death had been a murder because you spoke to him a short time before he died, and he'd been working in his office on his accounts, correct?"

"Yes, that's correct."

"So you didn't know that Augustus's body wasn't found in his office, but out on the gallery floor, is that correct?"

"It was?" he said. "He died in plain view?"

Ambrose's answer told me he knew exactly what the view from the sidewalk looked like when peering in through the big front window.

"He did."

"I . . . I don't know what to think about that."

"I thought not," I said. Then I switched topics. "One more question for you, Mr. Ariti, who's with you at your house right now?"

"Who's with me?"

"Yes."

"My ex-wife and Henrietta, but my cousins are coming over in about an hour."

"And Hermia?"

"No, she's not at the house. She's at her uncle's. She's more comfortable there."

"Good to know. Any security detail with you?"

"I've hired a private security firm. They've sent five armed men over to ensure my safety, and I've sent two over to Augie's place to watch over Hermia. My cousins are providing their own security as far as I know."

"Good. The last thing I need to tell you is that under no circumstances should you allow *anyone* else inside your home.

Tell your cousins not to come and turn away anyone else who wants to come calling."

"Why would I do that?"

"I can't get into it right now, but the life of everyone in that home right now is in danger if you allow even one more person inside. No family. No friends. You keep that door locked and everyone else out."

"All right. But I'd like an explanation—"

"Mr. Ariti," I interrupted. "Time is of the essence right now. Will you please put Henrietta on the phone? I need to speak with her briefly."

Another lengthy pause followed. Then, "All right. I'll go get her. I believe she's in the kitchen."

I put a finger over the phone's microphone, and said to Gib, "I know who's behind the murders. But there's a much bigger crime involved here too, and I'll need your help for that."

He studied me curiously for a moment before nodding. "Okay. I'm on board with whatever you need, Catwoman."

I smiled. "Thanks, Batman."

An hour later I stood in the middle of the warehouse waiting for everyone to show up. I'd set a trap that I planned to spring, and if I was lucky, no one else would get killed.

The trouble was, I didn't know that I was feeling especially lucky.

Still, there was no other choice in the matter. I needed things to play out how they would, and go from there.

In order to spring this trap, I also needed to make sure that Gib was well away from the area, so I'd sent him on a wild goose chase, and I hoped to make it up to him later when I presented him with the huge prize of breaking up an international drug ring.

While I stood in the very place where I'd been bound and

gagged, I heard a car pull up and the engine cut out. Footsteps sounded on gravel and the door from the outside opened.

"Hey there," I said, adding a wave.

"What're you doing here?" Konstantinos spat.

The man looked worse for wear, that's for sure. His face was wrapped in so many bandages it was like he was wearing a Halloween mummy costume.

"Waiting for you," I said casually, answering his question. My gaze fell to his wrist, and there, just like I knew it would be, was Gib's watch. "That doesn't belong to you," I said, pointing to his wrist.

Konstantinos pulled a gun from his waistband. "Who's gonna take it from me?"

I didn't answer him. On the one hand, I didn't need to, and on the other hand by the sound of another vehicle approaching we had more company arriving.

Konstantinos looked toward the door, the gun in his hand pivoting to aim it toward the exit, while keeping a shifty eye on me.

The door opened and all three of Ambrose's cousins walked in. "Hey there," I called to them. They all came up short, their gazes moving from Konstantinos to me and back again. "Come on in, you three. Enjoy the party."

Kyrie Ariti rubbed her bulging stomach. "What's going on here, Konstantinos?"

He shifted on his feet, not answering her.

"He hasn't told you?" I asked. When she looked at me blankly, I said, "His entire inventory has been confiscated by the FBI."

Kyrie gasped, her gaze snapping to Konstantinos, but her brothers' faces remained masks of confusion. Just like I'd suspected.

"*What?*" she roared at him.

For his part, Konstantinos seemed surprised, even though most of his expression was hidden by the bandages. His head whipped toward the pile of boxes stacked at the far end of the warehouse.

I grinned. "All those boxes are empty, Kyrie. He's played you."

"She's lying!" Konstantinos roared. "Kyrie, I swear! She's lying!" To prove his point he turned to hurry over toward the boxes, and she was right behind him.

"What's going on?" Lino Ariti asked.

"Your sister and your cousin's former husband have been running drugs behind your backs," I told them. "They've been selling narcotics on the black market."

Lino's eyes went wide as saucers while his brother's jaw fell open. "*What?*" they said in unison.

Another car pulled up outside and for this guest I needed to be ready. Pivoting my gaze toward the door, I waited for it to open, readying my amethyst ring to use lethal force if necessary.

But the door didn't open. Instead, there was the sound of another car coming in hot and the screeching of tires. "Freeze!"

An alarm went through me. That was Gib's voice. But he shouldn't be here. I'd purposely sent him across town so that I could take care of all of this myself.

"I said, *freeze,* Hermia!" he shouted again.

"No," I whispered. "No, no, no!"

I began to run toward the door. I didn't know how Gib had figured out that Hermia had been behind all the murders, but he'd obviously tailed her here, and he couldn't confront her . . . not when she held the Promise.

Racing forward as fast as I could run, I had my arm outstretched to push open the door when a lightning bolt hit my side and I flew in the air to land in a crumpled heap on the floor. "Thought you could hide behind a bunch of unbound?" Lavender called.

Belatedly I looked up to see her stepping out from behind a stack of shelving.

I sat on the floor, hugging my ribs. I knew for certain that some of them were broken. My breathing was ragged and, pathetically, I held up my hand defensively. "No . . . no . . . Lav . . . ender . . ."

"What?!" she snapped.

"Don't . . ." I whispered. She was going to ruin everything. She was going to kill us all.

"Don't what, Dovvvvvey?" she drawled. "Kill you? Kill them? Here's a news flash, toots, you're not the boss of me."

On that last word, Lavender unleashed another orb of power. It came at me hot and fast and I barely got out a defensive ball of my own to meet it three feet in front of me.

The explosion sent me back into the wall again where my head banged against the metal siding.

I fell onto my stomach, clutching my side, unable to breathe. Turning toward the oncoming threat as Lavender began to walk toward me with murder in her eyes, I saw the door open, and Gib walked in.

I shook my head, he couldn't be here, and then, to my utter horror, Gib withdrew his weapon, gripped it in his hand, and began to turn the barrel toward himself.

"St-st-st-stoooooooop!" I cried. It came out a whisper. Gib's eyes, wide and terrified, found mine. He shook his head as his hand began to pivot the barrel of his gun to his chest, right over his heart.

Meanwhile, Lavender had gathered another ball of energy between her palms, expanding it as she drew closer, ready to unleash it all on me.

The door opened again and in stepped Hermia, holding a small box in the palm of her hands. Calmly, she walked over to her cousins and opened the box to them. Immediately they both reached for the ring inside the box. Then they froze and began to walk away from her and each other . . . on a mission to kill themselves.

A popping sound startled me, and my attention darted to where Gib was standing.

Had been standing.

He crumpled to the floor, blood pouring from his chest, his eyes unseeing as he sank to the earth.

A cry escaped me, it was primal and raw, and it was the only sound I could get off before Lavender unleashed her deadly ball of energy, aimed right at my head.

Chapter 19

I will never know how Bits ended up in my pocket. All I know is that in the seconds before Lavender's energy was about to take my head off, he popped out of my pocket, and pushed the heart locket into my hand.

A moment later I stood in the warehouse, not quite alone and with the sound of a car fast approaching. Opening my palm, I saw the ruin of the locket which had crumbled on its last and final use.

Blinking, I realized I had only seconds to think through all of my next moves, and if I didn't get it right, I had only three minutes to live.

Sprinting toward the door, knowing Lavender was somewhere here but hadn't yet revealed herself to me, I ignored any common sense which demanded I deal with her first, instead bracing myself next to the door as it opened and waiting for Konstantinos to venture fully into the warehouse.

Winding up a small bundle of energy into my palm, I shot it forward to the back of his head, and he crumpled to the floor. Knowing that using my mystic power would alert Lavender that it was time to reveal herself, I bent low, grabbed Konstantinos's wrist, and unsnapped Gib's watch.

"Oh no, you don't," yelled Lavender, stepping out into the open to confront me.

"Oh yes, I do," I shot back, hurling a bigger ball of energy straight at her. She knocked it to the side using one of hers, and I took advantage of her defensive move to bolt outside and use another bundle of energy to seal the door.

Lavender hit it from the inside, and the power rippled through the door, knocking me backward to sprawl out on the pavement and narrowly miss getting hit by the car carrying Ambrose's three cousins.

Rolling out of the way, I clambered to my feet. "Get out of here!" I screamed at them.

All three stared at me with wide eyes from inside the car. I waved at them and yelled again. "The FBI is on their way! Go! Go now!"

Kyrie Ariti slapped her confused brother on the shoulder, yelling at him in Greek, and he put the car in reverse, speeding away.

In the next moment the door to the warehouse flew off its hinges and Lavender appeared. I brought up the hand with the amethyst ring, ready to end her when another car barreled down the road and swung in next to me, blocking Lavender from my view.

Hermia sat behind the wheel, staring evilly at me.

I guess she'd gotten the message I sent to her through Henrietta, who'd let me know that the day Hermia had been released from the hospital, she'd gone home with her father and stepmother, telling them that she'd take refuge in the guesthouse, and right before Gib and I showed up, she'd shown Cheyanne the Promise.

She'd been the one to also show it to her uncle Augie. I'd figured it out when I realized that Ambrose hadn't been told where in the gallery Augustus had died.

But Hermia knew. She'd told me at his house the day after Eleni died. She'd pretended to be distraught over the idea that her uncle died five feet from the front door. She couldn't understand why he hadn't gotten out.

She'd watched him through the window.

And then she'd murdered her aunt in much the same fashion.

She'd also told me she was living in Italy . . . where Vostov's court was based.

Nicodemus had always had a thing for black-haired beauties. My guess was that he'd met her and introduced her to our mystic world. For whatever reason, he hadn't bound her, but he'd shown her enough that she knew how to get around his wards, infiltrate his hotel room, steal the Promise, and use it on the guard at the door who likely thought nothing about letting Kallis's girlfriend inside his hotel suite while he was at the summit.

Hermia's gift of sight—something she'd inherited from her dad's side of the family—had allowed her to use the Promise with impunity, and she'd set off murdering her family to ensure that all that money finally came directly to her.

"It's over, Hermia," I told her, my gaze darting between her and Lavender, who was starting to head my way again.

Hermia got out of the car, holding the Promise, a sick smile on her face. Behind me a car came racing down the street.

Gib.

Lavender paused and Hermia did too, but I didn't have that luxury.

Spinning around I sprinted toward the fast-approaching car, and Gib had to turn the wheel wildly to avoid hitting me. He skidded to a stop, and I took the opportunity to jam some essence into his watch, then toss it through his open window.

He caught it just as Hermia came racing toward us, the lid to the Promise open wide. I turned my head away without getting a full view, but Gib's eyes centered on the ring and his gaze became unfocused and then his jaw fell slack.

"No!" I yelled at him. "Gib! *NO!*"

He blinked, and his gaze pivoted to me. "Fight!" I shouted,

willing his watch-turned-trinket to work against the magic of the Promise.

I was about to charge forward when a jolt of energy hit my back, sending me flying once again. I landed on the other side of Gib's car, taking the brunt of the impact on my shoulder. Rolling through the pain, I got to my knees, my gaze searching for Gib.

He'd gotten out of his car and was holding a hand outstretched toward the box that Hermia was bringing to him.

"*Fight!*" I screamed, but Gib raised his hand, his watch dangling for a moment from his fingertips before it dropped to the ground, as his fingers grazed the Promise's ring.

"Why will you not *die*?" Lavender screamed at me, right before hurling another ball of energy.

I saw it coming and an anger filled me like I've never known. It was as if I'd spent two hundred years being docile and coy and all the while I'd repressed a beast of a warrior within my soul, just waiting to be let out.

With a primal scream I unleashed a burst of energy that met hers, exploding them both but the shockwave went toward Lavender rather than outward to us.

As Lavender flew backward, my eyes roved to find Gib, trembling from head to toe, his hand shaking so violently that it seemed to have a will of its own.

He reached for the gun in his holster, and I knew I'd lost. There was no way to claim back three minutes of time for a do-over.

Hermia stood in front of him, holding the ring box open, nodding to him with a sadistic smile on her face. Her true nature was finally revealed. She was a monster who enjoyed killing.

Just beyond Gib and Hermia, Lavender rolled to her side and pushed herself up. She got to her feet and it was obvious she was gathering herself to unleash another bomb of energy at me.

Angry as I was, I didn't know if I had enough juice to hold her off and try to save Gib.

And then, I felt something heavy tug on my finger, and I looked down, realizing I still wore the amethyst ring.

I lifted my hand, curling my fingers into a fist, and took aim. Across from me, Lavender snarled, exposing teeth and a mad thirst to kill me, even if it meant she'd die in the process.

While I took aim with the ring, I raised my other hand, sending a burst of essence straight at Hermia, hitting her in the right wrist.

She nearly dropped the Promise, but that hadn't been what I'd been hoping for. Instead, what dropped to the ground was the golden bracelet I'd wrapped around her wrist. And then I flung another object at her.

My trusty Swiss Army knife.

It landed at her feet, blade down.

I'd figured out that Hermia was behind the stolen Promise and the murders within her family. The night of her uncle's wake, she'd gone to the powder room and set up the champagne glass and the Promise to be a surprise for someone else—likely for her stepmother or for her father's cousin, maybe Kyrie, but I believed that Hermia had accidentally exposed herself to the Promise, and it had ignited a suicidal compulsion within her that I'd blindly stopped and kept at bay with the bracelet.

She'd hidden the ring box in with the mop and bucket before the compulsion to kill herself had taken her over completely and in all the time since, she'd played me so well. But that was at an end. And as I looked at her, I knew she knew it too.

Meanwhile, Gib continued to struggle where he stood, his gun now free of its holster. He fought to get the grip right while fighting the urge with every ounce of his being.

Beyond him Lavender gathered her energy, and she began to run toward me, her hands cupped over the bright ball that would probably kill me within the next few seconds.

But I had to wait. Just a few moments more.

Hermia bent over and picked up the knife at her feet. She curled the blade toward herself and her gaze locked with mine, her eyes wide and wild, as wide and wild as I knew Gib's were likely to be.

Lavender pounded the pavement, coming at me faster than expected. She brought up one arm high above her head, her ball of energy ready to unleash, while I aimed the ring, centering all my focus on the target.

Hermia's hand clutched the blade and began to descend, straight for her heart.

The muzzle of Gib's gun turned toward his heart, his finger hovering over the trigger as he fought to keep it from squeezing it.

And still, Lavender came.

Hermia's grip on the blade tightened and she plunged it down into her chest, her grip on the Promise faltering.

In that instant I unleashed the amethyst ring, sending a blaze of white-hot energy that connected with the ring box as it started to fall.

The Promise exploded in a burst of energy I doubted we'd survive. Everyone flew away from the central mass explosion.

As my body lifted into the air, riding the wave of energy, I extended my hand, releasing a small current straight toward Gib.

It hit him mid-back, protecting him from slamming onto the ground while I flew clear across the street, to slam into the side of another warehouse.

And then, my world went black.

"Dovey," I heard. "Dovey, wake up. Wake up, honey. Come on. Stay with me."

My eyelids fluttered and streaks of light snuck in, sending tendrils of pain to the center of my brain.

"Ow," I whispered.

"Dovey?"

"What?"

I didn't know who was talking, or why. All I knew was that my head felt like it'd been used for a drum solo.

"Dovey, can you open your eyes?"

I sighed, wearily, but struggled to open them. My vision was blurry for a minute but then it cleared and I found myself looking up into startlingly gray eyes.

Gib.

"Hey," he said, a smile spreading wide. "There you are."

"Here I am," I agreed. My throat felt raw and ragged. "Where is here?"

Before he could answer I pulled myself to a sitting position.

"Whoa there, girl. Easy, easy. Don't overdo it."

I inhaled deeply. "Too late," I said, a wave of dizziness taking me over. Blinking into the light of day, I looked around me and saw nothing but bodies.

Hermia lay dead on the gravel road, my knife sticking up from her chest, and Lavender lay dead a dozen yards away from her, at the base of a lamppost, the hair at the back of her head matted with blood while her sightless eyes stared up in surprise.

"Are you okay?" I asked Gib once I'd taken in the scene.

He chuckled but it was less a mirthful sound and more one of relief. "Yeah. Yeah I am. I don't know what the hell happened, but one minute I'm thinking I'm about to kill myself, and the next minute I'm flying through the air, but instead of crashing onto the pavement, I just sort of landed lightly on the ground without even a bruise."

"Lucky you," I said, rubbing my shoulder and feeling black and blue all over.

"The crazy thing is, Dove, right before all of that happened, Hermia killed herself, right in front of me!"

"You don't say?"

"I think it was the guilt. She killed her aunt. I have proof."

I looked up at him. "Proof, huh?"

He nodded. "One of the tenants in Eleni's building sent me a video from her doorbell camera of the day Eleni died, not two minutes after she plummeted off the terrace. Hermia stopped in front of the camera and shoved a small package into her coat. It was exactly the same size package the building manager said he gave to Eleni on her way upstairs.

"Hermia must've grabbed it on her way out after tossing her aunt over the side."

I cupped the back of my head, feeling a raging headache beginning to form. "Yeah, that must be how it went down."

Gib looked over his shoulder toward the warehouse. "I also got a tip, you know."

"A tip?"

"Yeah, someone called in a tip about a boatload of prescription narcotics being in the warehouse that Konstantinos owns. I've called the cavalry. They should be here with a warrant soon. I don't know how I'm gonna explain all this other stuff to them, hell, I don't even know who that lady"—Gib paused to point toward Lavender—"even *is!*"

I puffed out a small chuckle. "She's probably part of the drug ring, Gib." It didn't matter that they'd never be able to identify Lavender. It only mattered that she'd never bother me again.

Gib helped me to my feet and right about then is when Konstantinos came stumbling out of the warehouse. "I think you'd better get over there and arrest him," I said to Gib.

"You okay for a minute?" he asked me, and I thought it was sweet that he didn't want to leave my side.

"I'm fine."

Gib got up and headed over to Eleni's ex-husband, who, I now knew, had convinced her that it was her brothers Augustus and Ambrose who were running a drug ring, and he'd been threatening her to go to the authorities over it if she didn't pony up some cash which he knew she got every month.

I also now knew that Eleni's cousin Kyrie was in on the scheme with him. I wondered if the baby she carried was his.

I watched Gib move to Konstantinos and waited for him to be preoccupied before moving over to find and pick up the ruins of the Promise and my Swiss army knife, then stumbled away out of view.

There was no way I wanted to be anywhere nearby when the rest of "the cavalry" as Gib put it showed up.

Luna was parked behind one of the other neighboring warehouses, and it was a relief to slide in behind the wheel and drive home.

Once there I showered, changed, fed Bits (and thanked him for saving my life), then I headed to SPL.

Elric greeted me at the elevator on the eighteenth floor. "Tortelduif."

I moved forward and wrapped my arms around him. He chuckled softly. "Did you miss me?"

"Yes," I said, knowing it was the truth. Maybe not the whole truth, but it was true enough.

Stepping back, I held out the burnt-out remains of what had been the Promise.

"It couldn't be saved?" he asked.

"No," I said. Because it couldn't have. I couldn't have let Gib die. It had to be done.

Elric eyed me keenly. I realized I had no idea what he was thinking. I didn't know if he knew the whole of what'd happened near that warehouse or not, but if he did know, he didn't let on. "Very well," he said.

I nodded to him and turned to go but he stopped me when he said, "Do you still love me, Tortelduif?"

I turned to him. “Always, Elric.”

And I meant it.

Just not like I used to.

I can’t be certain, but I think he understood, because there was a hint of sadness in his eyes as the doors closed between us.

Later I sat in my favorite chair, reading a book, when there was a knock at my door.

I knew who it was without looking. Opening the door, I said, “Hey.”

“You disappeared on me.”

I shrugged. “Sorry. I may do that from time to time.”

Gib’s expression shifted from worry to apprehension. “Will you always come back?”

I leaned against the door and reached out to settle my hand on his arm. “Yes,” I said.

And I meant it.

Just like I always would.